Harley Quinn™

REDEMPTION

— DC ICONS —

REDEMPTION

—DC ICONS—

RACHAEL ALLEN

Random House 🏠 New York

Copyright © 2024 DC.
BATMAN and all related characters and elements © & ™ DC.
WB SHIELD: ™ & © WBEI. (s24)

Harley Quinn created by Paul Dini and Bruce Timm

All rights reserved. Published in the United States by Random House Children's Books, a division of Penguin Random House LLC, New York.

Random House and the colophon are registered trademarks of Penguin Random House LLC.

Visit us on the Web! GetUnderlined.com

Educators and librarians, for a variety of teaching tools, visit us at
RHTeachersLibrarians.com

Library of Congress Cataloging-in-Publication Data is available upon request.
ISBN 978-0-593-42994-5 (trade) — ISBN 978-0-593-42996-9 (ebook)

The text of this book is set in 11-point Berling LT Std.
Jacket art by Kevin Wada
Additional jacket photos © 2024: vines by enviromantic/Getty, leaves by SondraP/Getty
Interior map art by Ansley Allen
Interior retro diamonds art by velikiyzayats/stock.adobe.com
Interior paper texture art by frenta/stock.adobe.com
Interior leafy border art used under license from Shutterstock.com

Printed in the United States of America
10 9 8 7 6 5 4 3 2 1
First Edition

To everyone who loves Harley Quinn and sees
a piece of themselves in her

PROLOGUE

Dear Harleen,

   You don't know me. You don't, but you will.

   I watch you. As you walk home to your dorm from the library at night. You really shouldn't look at your phone so much—anyone could sneak up behind you.

   I watch you. Drinking your morning coffee out of a dented black travel mug in biology class.

   Maybe I'm watching you now while you read this letter. I'm never very far for very long.

   Today, I decided I needed to do more than watch. And, so, a letter and a gift, the first of many, if all goes well.

   I watch a lot of girls. People. A lot of people. But not just anyone. Some of them don't look the way they're supposed to. Mismatches. It's so frustrating when the real world doesn't align with what's inside my head. I have to draw them the right way. One time, sometimes, many times. I draw them until I don't itch anymore. I know how to draw them correctly. That's not the hard part. Their insides sing blood songs. Did you know that? I don't choose. I never chose any of this. I was searching for something else entirely, and there it was—an article about a massive Arkham jailbreak and a Gotham U student who was injured at Ace Chemicals. The student sounded like someone I would like to watch. It wasn't hard to figure out it was you.

I put you on my short list. Could you feel it when I did that? Did you get a tingling feeling up the back of your neck when I wrote your name, like I was standing behind you, whispering it in your ear? I like to think that you did. The list I've curated is of people with unbelievable physical abilities, beautiful girls, canvases oozing with siren songs. People I need to acquire. Wait—I'm getting ahead of myself. How to explain this . . . ? It's so important that you understand me.

One time, I met a girl sitting on a bench outside the train station, and I wondered what it would be like to make her match the visions in my head.

And I found out.

I'm an artist, you see. Only instead of working in tired mediums like paints and pencils, I'm creating something entirely new. Stitching and slicing and welding and tearing and composing. I'm breaking the very idea of what art can be.

Imagine how it felt to learn that you—one of my most exciting potential pieces—were searching for me, were keeping tabs on me too. I knew you were special because your insides are so very loud, but when I found out you were looking for me, we became connected. It's clear now that you're meant to be my muse.

Someday, I'll acquire you too. But I have so many skills to hone first and so many girls to practice on. Do you want to see what I've been doing with them?

—The Dollmaker

CHAPTER 1

SCIENCE EXPERIMENTS THAT INVOLVE KISSING SHOULD BE A lot more fun. Ivy, my girlfriend, my G-I-R-L-F-R-I-E-N-D of exactly twenty-nine days and four hours, purses her lips and leans forward. Her hair glistens in the sunlight, and she smells like summer and overripe peaches. Her lips look soft and so very kissable.

And . . . I pull out a box of cotton swabs. (No. Fun. At all.)

"Think about me!" I tell her.

The puckering takes on a smiley shape. I run a swab across her lips and then carefully open her mouth so I can make small circles on the insides of her cheeks as I count to five.

"Perfect!" I remove the swab and stuff it in a tube filled with clear media. "Now think about Woodrue!"

I take another kiss sample with a fresh swab.

"Now think about kissing Catwoman!"

"Wait, what?"

"Kidding! Think about me again."

Another swab.

I vortex all the vials to homogenize the samples, and then I spin them down so I can run the toxicity assay. *Please work. Please work. Please work this time.* It's important to distract myself, because if I don't, I'll start thinking about the letters. And what comes with the letters. So I keep my eyes on the centrifuge as it works its way up to 10,000 *g*. While I'm doing my science, Ivy repots some begonias that she rescued (read: stole) from the nearby home improvement store because "the poor babies had root rot and they needed someone to take care of them." Her conservatory—the place where we're working—is unreal. Like a jungle ate a science lab and then settled down in a Victorian solarium. The walls are so thick with greenery, you can hardly see them, and the ceiling is retractable glass.

Also? There are lab benches with science equipment and a sitting area for relaxing and shelves filled so tall with books that you have to use a vine-covered ladder to reach them. (I honestly still haven't been able to decide if the ladder is alive—the last time I was stretching out my fingers to grab a book just beyond reach, one of the rungs SHOT OUT A VINE to help me.)

And then there are the flowers as big as people and the vines hung thick with mysterious fruit and the ones that smell like death or cinnamon or banana pudding. This place feels like a mythical parallel world—something hidden and primordial. Our own personal oasis on the outskirts of Gotham City. A break from the horrors that find their way to my campus mailbox. I have been here two days, and I never want to leave.

"Have your professors posted grades yet?" Ivy asks as she makes cuttings of her *Monstera deliciosa*. (It has a ton of white patches and streaks within its tropical green leaves, which apparently makes it some kind of celebrity in the plant community.)

I shake my head and do another rinse step for my assay. "No." I say it like I'm personally offended, because I am. "And refreshing every ten minutes doesn't make the grades appear."

Ivy smirks. "Cruel and unusual."

It really is. I've been working like a fiend to make all A's so I can get into a top-tier med school, even while the darkness at the back of my mind whispers that I could do more good by putting on my Harley costume and taking to the streets.

"What are you thinking about?" asks Ivy.

I blush. "Nothing."

It's not that I think she'd judge me, but it's one thing to do some fun and nefarious secret missions on the side, and it's entirely another to say you're considering them as a whole life plan/alternate career. Especially when all you have is some amorphous picture in your head of tearing through Gotham City by night with glitterbombs and truth bombs and actual bombs, and not, like, a specific plan of how this entire setup would work or what the point would be. It's better to tell her when I have a solid plan. Yep. I'm sure an epiphany about my life goals will strike any day now.

Just then, the Isleys' housekeeper bustles in with a monogrammed cheese board straight out of a magazine. Baked brie. Fig jam. Fruit I don't even know the names of.

"Thanks, Dorothy," says Ivy kindly.

I choke out a "thank you" too. I wish I could feel more

comfortable around this woman, who is almost like a mother to Ivy. But I don't know if I'll ever get used to people waiting on me.

The minute I leave the conservatory and set foot on the rest of the Isley estate (because it's definitely not just a house, this place), I'm reminded of exactly how different Ivy and I are. When she found out I didn't have a place to stay during that awkward week between spring and summer semester when they don't let students live in the dorms, she didn't hesitate—I just had to stay with her at Hawthorne.

Do I have to call it Hawthorne?

She rolled her eyes. "Only in front of my parents. I used to try to think up awful nicknames just to piss them off," she continued, and I grinned. "But they're going to be away at their Tuscan villa all summer, a fact that my mother has worked into conversation ad nauseam with everyone from the neighbors to our dentist, which means we'll get the house to ourselves."

Ivy looked positively gleeful. At the thought of them leaving? At the thought of me coming to stay? Probably both.

And because I adore her, I only teased her a little about how I didn't realize "to ourselves" meant us plus a staff of seven.

Ivy sprinkles the cheese board with edible flowers, and I abruptly stop spacing out because (A) Ivy, and (B) *cheese*.

I walk over to the sitting area to pop a bite of baked brie into my mouth and eat a couple of round berries the color of an egg yolk.

"So, you think it'll work this time?" asks Ivy.

"The cheese? It's definitely working."

I give my belly a comical rub, but she doesn't laugh.

"The experiment." Ivy tucks her legs underneath her and picks at some pomegranate arils.

"Are you kidding?! It's totally gonna work!" I hype myself up so I can hype her up. Don't let the doubts slither into my brain. The whispers that tell me we've been trying for months and we thought we'd have it figured out in weeks. The shadows that hiss that it may be impossible, and what are we going to do then? Oops, guess the doubts slithered in after all.

I leap up from the table. "HEY, WHAT'S THIS?"

Ivy glances at me. "Huh?"

"These flowers." I point at the furry pink cotton balls that strongly resemble the trees in a children's book my mom used to read to me. "I'm, like, fascinated by them. What are they?"

"I know what you're doing." The left side of Ivy's mouth curves upward.

"What? Showing an interest in your hobbies? Being curious about nature's wonders?"

"Distracting me."

"Is it working?"

She can't help but crack a grin. "Yes."

"So . . . what are they?"

"Mimosa trees." She walks over and plucks one of the fluffy pink flowers. She holds it out to me. "Smell it."

I breathe in, and then I sigh out because these flowers, wow. "They're amazing. Like honey and almonds and a summer breeze, and something spicy I can't quite put my finger on."

"Ginger," says Ivy, looking incredibly pleased with my assessment.

"Yeah, that." I sigh again because I still feel a little day-dreamy after inhaling the flower.

"When I was little, I used to call them powderpuff trees, and I'd pick the flowers and pretend to do my makeup with them." She brushes the flower along my cheekbones like a blush brush, and I shiver.

"I bet you were the cutest kid ever."

Her smile falters, but just for a second. She doesn't like to talk about her childhood.

"You can make a tincture with the flowers that alleviates depression. Well, that's the folklore anyway, but I think there might be some scientific merit to it." (Classic Ivy recovery.)

I move along to another raised flower bed, and Ivy pushes the flower into the soil next to me with her hand, then swoops her fingers around it gracefully like a ballerina until it grows into a tiny mimosa tree.

"I will never get over you doing that. It's like magic."

Ivy narrows her eyes. "Science."

"But in some ways, aren't they the same thing?" I skip along to some shiny-looking blueberries before she can get too ruffled. "Oh! How 'bout these?! Let me guess! They turn you into a blueberry. Nope, too obvious. Temporary telepathy? I've always wanted to know what Officer Montoya thinks about when she's not interrogating people." If I could really have that, the ability to break into people's minds, I could find the location of the man stalking me in the time it takes to snap my fingers. I open my mouth wide, ready to eat a berry right off the branch.

A giant elephant's ear leaf leans over, forming a bright green barrier against my face. "Um, those are belladonna, and they can kill you," says Ivy.

"Oops." And then I eye the plant skeptically. "Just one of those little berries?"

"I mean, maybe if you're lucky, it'll just be delirium or hallucinations, but yes, deadly nightshade. Poison of the ages. Used to make witches fly and women's eyes dilate."

"Wut."

"It was a whole thing to look prettier in medieval times. Zero out of ten. Would not recommend."

"Oh-ho-kay. No belladonna for me."

But what if it wasn't just poison? What if it was poison and powers? Would the juice be worth the squeeze?

My timer buzzes from across the room.

"Oh! My experiment!"

I run over and eyeball the toxicity levels and then export the results so I can analyze them. Ivy buzzes around me while trying to pretend she's not hovering.

"Huh. It's still showing high levels of toxins when you think about me. Or when you think about anything at all, really. Not as high as when you think about Woodrue, though, so that's something!"

Ivy takes a step back and sits on the table. "Yeah. For sure." But her voice is hollow, and I know no amount of excited plant questions are going to fix this.

I sit next to her and press my shoulder against hers.

"It's okay. We'll keep trying."

She nods.

I have another idea I'm working on—one where I try to isolate exactly what it is in Ivy's saliva/body/whatever that's keeping her from dying from her own toxin, but I've had absolutely zero luck finding it so far, so I don't mention it. It's been hard to keep our hopes up lately.

It's not just our kissing problem. We've hardly made any progress on trying to find the missing girls or the trafficking gang either. I remember how powerful I felt last semester watching The Scarecrow get arrested during grand rounds. Realizing that I hadn't been pushed into those chemicals—I'd jumped so that the very last of the mind-control chips would be destroyed. And even though I knew it wasn't over, that The Scarecrow had intended to supply those chips to a bigger operation that had been kidnapping girls all over the city, I wasn't worried then. I told Ivy we'd cure ourselves and find the missing girls in a single spring-break road trip. And now it's summer, and we're still right where we started. No progress. And that's *with* the mastermind behind the missing girls sending me serial-killer letters in the mail for the last two months.

Sometimes the letters aren't all he sends. Sometimes there are "gifts." Packages tied up with twine. Dolls nestled in tissue paper. Horrific, ugly little things with bat wings sewn into their backs and tentacles coming out of their faces.

And the letters that come with them . . .

I discovered the most intriguing girl in a back alley yesterday. Her face is plain, and I think she may be addicted to a couple of vices, but I already have ideas for how to transform her. What do you think? Beautiful, no?

Because it turns out the dolls he sends me aren't just dolls. They're *plans.* Blueprints. This isn't your usual human-trafficking operation. He's taking the girls because he wants to make them "transcendent." Turn them into what his sadistic brain thinks of as art. I shudder just thinking about it.

Every time he takes a girl, I get a letter and a doll. Every time. He used to keep them on a shelf in his (no doubt dreadful) lair, but now he sends them to me because apparently I'm just that special. And every time I get one, I feel that much more like a failure. Another girl mangled. One more I've failed to save. It got to where my hands shook every time I checked my Gotham U mailbox.

Another benefit of staying at Ivy's? The Dollmaker doesn't know where I am. I'll get a break from his ghastly presents, if only for a week.

When I got that first letter, and the first doll that went with it, I was disgusted. Panic-stricken. But it gave me something to follow up on. The man behind the trafficking gang, one of the two men who were collaborating with The Scarecrow, had revealed himself to me. Named himself, even— The Dollmaker. And I already knew one of his other aliases, Anton, from his emails to The Scarecrow. He wasn't being nearly as careful as he should have been.

Why is it so hard to find him, though? I've been to every dive bar and hole-in-the-wall in the East End, seeing if I can get some drunk person to spill that they maybe thought they saw something a few days ago. I've pumped my underworld connections for any information they might have on a guy named Anton or someone who goes by "The Dollmaker." I've asked all the girls in my old neighborhood if they've noticed anyone more suspicious than usual lurking around. But other than the confirmation that, yes, girls are disappearing more rapidly than normal, and a couple people claiming to have seen the same idling black car, I've got nothing. I think back to my gap year, when I was part of the Reckoning. How much the five of us accomplished in such a short amount of time. Sometimes I wonder if the reason Ivy and I are having trouble making progress is because it's just the two of us.

I never ended up hearing back from Jasmin and Bianca last semester, even though I sent them a bunch of texts. Jasmin's still a grad student at Gotham U for another year, so I guess I could find her on campus taking summer classes. I want to find out how Bianca's back surgery went too. It was months ago that she broke her back trying to follow a trafficking gang on a mission that I couldn't risk helping with. Months ago that they flew her to Santa Prisca for experimental surgery.

The fact that I haven't heard from her since before the surgery worries me. So, I guess I could try to track down both of them, but I don't know. They could easily get in touch with me, and they haven't. Maybe I need to respect their boundaries. It is my fault we're not talking, after all. The result of me damaging our friendship by not being there for them when they needed me. Being too laser focused on what I thought my future was supposed to look like. Trying so hard to do things the "right" way that I wronged everyone around me.

Turns out the right way doesn't work for me. I'll take the way that gets results any day. Though it may be too late to get my friends back.

I shake away the thought. Thank goodness I've got Ivy.

Our eyes meet and she says, "You want to do our nails? Or go swimming? The sunlight always makes me feel better."

I blink. Wow, if Ivy is trying to cheer *me* up, I really must look deep in my feelings.

"Yeah. That would be awesome," I say.

She frowns. "Which one?"

"Both," I answer quickly, jumping up from the table. "Um, in whatever order would make the most sense."

She rolls her eyes. "You are so weird." She starts to move from the table to a flower bed, but I grab her hand and pull her closer to me before she can turn away.

"You like it."

"Maybe I do," she says in a teasing voice that makes me think all kinds of dangerous things. Her thigh is touching my hip bone. Her peaches-basil-summer-rain smell feels like a drug. Kissing her would be like eating a fistful of belladonna berries, but I'd do it. Cure or no. If she asked me right now, I'd—

Ivy pulls away, panting, which is good because the rational part of my brain would actually like to live to see tomorrow.

"We have to be careful," she says.

"Yep." I close my eyes because the being-careful thing is a whole lot easier if I can't see her.

Especially now that we spend almost every second with each other, working in the greenhouse, elbows touching, waking up in Ivy's bed. Double especially if we're about to go swimming and I'm going to see her in a bathing suit for the first time.

Ivy. In a swimsuit.

"Definitely gotta be careful," I squeak out.

There's a knock at the conservatory door, and THANK FREAKING GOODNESS, because I'm not sure how I was supposed to survive the next five minutes.

The Isleys' butler enters.

"I've got a package for Miss Quinzel."

And I tear my eyes away from Ivy long enough to really

look at him and what he's holding. Not just any package. A pretty white box tied with twine. Big and rectangular— the same size as the others. The feeling of safety I had here evaporates. Dissolves like cotton candy in a rainstorm.

I glance at Ivy, and the dread I'm feeling is mirrored on her face.

"Thank you, Mason," she says with only the tiniest quaver in her voice, and he nods and places the package on the table gently and obliviously because he doesn't know there's a time bomb of suck inside.

As he leaves, I walk over to the table so I can look at the tag.

I confirm what Ivy and I already suspect.

"It's from him." The pieces connect in my head, a horrible puzzle taking shape. "He knows I'm here."

On Dollmaking

There are five steps required to make a doll.

First, the Taking.

Second, the Trials.

Third, the Metamorphosis.

Fourth, the Calming.

Fifth, the Engraving.

Most of the deaths happen during the third step.

CHAPTER 2

I SLIDE THE LID OFF THE BOX, WINCING BECAUSE I DON'T know exactly what version of cruelty is waiting for me today, but I know it will feel like a punch to the gut. That's what it always feels like. I hiss when I see the doll's face. Is that . . . real skin? I touch her cheek because I have to know, and no, (mercifully) it isn't. She's made of plastic or rubber or whatever it is dolls are made of. But her cheek and forehead are charred on one side, and the skin-like material is burnt and has bubbled in such a way that for a split second, I thought it might be real.

Ivy leans closer, her hair brushing against my shoulder, so she can see the doll. That one small act pulls me out of this living horror show for a moment, and I'm grateful.

"Do you think he really burned her face like that?" asks Ivy.

I shudder. "Either he did or he's planning to."

I pick the doll up carefully because sometimes they contain hidden surprises. I still haven't gotten over the one that sliced into my finger when I touched her arm the wrong way. The tag next to this doll's head reads *Firefly*, and she's dressed in a black suit and helmet that look flame-retardant. There's a tank on her back, and one of her arms holds a big black flamethrower. Or maybe it's fused to her sleeve? I inspect the doll's forearm more carefully. No, not the sleeve. It's fused to the doll's arm. Does that mean it's fused to the real-life girl's arm?

I bring the doll closer, and the motion of it sends a wave of air wafting toward me. A particular brand of noxious. Between an ill-fated sleepover when I was thirteen and the number of curling irons and flat irons I've used over the years, I recognize it immediately. Burning hair is the kind of smell that gets in your nose and doesn't let go.

I turn the doll over, investigating the ponytail coming out of her helmet, the hair shiny and oh-so-real and ending in a burnt tangle. Against my better judgment, I sniff.

And then I gag.

"It's hair. He used real hair." I drop the doll into its box, and Ivy slaps on the lid like it's going to come alive and murder us.

"Do you think—?" begins Ivy, but she can't finish her sentence.

"Do I think he set this girl on fire and used her real, actual, burnt-to-a-crisp hair to make me Little Sally Burns-A-Lot here? Yes. Yes, I do. What the actual eff is wrong with this guy?"

"*Everything.*" Ivy shivers and pushes the box farther away from us like it's filled to the brim with black widow spiders and venomous snakes.

And now that we've done the worst part, the inspecting-the-doll part, our brains start to work again. We pace back and forth in the conservatory. We talk only in questions.

How did he know you were here? (Ivy)

Do you think he has people following me? (Me)
Has he been watching us this whole time? (Ivy)
What if he has people outside right now? (Me)
Or drones? (Ivy)
Do you think I should check the security feed? (Ivy)
You have a security feed? (Me)

The fact that he's found me—here—in this place where I thought I was safe makes this whole thing feel like that much more of a violation. I've only been here *two days.* It makes me feel like I'm never not being watched. Can I change my clothes and feel safe? Or take Ivy's hand without him seeing? I *know* we were alone in her dorm room when we talked about me staying here—but he could have bugged our rooms! Or maybe he just saw us hauling my stuff to her car and followed us here. I search the grounds outside the window like I'm expecting to see him hiding behind a bush or hanging from a tree. Not that I know what he looks like. Not that I'd be able to tell if he was standing in line behind me in a coffee shop or walking his dog past me at the park.

"Hey." Ivy wraps her arms around me from behind and rests her chin on my shoulder. "It's going to be okay. You're safe here. We have really excellent security."

I nod, even though I can't shake the feeling that I could be anywhere, and if he really wanted to get to me, he would. He takes these girls like it's nothing, and the police don't even care. Because he's smart—he takes the right kinds of girls. The ones the police don't look for. And every time, he taunts me with how he's taken another, and I'm not one bit closer to stopping him.

I pull away from Ivy's hug and turn around to face her.

"I'm just—I'm over it. It's been months. I want to find

this guy and take him out already. I'm sick of him toying with me."

I think of the letters he's been sending. That very first one and then the ones a few weeks ago:

There were times when I doubted myself. You've no idea the struggle white men face in finding their footing in the art world these days. But now I know that all those years of toiling without so much as a scrap of recognition from the critics were worth it, because I've hit upon something next-level. It's genius or madness. Probably both. I'm enclosing a model of one of my most recent pieces here. I've only ever trusted one other person with my ideas.

Today I was doing some digging, and I discovered your connection to Talia al Ghūl. You were Talia's sidekick, but she didn't value you. She didn't treat you the way I could. I'll put you on a pedestal. You'll be my inspiration. My right hand.

I fear I've hit one of those low points that we creative types are wont to have. Two of my pieces weren't working this week, and I had to completely discard them. I suffer a great deal for my art. The only thing that could cheer me up was you. I went to campus and waited in the building where you have your biology class. We shared an elevator ride, and for three floors we were breathing the same air, and your energy was contagious. It gave me the strength to get through the day.

I haven't been able to stop thinking about you since.

Tonight I tried something with one of my pieces: genetic manipulation. Like that old movie about the scientist who turns himself into a fly, only nothing as coarse and ugly as that. The end result gave me chills, and even though she only lasted for a few days, I knew I had to explore that idea some more.

I was actually able to find a photo of that particular missing girl. At least, I'm pretty sure it was her. Her resemblance to the doll was remarkable—from the nose up. Blue eyes and curly brown hair. But poking out of her body in every direction were jagged black legs. Insect legs, bending in impossible angles. And where her mouth should have been, another set of legs. But strange ones. A cross between spider legs and mantis arms. Able to unfold and snap back just as quickly. Ivy searched the internet and figured out the girl had been genetically crossed with a whip spider. Was he really able to do this? To make someone look like this? That letter and that doll coupled with a picture of the girl before The Dollmaker had gotten to her—it was one of the worst days I've had in a long time.

His most recent letters, though. They're different. More urgent. There's been a shift in him.

I've created so many mock-ups of you, but none of them are right. I can't sleep. I can't eat. I'm obsessed with the idea of turning you into something that will become the model for all of my future creations. I've decided I need to increase my doll output to better determine what I'll do with you when you come to me. I'll take as many girls as I need in order to perfect my methods. It makes me itch all over that I haven't figured it out yet.

I hate how I can't simply discuss these things with you. Our creative partnership feels so one-sided. Don't you understand? We are nothing without each other. Our greatest heights can only be achieved together. What do I have to do to get you to return my attention?

I shake my head, trying to block out the letters playing over and over in my brain. The ones where he describes what he's doing to the girls. The ones where he calls me Talia's sidekick. It bothers me that an outsider would see it that way. I'm so much more than someone's sidekick. But I think that's really what he's looking for when he says he wants me to be his muse. What is he like with the others, the ones he doesn't want to be his muse?

I grit my teeth.

"Every time he takes one of these girls, I feel so much worse," I tell Ivy. "And the letters, they're getting worse too."

Her head shoots up. "Wait a minute. Why doesn't this one have a letter? They always come with a creepy letter."

"You're right. I got all freaked-out by the hair and forgot."

I hurry to remove the lid again. Try not to inhale or think about the charred hair as I pick up the doll from the box.

Ivy sorts through the tissue paper. "I don't see a letter."

I flip over the tag that says *Firefly*, the only writing I noticed in the whole box, but there's nothing there either.

We comb over the box and the doll and the tissue paper one more time. And then it hits me.

"Ivy, the doll. What if it's *in* the doll?"

Ivy stares at the pint-sized monster in front of us.

"You think we should rip her open?" Ivy eyes the doll like

a bunch of centipedes are about to come pouring out of her insides.

I pick up the doll and try to gauge whether she feels weirdly heavy or something.

Ivy is scrutinizing the lid to the box. "Does it seem like there's just the faintest outline of something? Like words or pictures?"

I frown. "Like invisible ink?"

"Maybe?" Ivy runs off and comes back with a black light, which she just happens to have in her conservatory because of course she does. She tries a UV light too, and we see a little more, but it's still hard to make everything out.

"I wonder . . ." Ivy purses her lips, tilting the box lid this way and that. "Well, the black light could suggest something organic, and the fact that it's paired with that fire doll. . . . What if we're supposed to burn it?"

"You mean set the box lid on fire? Don't get me wrong, setting things on fire is my eighth favorite activity, but—"

"Not the whole lid. Just, like, hold a small flame against the letters."

"Lightly burning the letters. Huh." I narrow my eyes at the doll. "You don't think—?" I inspect the tiny flame-thrower and the tiny black button that I thought was just for show. And then I push it.

WHOOSH.

I dodge the flame, but only just, almost losing an eyebrow in the process.

This time I aim the doll and her flamethrower at the message on the lid, carefully sweeping back and forth. Close enough that words start to appear in a color that makes me think of French toast but not so close that the lid catches fire. I get to the end and lean in to read the jagged letters, and my entire being fills with dread at the words silhouetted on the lid. At this newest message from The Dollmaker.

I've given you so many gifts, and I haven't received anything in return. Maybe it's time I take something of yours.

I Used to Be a Person

Once upon a time, I was a toddler, playing with my blocks as my mom's boyfriend screamed in the background.

Once upon a time, I was in second grade, and I looked forward to school and a hot lunch and markers and a hug from my teacher.

Once upon a time, I was fifteen, and it seemed better to walk the streets at night, sneaking cheap wine with a pack of girls, than to stay in my apartment.

Once upon a time, I got in the wrong car.

Her memories are all there, right alongside my new ones, but I keep them to myself.

Mr. Tetch doesn't like to talk about her.

CHAPTER 3

I PAW THROUGH MY DUFFEL BAGS LIKE A DRUNKEN RAC-coon, flinging clothes and shoes in every direction while Ivy meticulously inspects her jewelry box.

"If you were The Dollmaker, what would you take?" I ask as I completely upend my makeup bag.

"I don't know," Ivy calls back. "Do you think you'd notice if anything was missing?"

It's a good point, but he seems like the type to take something that would make a statement. (You better believe Bernie was the first thing I checked.)

"What are you girls doing?" That last question comes from Ivy's mother (who, honestly, cannot leave for the Tuscan sun soon enough), and it barely meets the grammatical requirements because while it is technically a question, she means it as a command. A judgment. *Whatever it is, you shouldn't be doing it.*

I glance up from my duffel, wishing I hadn't thrown the clothes quite so far and with quite so much vigor. A white

T-shirt punctuated with holes rests directly in front of Ivy's mom's Chanel flats. She eyes it the way you would a pile of dog poop.

Every time. Every damn time I am in this woman's presence, it's like I can feel the poor radiating off me.

Poor-people things I have learned are poor-people things because of how scandalized they made Ivy's mom look:

1. Eating chips directly from the bag instead of putting them in a bowl first. *(I've just never seen anyone do that.)*
2. Taking public transportation. *(Oh gosh, how many times were you mugged?)*
3. The way I talk. (I swear her nostrils flare every time I say "ya know.")
4. Keeping perfectly good things like my laptop charger that I repaired with electrical tape. *(Why don't you just buy a new one?)*

"I'll have one of the maids come up and sort through this for you. She can get rid of the old things." Her eyes drift from the shirt to a pair of (artfully) ripped jeans. I grab them to my chest protectively.

"It's no trouble. I can do it myself." If I let someone throw away every piece of clothing with holes or stains, I'd have about two outfits left.

"Mom?" Ivy gently interrupts us. "Did you need something?"

Mrs. Isley shakes herself back to her freshly-starched-clothing reality. "Right. Your father and I are leaving for the villa soon."

As she says this, he passes behind her in the hallway, a quick blur.

"Charles?"

"Yes?" he calls from down the hallway.

"We're saying goodbye to Pamela?"

(Ivy has asked them repeatedly to call her Ivy.)

"Yes, right."

He backtracks and stands next to Mrs. Isley in the doorway.

"We'll see you in a few months," says Ivy's mom.

"If you need anything, be sure to tell the butler," says Ivy's dad, even though Mason has literally worked for them since before Ivy was born, and he clearly has a name.

The moment stretches. I wait for some embraces or "I love yous" or, at the very least, a pat on the shoulder. Ivy's waiting too. I can tell by the way she straightens her back, like if she can appear perfect enough, they'll decide she's worthy of their affection.

And when she realizes that it's not coming, that she's going to have to stand up and walk across the room and make them love her on their terms, it is the saddest thing I've ever seen.

Ivy rises from her chair, defeated. This walk is going to take eleven hours—I want to look away, but I feel like I should witness her getting these goodbye hugs, even if they are sad, brittle ones.

And then her father checks his watch. "Oops. Better get going. Private planes wait for no man."

Even though, isn't that the whole point of a private plane?

Her parents deliver the most robotic goodbyes possible

and disappear from the doorway. *You're on your own, kid. Nice knowing you.* Ivy sits back down, but she doesn't even sigh.

I—I can't. I just can't.

I fly across the room and pick her up off her chair and hug her as tight as I can.

"What's that for?" she says.

I squeeze her even closer. "Because they should have done it."

Her body relaxes (collapses?) into mine, and we stay like that for a minute or two or ten. Like if I hold her long enough I can mend all her broken pieces.

Ivy grips the steering wheel tightly, navigating her berry-pink convertible through the heart of Gotham City and into a seedier part of town. The brick buildings shoot toward the sky proudly, but they've seen better days. A rat with a gnarled tail fights a squirrel over who gets to be king of the trash can.

My eyes slide over to her. "Where exactly are you taking me?"

"On a date," she answers back quickly, but she can't hide her smile, even though I can tell she's trying to.

"Uh-huh. And what are we doing on this date? Searching for the best ice cream truck in Gotham City? It's a couple blocks that way. Oh! Or are you taking me to my high school, so we can break in and re-create prom?"

"You'll see." She pulls through an alley and into a decrepit parking lot that is empty of all other cars.

Then she grabs a ginormous backpack from the trunk and ignores all of my other totally helpful date-night guesses as we climb down a rusted set of stairs that end at an even rustier set of doors attached to what I'm assuming is the basement of a factory or a warehouse or something.

Ivy pulls a crowbar from her pack, and I realize that she's about to break the lock and also that I suddenly feel tense all over.

"Holy crap, Ives, did you find out where the trafficking gang was hiding?"

She turns. Winces. "No, sorry. I was actually bringing you here to take your mind off all that."

"Oh! I mean, yeah. Good thinking. I love abandoned factories. Especially rusty ones. The rustier the better. This one looks like it's got some good ghosts living in the attic. Maybe even a couple raccoons too, and—"

"It's more than just a factory."

She smiles that sly smile again. Just as she slams the lock with her crowbar. HOT. Turns out my type is "girls who smile wickedly while wielding crowbars."

The lock falls to the ground, and I find myself getting entirely too turned on for someone standing outside a giant industrial eyesore and sweating through their tank top.

"She's a ten, but she knows her way around a crowbar," I joke.

Ivy wiggles her eyebrows at me and completely shoots off all human standards of rating scales. She's a damn fifteen, I swear it.

She pulls open the rusted door (it screeches like a dying cat), and we go inside, and then she pulls it shut behind us like she has never seen any horror movie ever. But whatever, it's cool, I follow her and the feeble light of her phone upstairs to certain doom anyway.

I can tell that the room we're in is huge—spacious, tall ceilings, painted concrete floor that spreads in every direction. But it's so dark, I still have no idea what kind of place this is. Ivy rustles around in her backpack beside me, pulling out two solar-powered lanterns that I vaguely remember seeing on her back porch this afternoon. She hands one to me and clicks a little button to turn it on.

Oh.

I raise the lantern higher, taking in the equipment around me. Huge metal hoppers and drums and vats forming a skyline. Paint peeling paper-thin in snowflakes that litter the floor.

"What is this place?" It reminds me of Ace Chemicals, only the feel is different. You know in just a glance that this place isn't sinister. Maybe it's the white ceiling striped with candy-apple red. Or the vibrant colors of the metal tanks. No industrial gray-green-yellow-beige here.

I spot heaps of white powder under some equipment in the corner. "Whoa, is that—?"

"It's flour." Ivy smirks at me. "Or confectioners' sugar. I haven't actually tried it."

I run closer. "But it's in piles like snow. Why would you ever need that much sugar?" I eye the nearest pile. "Or flour." I touch my finger to the tippy top of the powdery mountain and lick the mystery substance off. "Nope, definitely sugar."

Ivy looks horrified. "I cannot believe you just ate that."

"Well, I had to know."

"It's probably ancient."

"Still standing by my decision." I shrug cheekily.

"There could be bugs inside!"

I feign surprise. "Is that what that extra crunch was?"

"OHMYGOSH." Ivy rakes a hand down her face. "Look, I'm going to show you the rest of the place, but no more eating things off the floor."

"But what if I find a trail of macarons? Or a gravity cake? Or an entire case of Girl Scout cookies?"

Ivy narrows her eyes, but I can tell she's not really mad. "I'm going to hold your hand, just to be safe."

She laces her fingers through mine. That familiar heart-stopping, electric-jolt feeling chases through me. Thirty days and eleven hours later, and it still hasn't gone away.

"You know you're just rewarding my bad behavior?" I squeeze her hand as I say it, and my voice is no longer playful. It's soft like velvet and dark with longing.

Ivy's cheeks turn pink, and my stomach flips.

"C'mon," she says, pulling us through a series of hallways.

She stops only once, consulting a hand-drawn map tucked in her back pocket. "Almost there."

"You've been here before?"

"Mmm-hmm," she replies in a voice that hides VOLUMES.

She pushes open another deliciously creaky door, and then we're in a big open room again. Ivy lifts her lantern higher, and a jelly-bean-shaped desk and lollipop swirl of a floor and huge see-through pipes full of every candy you could ever want take shape.

"CANDY FACTORY!!!"

I yell it like a five-year-old. I can't help it. But Ivy just grins like this is exactly the reaction she was hoping for.

"I thought it would be fun to do some urban exploring

as a date, and then I found out about this abandoned candy factory, and I may have snuck in here yesterday and set up a picnic. . . ."

She lifts her lantern higher, and I realize there is a whole-ass picnic laid out in the center of the lollipop swirl. A thick celery-colored blanket. Bohemian throw pillows. A small wooden folding table, just the right height for eating on the floor. And there are plates and real cloth napkins and silverware and a candelabra and the most beautiful flowers growing through all of it. Live ones, I can tell.

"This is gorgeous." I run closer, still holding her hand. "How did you do all this? It must have taken you a million trips." A realization. "Wait, but the door was locked when we got here. How did you get in the first time?"

"Oh. Well." She hesitates, but she's proud of herself. I can see it in the set of her shoulders. "When I said *I* set up the picnic, what I really meant is that I sent some of my vines in through a second-story window."

"You did all this with plants?!"

She nods proudly.

"Wow. I mean, that is some enchanted-castle-level stuff right there." There are heart-eye emojis radiating from my pores, and Ivy can see each and every one of them, but I don't care.

We snuggle into the pillows and blankets, and Ivy removes our dinner from her backpack: fizzy water and trail mix and ants on a log because she "sucks at cooking." We talk about everything except The Dollmaker and our kiss problem while we eat. Like, it's clear we are conspicuously avoiding those subjects. It's nice, though. To have a break.

Ivy tucks her red hair behind her ears. "You ready for dessert?"

My eyes go straight to the transparent towers of candy across the room. "YES."

Ivy rolls her eyes. "Please promise me you will not eat any of that candy."

I cross my fingers behind my back. "We'll see."

She unzips a lunch-box-sized cooler and pulls out a glass bowl. "It's homemade whipped cream," she says, removing the lid. "It's one of the only things I *can* make because Dorothy taught me how when I was a kid, and once you try it, you'll never be able to eat store-bought whipped cream again."

"Ohhhh." I am intrigued. Plus, I never say no to sweets.

"And I thought . . ." She gestures toward one of the plants on the table, and it sprouts dainty white flowers that turn into full-grown strawberries in seconds.

"I am never going to get over you doing that. It's so freaking cool."

She picks the reddest, most perfect strawberry and dips it in the whipped cream. "Do you want to try one?"

She's holding the strawberry in midair, waiting for my answer.

"Oh! Oh, you mean with you feeding me the strawberry and me eating it out of your hand. Yes. Sure. Definitely. I would definitely like to try that." I think about how nice it would be if my inner monologue actually *stayed* on the inside like everyone else's.

But I don't think about it for long because Ivy's hand has already started moving toward me, and there's something so intimate—so *charged*—about the act of feeding another person. And it's not just any person feeding me—it's Ivy. And we're in the middle of a candlelit picnic in a haunted candy factory surrounded by a bevy of flowers that I swear just leaned forward in anticipation.

Her hand shakes ever so slightly as I take a bite of the strawberry. The whipped cream literally melts in my mouth, and the berry—it's tart, it's perfect, it puts every weekend farmers market strawberry to shame. I close my eyes so I can fully enjoy the out-of-body experience this dessert is making me have.

"That is the best strawberries and cream in the whole wide universe," I tell Ivy.

"Thank you." She looks down at her lap. "Also, there's something I've been wanting to ask you."

Oh? I sit up straighter. What could it be? She's already my girlfriend. "Shoot!" I say, sounding way more flippant than I feel.

Ivy does not shoot. In fact, she looks like she might be mildly hyperventilating.

"Ives?" I say it so very gently.

"Right, well, I was thinking about how much I've loved having you stay with me these past few days."

Loved. She said *loved.* Did anyone else hear her say *loved?* I know she didn't technically say she loves me, but there were undercurrents.

Ivy blushes and continues. "And then with the thing with The Dollmaker happening yesterday. I was just thinking . . . what if you move in with me for the rest of the summer? For safety. Yeah, yeah, just to be safe."

My first thought is that this is going to be the best summer ever. My second? I don't know how I feel about living in someone else's mansion all summer. I'm scared it'll give me that grimy feeling I get when I know I'm taking a handout. Ivy's mom would see it that way for sure. I don't even want to imagine their conversation when Ivy asked her.

"You don't want to," says Ivy quietly, and I realize her face has crumpled in front of me.

"No! I do! I totally do!"

"But?"

"I would love spending the entire summer with you." I don't miss how Ivy's heart clings to the word *love* the same way mine did. "But I guess I worry I'd be freeloading or something."

Ivy's face floods with relief. "Oh, no, it wouldn't be like that. Honestly, you'd be doing me a favor. I'll be super lonely in that big house all by myself while my parents are away."

I give her a hesitant smile. "Well, I don't want you to be lonely."

"Terribly, horribly, *tragically* lonely."

"And it would be really fun to live together."

"So much fun."

"And probably safer too."

"Definitely the safe decision."

The pause stretches out between us like pulled taffy.

"Yes," I finally say.

And I know it was the right decision by how my blood is singing in my veins and by how warm and happy Ivy's arms feel when she throws them around my neck.

I guess it would also make it easier to focus on the kiss problem, having round-the-clock access to Ivy's lab equipment. I pluck a strawberry from the plant in front of me and swirl it around in the whipped cream. We'll have to be extra careful, though. These past three days have been torture. Exquisite, delicious, magnificent torture, but torture all the same. Like a lavender haze I don't want to escape from.

I try not to think about that as I bring the strawberry

to Ivy's mouth. She smiles as she takes a bite, and I have to close my eyes again because it's an out-of-body experience of a different sort. I pull my hand away, only I guess I'm not as dainty and controlled as Ivy when it comes to feeding strawberries because there's a dash of whipped cream on her face, just at the corner of her lips.

I inhale sharply. I know what I want to do. What I can't do. It's impossible to look at that dot of whipped cream without imagining what it would be like to make it disappear. And I wouldn't use a napkin.

"You have some whipped cream." I touch my own lip in a mirror image to hers. My voice is raspy. Desperate. "Right there."

"Oh." Ivy's eyes widen because she can tell what I'm thinking. People two states away can tell what I'm thinking.

I crawl closer toward her on the blanket, and she leans backward but not nearly far enough.

"Harley."

Her chest is rising and falling so quickly. Her eyelashes flutter delicately. I lean closer.

"You can't kiss me."

All I can do is stare at that spot of whipped cream on her face and think about what it would taste like. Better than all the whipped cream in the bowl, that's for damn sure.

"I know," I say back.

Instead, I find reserves of strength I didn't know I had, and I move my index finger to her mouth, and I wipe the whipped cream away. It takes more strength than completing a killer vault routine.

Ivy sighs in relief. Then she grabs a napkin from the table and wipes my finger off, quick as a flash, because she knows me better than I know myself.

"I think—" I say between breaths. "I think I need to go sit on the other side of the table from you for a minute."

"Yeah, I think that's a good idea too." Ivy has her lips pressed together in one straight line, and she's gripping that napkin like she's about to tear it in half. I think I'm not the only one who almost got carried away just then.

I crawl around to the other side of the table and lie on the blanket, panting. What in the poisonous hell is wrong with me? I saw what happened to Ivy's last girlfriend (dead from a single kiss). I've performed the experiments myself (not close to a cure, not even a little bit). Why is it so hard to hold myself back from her?

I press the heels of my hands against my eyelids until I see stars. "Ivy?"

"Yes?"

I don't want to say it. I don't want to, but I have to.

"I don't know if it's a good idea for us to live together this summer."

I feel her flinch from three feet away. I've hurt her, and I hate it.

"I'm just worried about what a temptation it will be." Us living together when we can't kiss without my imminent death.

Ivy takes a long time to answer. "I know that part is hard, but—don't all the other parts make up for it?"

"Oh, they do." I rush to get the words out. "They absolutely do. I'm just frustrated with myself because I'm the one who's having such a hard time with this. I'm the one ruining things."

"Hey." Ivy leans over the table so she can look directly into my eyes. "You are not ruining this. You're not ruining anything. We are both coping with a difficult situation the best we can." Her gaze lingers on my lips. "And you're not the only one having a hard time with this."

I smile in spite of myself. "No?"

"*No.* You don't think I want to kiss you all the time? Some days it's all I can think about. Yesterday, I pruned a tree fern."

"I imagine that's a bad thing for people who love plants?"

"Terrible," Ivy shoots back.

"But." Okay, I'm not saying she wants to kiss me as much as I want to kiss her, but mayyyybe. "What about the other thing?"

Ivy blinks at me.

"The Dollmaker thing? I don't want to put you in danger."

She doesn't answer. In fact, she turns and starts digging around in her backpack, which is honestly kind of concerning.

When Ivy turns back around, she smacks a pen and a piece of paper onto the table. "Look, we may not be able to kiss, and you may have a creepy stalker who knows where I live, but we can still have a lot of fun this summer."

Oh, I like it when she gets all intense about things.

"Okay, yes," I say. But she's already scribbling something on the paper. "Is that, like, one of those relationship contracts where I have to promise to eat only fruit or something? Because vegetables make perfectly good snacks too!"

She narrows her eyes at my joke because apparently this is Serious Business.

"This," Ivy says, "is a bucket list."

"Oh!!"

I! Love! Bucket Lists!

Ivy knows this. I know she knows this. I glance down at what she's written: *Harlivy Summer Bucket List.*

"Are you in?" Ivy flings the words like a gauntlet, and I think for a second about how lucky I am. To have a girlfriend who put together an elaborate date in a place that she knew I would find absolutely captivating. Who knows just how to cheer me up when I'm having a hard time with things.

I scooch around the table next to Ivy so I can help. "Always."

Harlivy Summer Bucket List

1) Adopt a pet
2) Go to Pride
3) Find a cure so we can kiss for approximately forever
4) Find the girls. Defeat the bad guys. Save the world.
5) Liberate the hyenas at the Gotham City Zoo
6) Mani-pedis
7) Road trip!!!

What If

What if I hadn't gotten into a fight with my mom that day?

What if I had left the apartment a second later?

What if my shoelace had come undone on the stairwell and I had stopped to retie it?

What if there had been a red light that kept the black car from arriving in the street at the same time I did?

What if he had asked some other girl to get in instead of me?

What if I hadn't been angry enough to say yes?

CHAPTER 4

IVY LEANS OVER ONE OF HER ORCHIDS, SMILING AS SHE mists it with water, her head nodding along with whatever is playing in her lavender-colored headphones. She looks like she could be listening to a bop. I know better. I tap her on the shoulder and try not to snicker when she startles.

"Are you listening to another one of those cold case podcasts?"

She smiles sheepishly. "Maybe."

"You can listen to them without headphones, you know. They don't bother me. I actually kind of like picking the killers' minds apart."

Ivy looks even more sheepish. "I think they scare the plants."

I choke-cough. "The plants, huh?"

"What? I like to keep them on a steady diet of classical and Bono." She caresses one of the orchid's leaves and puts the pot back into place. "Plus, this one's extra scary. Can I tell you about it?"

"Sure." Her eyes are so bright that I can't say no. Plus, do you know how many times I've monologued to her about U.S. Women's Gymnastics Nationals and neuroscience research and how a hyena is really the ideal house pet?

She leans forward. "Have you ever heard of the Looking Glass Killer?"

"That guy who killed all his victims at tea parties?" I remember seeing something about him on TV. How he'd set up an elaborate tea party and leave shattered-mirror shards all over the place like you were supposed to peer through the empty frame and view the crime scene that way.

"Uh-huh. Only that's not the weirdest part. Forensic analysis of the crime scenes suggests that the victims actually killed *each other*."

"Wait, how is that even possible? Weren't the victims usually entire families?" I think back to a couple of the leaked crime scene photos. Scissors through the base of someone's skull next to a bowl of clotted cream. And there was one with power tools that he staged in a public park. I shudder. I don't even like to think about that one. "How would you get someone to do that to their own family?"

"I don't know. The podcast I'm listening to thinks he was controlling his victims somehow. Hypnosis, maybe. Or some kind of brainwashing. They don't have any proof, though." Ivy shivers. "I still remember when the last one happened. It was over a year ago, and I had gone to get a chai that morning, and a few hours later, they found broken mirror glass leading into the art gallery right next door."

"Ohmygosh, are you serious? It could have been happening while you were there."

"I know."

That was the creepiest thing about the murders. You

never knew where he would stage them. A park. An upscale boutique. The roof of the GCPD. He wanted to make all of Gotham City a part of the show. Everyone from the diamond district to the East End grew to dread the day they'd be living their life as usual only to find pieces of mirror glass waiting for them.

And two empty chairs around the tea party table, complete with their own table settings. Always two empty chairs. For what? Were they supposed to seem inviting?

"That last one was weird too," says Ivy. "It was just one victim, some guy, and it seemed to connect to all the other tea parties."

"Wait, seriously?"

"According to this podcast, the man was the father of two runaways, and every tea party prior to his included at least one victim who'd been working on the runaway case in some way, whether they were part of the police force tracking them down or a journalist who reported on it or whatever. And another weird thing—this was the only tea party with a written message. The victim had written the words *I'm sorry* on the tablecloth. In his own blood."

"OHMYGOSH."

"RIGHT?!"

"How does a person do all that and not get caught?"

Ivy shrugs. "No one knows what happened to him. The killer just . . . vanished."

I glance at my phone and realize that while Ivy has been regaling me with Serial Killer Story Time, I really should have been getting ready. Freaking ADHD time warp.

"Oops! Running late!" I rush back over to the main house to get dressed for my internship.

A few hours later, I'm leaning over the console and

air-kissing Ivy goodbye before I head into Arkham Asylum. I love how it feels—us sipping coffee as we drive into the city together in the mornings, her dropping me off, our schedules and lives folding into each other. We're together-together. Not just dating. We have morning rituals and habits, and I love that she starts each day with a five-minute meditation and that she uses coconut oil instead of mouthwash and even that she leaves tangles of red hair in the shower. Every day I discover something new—that she has a freckle on her left shoulder blade, that she marks her favorite parts of books by pressing flowers between the pages—and I take each new discovery and file it away like something sacred.

I watch Ivy's convertible until it zips back through the Arkham gates and out of sight. And then I enter the asylum.

It hits different than it did this past school year. First of all, there's no more Dr. Crane leading the program with his creepery and pomposity. No Scarecrow haunting the halls at night and drugging people with fear toxin. But there's also no King Shark, Talia, Riddler, Two-Face, or Joker. They escaped during Arkalamity, and they haven't been recaptured. I let out a long-suffering sigh as I pass through the security checkpoint. It feels like Arkham is going to be no fun at all this summer.

"Hey!" a voice calls from down the hallway, and I look up to see a person who actually could make interning this summer pretty cool after all.

"Shiloh!!!"

I tear down the hallway and practically tackle them, startling a couple of baby interns in the process. I can't believe I almost forgot Shiloh would be here this summer. "How's your summer going? I love your new hair! Do you want to go get coffee before the intern meeting?"

I guess it's technically only been a couple weeks since I've seen them, but also, we both got girlfriends in the past two months, so I feel like there hasn't been enough Harley-Shiloh time.

Shiloh grins and runs a hand through their newly dyed purple hair. "Hey, thanks."

I put my hands together and make the pleading face. "Also, coffee?"

"I feel like an enabler."

"Pleeeeease."

Shiloh rolls their eyes. "I guess, but you should really see someone about—"

"I'll take it!" I grab their arm and start power walking in the direction of the staff cafeteria.

Shiloh stops, and my arm jerks backward. I turn, confused.

"I thought you said yes."

Their eyes dart toward the intersection of hallways up ahead. "I did, but we should take the back way."

"Uh-uh. This way's faster."

"Yeah, but there's something I really need to do on the—"

"We can do it after the intern meeting! We'll be late if we take the back way AND stop for coffee. And I don't know about you, but—"

SMACK.

I smell Winfield before I see him. That should give you an idea of just how thoroughly my body crashed into his when we rounded that corner. It occurs to me that this is why Shiloh wanted to take the back way.

I peel myself away from Winfield's ocean breeze-y polo and try to extricate my limbs as gracefully as possible.

"Hiya!" I say, putting on the biggest, fakest smile you have ever seen.

"Hi," replies Winfield in this deep, husky voice that suggests he has been handling our breakup with lots of brooding and possibly some emo poetry.

I tone down the smile a bit. "How are you doing?"

"I'm good, yeah. I'm working on my secondary essays for med school right now. They haven't asked for them yet, but I wanted to prewrite as many as I can. And other than that, yeah, just interning and living at the house this summer. Hey, are you living at Alpha Nu?"

No, no, no, no, no. Of all the possible questions. My stomach drops. My mouth goes so dry I can barely open it.

The pause gives me away before I even say it. Winfield looks like he would trade a kidney to retract his question.

"I'm staying with Ivy this summer," I finally say.

Hi there, open breakup wound, I'd like to introduce you to a metric ass-load of salt. The words hang between us like a betrayal, even though I haven't done anything wrong.

"Of course you are," he chokes out.

I open my mouth to say something back—I don't even know what—when Shiloh, patron saint of awkward girls everywhere, grabs me by the arm and says, "So-sorry-gotta-get-coffee-running-late!"

"See you, Win. Have a good day," I say by way of apology as Shiloh whisks me away.

"Bye, Harleen."

I don't bother telling him I go by Harley now, because (A) that would involve remaining in this woefully awkward situation for additional seconds, and (B) I'm still not totally sure if I should change my name at work yet. People are already weird enough about my ghostly skin and Technicolor hair.

"Have a good day?" Shiloh repeats, elbowing me in the ribs.

"You try telling your golden retriever ex-boyfriend that you're living with the girl of your dreams."

"And while we're on the subject, why didn't I know you're living with Ivy?" Shiloh pretends to be mortally offended. Even the flamingos on their button-down appear to be judging me.

"It was just decided! And it's amazing," I squeal.

Shiloh squeals too, and then we order our coffees, and I spill every last detail about Ivy and our candy-factory date. "She's so wonderful. Like, it almost feels weird to be this happy."

There's this part of you, when you grow up the way I did, that can't help feeling uneasy during the good times. Like they're just a temporary place you get to visit before the other shoe drops.

"That's really cool," says Shiloh.

Our lattes still aren't ready, so I ask what they've been up to lately. Ultrarunning, it turns out. (That's, like, running for people who think a marathon is a nice jaunt. Like, one hundred straight miles of running. Running to the *n*th power.)

"Do you think you could run all the way to Metropolis? Also, how do you eat? And sleep? And, like, poop?"

Shiloh answers all these questions and more, chest puffed up on their skinny frame. Wiry frame, though. All hidden muscles and tendon strength.

"I never realized you were such a jock," I say.

And Shiloh grins, pleased. "It's really challenging. But fun at the same time, you know? And kind of complicated, too, when you factor in having to have a support team for each run."

"I would be SO good at being on your support team! I could tape little messages of encouragement to your protein bars. Oh! And we could get shirts with your face on them!" (I will never forget how it made me feel when the Reckoning showed up with those at my gymnastics meet last year.)

They laugh. "That would be great. Especially because last time, I . . . didn't have as many people as I thought."

There's something about the way their voice dipped on the word *people*. "You still seeing Natalie?"

They sigh, one big whoosh that expels all the air in their body. "Yep."

"That good, huh?"

"No, she's great. It's just complicated, you know? She doesn't want to be exclusive, and I get that."

"She still going on dates with her boyfriend?"

"*Ex*-boyfriend."

"And she's the one who bailed on your ultrarunning thing, right?"

Shiloh's shrug and lack of eye contact tells me everything I need to know.

"When are we getting rid of her?"

"Hey!"

I throw up my hands. "I'm sorry. I'm sorry. I just think you deserve better than a situationship with a girl who doesn't show up for you."

"Harley . . ."

"I'll stop, I swear. I know I can be annoying about this, so instead of stealing your phone and using it to kick Miss High

Infidelity to the curb, I'll just say this: You're one of the most amazing people I know. I hope you end up with someone who sees that and appreciates you and would scream themselves hoarse at your races."

"Thanks," Shiloh says softly. They smile, and I feel a million times better knowing I might have made them feel even just a little bit better.

That is, until Graham appears next to us. Graham always gets Shiloh's pronouns wrong, and I swear the guy does it on purpose.

"Ugh, does he still intern here?" I say to Shiloh, not at all quietly.

Graham's ears turn red, but he pretends he doesn't see us.

Last fall, Graham and a bunch of the other interns used to talk crap about me because there was a rumor I'd slept with a professor. This summer, they're terrified of me.

Or impressed. Honestly, it's hard to say, and I'll accept either coming from them. I was never technically arrested for the events of Arkalamity this January—the security camera footage of Talia with a knife to my throat made me look innocent enough. And besides, Dr. Crane was the main person who knew about my involvement, and when he got arrested, the secrets went with him. Anything he might have tried to say about me would have looked like he was retaliating on a whistleblower.

Our coffees are ready, thankfully, so we leave Graham in the transphobic dust.

We find ourselves walking down a hallway alone, and Shiloh lowers their voice. "Hey, what's going on with that guy sending you those dolls last semester? I can go with you to check your mailbox if you want."

"Still no leads," I say, fretting with the sleeve of my coffee cup. "And. He knows I'm at Ivy's."

I explain about the most recent doll, about The Dollmaker's promise to take something from me, about how I wish I could predict what he was going to do next.

I'm still thinking about it later that week as I get off the shuttle at Arkham Acres. The longer I go without solving this, the more anxious I feel. We pretty much tore apart Ivy's room after we got The Dollmaker's message. And I don't really own anything that wasn't there. Maybe he was just threatening to take something so I'd stress over trying to figure out what it was?

I try to shake the thought away because I'm here to visit Remy and Stella, and I want to be in the right frame of mind for that. I see Remy across the rec room doing some kind of powdery craft project at a table by the window, pink hair shining in the sunlight.

"Whatcha doing?" I ask, plopping down beside her.

"Harley!" Her eyes light up when she sees me. "I'm making bath bombs. Wanna help?"

"Is there glitter involved?"

"Yes."

"Then always."

Remy shows me how to mix the baking soda, citric acid powder, Epsom salt, and cornstarch. We pick scents carefully because Remy wants to make a signature bath bomb for each of the girls on her floor. We debate the merits of lavender, campfire, eucalyptus, magnolia.

"What about Stella? I'm feeling toasted marshmallow," I say.

"Definitely toasted marshmallow," Remy replies, picking up the brown glass bottle and taking a sniff.

"Hey, where is Stella today, anyway?" I scoop up some of the mixture and clamp the two halves of the metal bath-bomb sphere shut, which is so not as easy as it sounds.

"Oh, her family came to visit her today."

"Aw, I'm sorry I missed her." It's been a few weeks because of finals. I wish I could have gotten over here sooner.

I decide to shoot Stella's mom a text:

> Harley: Hey, I know y'all probably want to spend every minute with Stella but let me know if she wants a friend to hang out with.

I scroll through my texts until I find Jasmin's name. It's been a while since I texted her or the Reckoning Secure Chat. I glance at Remy, but she's still up to her elbows in bath bombs, so I dash out a text to Jasmin, quick, like ripping off a bandage, before I can second-guess myself. I send almost the same one to the Reckoning Secure Chat. All the messages on both for the last few months are from me. But I try not to let it hurt me too much. It's possible Bianca is still in Santa Prisca for her experimental treatment. I just wish I knew.

"Do you want to make one for Ivy?" asks Remy, and I tuck my phone under my leg, fast.

"Definitely!"

Remy and I sniff all the vials of essential oils that make us think of plants, ultimately going with orange blossom, ginger, and a hint of grass.

I inhale until I'm dizzy. "Mmmm. Ivy is going to love this."

We make it pale green with peach sparkles, and then we make a whole bunch of other ones, and Remy's voice grows brighter, and she talks more and more the longer I sit next to her. I know that's the whole point of my visits—to see how she and Stella are, to spend time with them. But today I can't help but feel like she's helping me as much as I'm helping her. I'm so grateful to Remy for keeping my mind off Jasmin and Bianca and The Dollmaker and what he took. It feels like having eighty billion pounds of weight off me.

But as I'm hugging Remy bye and walking down the corridor to the front of Arkham Acres, I pick the weight back up, think about him again.

I've given you so many gifts, and I haven't received anything in return. Maybe it's time I take something of yours.

What could it be? The receptionist (Gary, with the lumberjack beard) says goodbye as I walk past, and I wave back. Pretty much everyone knows me here now (and luckily, no one ever found out I stole that nurse's list).

As I'm waiting for the shuttle, Mrs. Watkins texts back:

> Mrs. Watkins: I'm sure she'd love to see you.
> But Stella's not with us right now.
>
> Mrs. Watkins: She's still at Arkham Acres.

The Taking

It's not like being mugged.

You go with The Dollmaker because you want to. Trying so hard to run away from something that you don't realize what you're running toward.

He told me: You're so beautiful.

And his eyes weren't the kind they warn you about.

He said: I'm an artist. Would you like to come with me and be the subject of my next piece? I'd pay you.

I felt like he could see something inside me that I didn't have the confidence or imagination to see myself.

I felt like a model. Being scouted and whisked away in a fancy car.

Like a princess. When he took me to this factory-looking place called the Tower and said I was getting all new clothes. That I could live there the whole time until the piece was finished. The car ride wasn't terribly long, and something about still being in Gotham City made me feel safer. So I said yes.

He said I had to throw away all my old clothes, my phone, my old everything. Which I thought was weird, but he said it was better for the art. Like a kind of method acting.

He didn't even try to stay in the room when I changed into the new clothes—white cotton pants and a white tank top (a blank canvas). He wasn't the kind of man they warn you about.

He was so much worse.

CHAPTER 5

I RUN BACK INSIDE TO THE FRONT DESK. LUMBERJACK GARY is on a call with a phone that looks like it's straight out of the seventies. C'mon, c'mon, c'mon. I tap my gold-tipped finger-nails on the counter between us, and he makes a pinched face but continues his phone call.

"No, I'm sorry, staff can't accept spirits as gifts. Yes, Tues-days are fine."

After several seconds (minutes? millennia?), Gary places the phone back in its cradle and turns his attention to me.

"Can I help you, Harleen?"

"Who came to visit Stella Watkins?" The words burst out in one breath.

Gary consults some sort of record, typing things into an antiquated computer system. His hands are not moving nearly fast enough.

And I have the worst kind of feeling, like a moment's delay will change her fate.

His mouth finally opens. "Here we go. Stella's uncle came to visit her—he should still be here. Let me just— Ah."

I lean over the counter. *"What?"*

"The system just crashed." He smiles apologetically.

"Noooo." I rake my hand down my face.

"I'm rebooting it now," he says. "What is it you're concerned about?"

"I just—" I sigh. I can't bring myself to say it. Because I'm worried it sounds ridiculous? Because I'm scared if I say it it'll become real?

"I'm worried," I finally say. "Stella's not here, and Remy said she was visited by family, and Stella's mom didn't know about it when I texted her."

Gary's head snaps up. "You're certain?"

I nod, and his fingers fly. This is the kind of action we need right now. Machine-gun typing only, Gary.

Gary's brows suddenly scrunch together. "Weird, it's like the system changed, and now she's showing as checked out. But I know I didn't enter that."

In response, I take off running down the hallway.

"He's on the approved visitor list," Gary calls after me.

I sprint the entire way to the rec room, dodging an orderly who calls out, *"Hey!"* as I pass. I skid to a stop in front of Remy.

"Did you see Stella's uncle check her out? Was it a man you've seen before?" I grab on to the table, chest heaving, waiting for her answer.

Remy seems puzzled by my intensity. "No, he just stopped by our room, and I told him she was outside. But I've only met her uncle a couple of times anyway. I figured maybe he got a haircut or something."

Not a good sign. Not a good sign at all.

"Is there anything else you remember about him?" Like that he was a whole different person??

Remy bites her lip. Tilts her head to the side. "Yeah. There was something strange," she says after a second.

Strange like he gave off serial killer vibes?

Remy glances in the direction of their dormitory. "He brought her a doll, but he left it on her bed. I remember thinking it was weird that he didn't take it to give to Stella himself."

My heart falls through the floor and plummets all the way to the subbasement. It's him. He was here.

Maybe it's time I take something of yours.

I want to fall apart, but it's important to stay strong for Stella right now.

"Show me the doll."

The Trials

He wants to know how fast you can run and swim and climb. How smart you are. If you have any special talents or abilities.

He measures your height and weight and the length of your limbs and takes X-rays and dental scans and a million photographs.

It felt like trying out for a sports team at school. Or auditioning for a talent show.

He wasn't mean when he held me underwater and asked me to squeeze his wrist when I couldn't take it anymore. He always spoke in the most refined voice, even when he asked me to go into the walk-in fridge without a jacket and see if I could make it longer than the last girl.

I knew to be wary by the way the other girls avoided his eyes. By the way they hushed when he entered a room. And whispered after he left.

But one day, I just couldn't help myself. He wanted to see how well I could handle an electric shock, and I asked what in the world that had to do with being a model or an art piece or whatever. He said it made him sad that I didn't trust his creative vision.

And that night when we filed into the dining hall for dinner, the other girls' plates had pork chops and potatoes. Mine was empty. It stayed that way for the next two days.

"Let me guess," whispered the girl next to me, Londyn, a tall girl with dark skin and curly, natural hair. "You asked a question."

I glanced around to make sure the guards weren't looking and then nodded.

She passed me an understanding smile. "It happened to me my first week too."

I watched the other girls at the table mentally file the information away so they wouldn't make the same mistake. And later that night, when I went to put on my nightgown, there was half a baked potato inside. "We have to stick together," Londyn whispered to the mirror as we brushed our teeth. A train whistled in the distance, and I nodded.

This was in the early days, when we were the first girls to live in the Tower, back when it was just girls and there were only eight of us.

The Alices. And the rest.

The Alices kept to themselves, sat at their own table, just the two of them. But the six of us were thick as thieves. *Do you want this extra roll I stole at lunch?* and *Here, let me help you bandage that* and *What was your life like before?* and *Don't you think it's weird that he keeps the Alices separate?* and *What do you think they do all day? Have you ever seen the other one, his partner? Did he burn your skin too to see how fast it would heal? Why do you think he's doing all these tests?*

And most of all: *What do you think's going to happen to us?*

Maybe you'd be more scared. Maybe you'd even try to escape. But we weren't, and we didn't. For a lot (all?) of us, it was better than where we'd come from.

But then we didn't know what was next.

CHAPTER 6

REMY FUMBLES WITH THE DOORKNOB, AND I STEEL MYSELF for what I know is lurking behind that door. I need to see what he's planning to do to Stella, and I'm terrified at the same time.

> I discovered the most intriguing girl in a back alley yesterday. I already have ideas for how to transform her.

> I'm creating something entirely new. I'm breaking the very idea of what art can be.

> Two of my pieces weren't working this week, and I had to completely discard them.

> Tonight I tried something with one of my pieces. The end result gave me chills, and even though she only lasted for a few days, I knew I had to explore that idea some more.

His designs have been getting more horrific by the week. More daring with each iteration that survives.

Remy turns the handle. The door creaks open. And there, on Stella's bed, is a doll that looks eerily like her—in some ways. Light brown hair and freckles and birdlike shoulders. Wearing a pair of wide-leg jeans and a lightweight sweater and a silver bracelet like the one Stella always wears. His thoroughness is unnerving.

And then there are the modifications.

I want to look away, but I force myself to bear witness to his grotesque creation. Claws and fangs and slits for pupils. And a nose that isn't even a nose anymore—more of a snout. She's a wolf-girl, I realize as I move around strands of her hair and find furry, pointed ears.

I run my fingers over the modifications and try not to throw up. When is he going to start doing this to her? Has he already begun? I gulp down a sob. Whatever he does to her is my fault. He took her because of me, which means she wouldn't have even been on his radar if I hadn't gone searching for him. Stella is more than just my friend. With me filling the blank space Bernice left, Stella has started to feel more like a sister. Who lets something like this happen to their sister? If Mrs. Watkins knew—

Don't think about that.

The guilt will swallow you whole, and you won't be able to help anyone with anything.

Think about how you're going to fix this. Focus on what you're going to do to help. There's a reason you know deep down you'll never be able to go back to being Harleen again. And the reason is people like him.

I take a deep breath and turn the doll over to see if there's a bushy tail, but instead find the tail of a scorpion, huge and sharp with a tiny scrap of a note staked onto the point.

She'll do.

There's a white envelope resting innocently on the bed next to where the doll was sitting, and I pick it up and tear it open and fight back the nausea as I read.

Dear Harley,

I've been agonizing over how to remake her. She isn't singing to me the way they usually do, but maybe I could make her sing. Please don't worry. This is just a mock-up. I think I'm stumped on this one because it's so important that she be special. This time, I intend for her to be more than just an art piece. She's going to be a present.

For you.

Of course, it's possible you don't want her to be changed (though I can't imagine why a friend wouldn't want another friend to become transcendent). Or perhaps you have your own ideas on what she should become. I'd love to hear them. I could teach you how to do it, you know. You could design them with me.

I think it's time we arrange a meeting.

Tomorrow.

I'll send further instructions.

I'm able to leave Remy in the hands of one of the staff psychologists (one of the ones I really like), and as soon as I'm sure she's going to be okay, I rush back to the front desk, where Gary is pulling up security footage.

"I found this doll on her bed," I tell him, placing the doll on his desk. I do not mention the letter burning a hole in my pocket.

He can't help but recoil at the sight of the doll.

Then two nurses and a staff psychologist rush between us, and I might as well be a ghost.

"I already called the police. But look," he tells them, rolling to the side in his chair so they have room to see his monitor. I take a step backward. Pretend to be texting. If that one nurse could just. Move. Her. Shoulder.

There.

There are multiple video windows pulled up.

"This is the guy who took her." He clicks Play on the first one. "I wasn't on duty yet, so I never saw him."

They watch a clip of the front desk as a woman, one of the other administrative assistants, sits there going about her workday. The lighting in the room is different than it is now. It must have been a lot earlier.

And then a man in a collared shirt and khaki pants enters, his hat pulled so low that I can't get a good view of his face. In his left hand is one of those canvas grocery bags. He pauses to talk to the woman at the desk. Makes her laugh as she helps him fill out some paperwork. He tips his hat as he leaves, and then he walks out of the camera frame.

The little cluster of them is watching so intently that they don't register me craning my neck to get a better look. Gary moves to the next video. The Dollmaker walks down the hallway to Remy and Stella's room. He pulls a doll from the canvas bag and stuffs the bag in a trash can.

And the next video. He's saying something to Remy, and she's saying something back and pointing. He nods and leaves the doll on Stella's bed.

Gary clears his throat. "This is when it happens."

I take a step forward. I don't care that I'm risking them seeing me. I need to see it happen. Because I don't care how charming this guy is—I just don't believe Stella would go with him willingly.

Gary clicks Play.

Stella is sitting on a bench under a tree, reading a book in the dappled sunlight. Her small smile has no idea what's about to happen to her. She's in the bottom right corner of the video. The rest of the yard is filled with half a dozen other Arkham Acres patients and staff. How in the world? The Dollmaker crosses into the frame. Walks down to that one small corner of the video. He and Stella are mostly obscured by bushes from the rest of the people in the yard. He waves and says something to her, but unlike Remy and the receptionist, her posture goes rigid.

He sits down next to her. She startles and closes her book. He keeps talking, and she keeps scooting away from him, the balls of her feet pressed against the grass like she's readying herself to leap up at any moment. His smooth talking isn't working on her.

He fans himself with his hat, a distraction, as his other hand reaches into his pocket.

He knows.

C'mon, Stella. There's staff just on the other side of those bushes. You can do this.

She tries. And he fires something that looks like a miniature crossbow just as Stella hops up from the bench. Instead of darting away to safety, she crumples to the ground. He puts his hat back on and drags her behind a tree before anyone notices.

I wait, but nothing else happens.

"Is that it?" the psychologist asks Gary.

"No, hang on." He puts the video at quadruple speed, and at first, it's still largely the same, but then one of the staff members supervising the yard puts their hands to their mouth, calling out something, and people start zooming inside. Gary restores the video to regular speed, and the people return to walking at a normal pace, leaving the yard one by one by one.

When it's empty, The Dollmaker emerges from his hiding place. He throws Stella over his shoulder and carries her out through the gate.

The Six

Londyn, nineteen, our leader. Gorgeous and talented, with coltish legs and cheekbones for days, the only one of us with actual singing and modeling experience. When he recruited her after an open mic night at a dive bar in the Bowery, she thought she was making her big break, that this could be her ticket out.

Cecelia, sixteen, honestly too sweet to be here. I know she used to live in an abandoned building and run with a pack of other kids who had dropped out of that hellhole of a high school down by the docks, but it's still hard to believe. She sings while she makes her bed and smiles like it's a pastime. Like she's the princess in one of those cartoons and all the squirrels and sparrows are her friends.

Jett, seventeen, a thief and a good one. Doesn't talk much. Midnight hair. Midnight heart to match. Don't accidentally sit in her chair at breakfast. Don't rub her wrong/look at her wrong/breathe wrong. Sometimes I wonder what happened to her to make her this hard.

Fallon, six at the time he took her, the youngest person here by far. He found her hiding under a pier in Gotham Harbor. She barely speaks. Is practically feral. But she has huge brown eyes that draw you in. Make you want to help her. Londyn has taken to tucking her in at night, and Cecelia and I braid her ginger hair and dote on her like a little sister.

Angel, seventeen, a runaway with a waiflike frame and a wicked sense of humor. Shaggy bleach-blond hair with an inch of dark roots. I bet she lived entirely in black concert T-shirts on the outside. I can picture her sneaking into bars and music festivals. Pocketing liquid black eyeliner at the makeup store.

And me, Everly, a fifteen-year-old girl from the East End with a sociopathic, codependent mom who can't keep an apartment but sure knows how to keep a string of bad boyfriends. I should have known this was too good to be true by how painfully ordinary I am. But everyone wants to believe they've secretly got main-character energy on the inside, somewhere, and then something will happen, and everyone will see, everyone will know, that you were meant to be more.

CHAPTER 7

MRS. WATKINS SOBS INTO MY SHOULDER AS THE POLICE OF-
ficer across from us takes a slow sip of his coffee. His desk is
piled with papers, and his eyelids are piled with exhaustion,
and he is going to do nothing for us. I can feel it.

"Tell me again what the individual looks like," he says
without actually looking away from his monitor.

I really hope Montoya gets back soon.

"Brown hair. Blue eyes. Freckles. Same height as me,
maybe shorter." This is a waste of my time. They're not going
to be able to find her. They never did anything about Dr.
Nelson until we took matters into our own hands. Until it
was already too late.

Mrs. Watkins pulls her head up from my shoulder so
she can dig through her purse. "Here." She slides something
across the desk. A photo. "It was taken a couple years ago,
but it still looks like her."

"Thank you," says the officer, placing the photo to the
side, like maybe he'll use it or maybe he'll accidentally put
his coffee cup on it and forget it's there.

"Is it possible this is related to the other girls who have disappeared?" I ask him.

(I know it is, but if Mrs. Watkins knew what I know, she wouldn't be able to sleep tonight or any other night.)

"What girls?" He raises his bushy eyebrows in a way that suggests he genuinely doesn't have a clue.

Wow. This is even more hopeless than I thought. A couple desks behind him, there are posters of uncaught criminals lining the wall—King Shark, The Joker, Talia al Ghūl, the Looking Glass Killer (no picture for that one)—and it makes me want to give up, but I try to explain anyway.

"Girls in the East End have been disappearing lately. Like, more than usual. And other girls too."

"We tend to see a high number of disappearances from the bad parts of the city," he says in this exhausted freaking voice.

"What about a . . . gang taking girls? Have you heard anything about that?" I narrowly avoid saying the word *trafficking* in front of Stella's mom, but only just.

"I don't know what you're talking about."

I sigh. Deeply. Apparently, he takes this as a judgment. (Possibly the first perceptive move on his part?)

"Miss, if you could just—"

You know what, we're done here. "I need to talk to Montoya," I say sharply. I don't care if she's still not here. I'll sit in front of an empty desk.

The burnt-out officer looks only too happy to comply. He drops us in front of Montoya's (non-empty!!) desk with a not-my-circus, not-my-monkeys kind of shrug.

Officer Montoya's eyes may not be bright and hopeful, but they're a hell of a lot more alert than that last guy's. Plus, she has the wherewithal and empathy to get Stella's mom a cup of tea. Montoya lingers on Mrs. Watkins's face as she passes her the steaming paper cup.

"You look familiar," she says.

"This is Mrs. Watkins," I say by way of introduction. I know exactly where Montoya knows her from. "Her daughter Stella has been abducted."

Montoya's eyebrows twitch at the name Watkins, and I nod as if to say, *Yes, in fact, this is the mother of my girlfriend from last year, the one who tried to kill our professor and was put away for it.*

"Ah," says Montoya. She's good with the words, this one.

"Remember what I told you about? A few months ago. About the girls being kidnapped?" I glance at Mrs. Watkins and really hope Montoya gets the message. "I think this has to do with that."

Montoya frowns. "Why do you think that?"

I take a deep breath. How to do this without letting her know I totally lied when I said I'd leave it to the police. That I've been searching for the trafficking gang ever since. "He or they or whoever, I've heard they're taking girls and making them different. Turning them into dolls. People have been calling him The Dollmaker."

I do not mention the fact that he has been sending me dolls for the last two to three months. I don't want to implicate myself. Not that it matters. Officer Montoya narrows her eyes at me like I am guilty as sin.

"And how do you know all this?"

"I'm smart that way? It's a hunch?" Why can't anyone ever believe I'm some good-girl detective like Nancy Drew? Is it that unthinkable? Apparently, it is, because Montoya continues to stare right through me like I'm made of pure malevolence. I sigh. "Look, just ask around about The Doll-maker, okay?"

Officer Montoya reluctantly agrees, but her eyes still say I'm guilty.

"Do you think you know who did this, Harleen?" Mrs. Watkins pipes in, and Montoya and I jump. It's not that I forgot she was there, I just . . . overlooked it?

I wince. "It's just a lead. I wish I had more."

She nods in a way that breaks my heart.

"Montoya is the best," I say. "She'll find Stella."

And if she doesn't, I will.

My words seem to give Mrs. Watkins hope, though, because now she's sitting up straighter and wiping her eyes, and she's thinking things. I can see it.

"And someone probably saw something," she says hopefully. "We could issue one of those alerts. A Violet Alert."

Now Montoya is the one wincing. "I'm really sorry, ma'am, but I can't issue a child-abduction alert, because Stella is twenty-two years old. I assure you, though, I will do everything I can."

"Well, except issue a Violet Alert." I don't try to keep the snap out of my voice.

"Harleen." Montoya goes on to spend several minutes pledging the devotion of Gotham City's finest to Stella's case, but I'm already over it. I said people like The Doll-maker were the reason I could never go back to being Harleen, but there's a second reason. Bureaucracy and politics and BS protocols and apathy. I don't have time for things like that. Neither does Stella or any of the other people I'm going to save. And I guess I could try to fight the bureau-

cracy, but I'd much rather fight the bad guys, which brings me to the third reason I'm going to keep being Harley for the rest of my life: *I just want to.*

The police are going to be exactly as ineffective as I expected. It's all the motivation I need.

I am going to that meeting with The Dollmaker tomorrow.

I Didn't Throw Everything Away

I had a rainbow scrunchie in my hair when he took me. And I used to love to write—little stories and poems and things.

So, I tucked those two pieces of the old me into the air vent in our room. The scrunchie and a journal I pocketed from one of the classrooms here.

It became harder for me to write. After the Calming. Mr. Tetch saw to that. But sometimes there are lapses, and the lapses are when I pull my journal out of that air vent and hide in the bathroom and write everything my heart and brain and fingers can remember.

It's dangerous. Londyn says it's reckless. Jett says it's stupid. But I like to think this small act of rebellion keeps the old me alive.

CHAPTER 8

IVY HOLDS THE LETTER FROM THE DOLLMAKER THE WAY you would an active grenade.

"I don't want you to go," she says quietly. "Do you have to go?"

A ficus tree bends close in the conservatory behind her, almost like it's trying to give her a hug.

I can imagine exactly how much I wouldn't want her going if the roles were reversed.

"He's got Stella," I say by way of apology or explanation, maybe both. He took my friend, and he wouldn't have gone anywhere near her if he didn't have some sick obsession with me. It's my fault that Stella got taken. So, it's my responsibility to fix things.

I've already filled Ivy in on everything that happened at Arkham Acres and everything that didn't happen at the police station after. She crosses the room and holds me tight and sighs.

"I know why you have to do it. But I still hate it."

I hug her back for a few more moments and wonder if

now might be a good time for the Other Thing I need to tell her. There's a piece of my identity I need to be honest about. I know I don't have it all figured out yet, and I originally wanted to wait until I did, but after what happened with Stella, it feels important to tell Ivy now. Immediately.

"Hey, Ivy?" I take a step back.

"Mmm-hmm?"

"There's something else I need to tell you."

"What is it?" Her eyes move over me like there are clues safety-pinned to my leather jacket or braided into my hair, and if she only looks hard enough, she'll find them. She's not exactly wrong.

This is going to be fine. It's all going to be just fine. Right? I mean, Ivy is my girlfriend. She asked me to live with her and everything. Finding out something like this isn't going to change the way she feels about me.

I hope.

"Harley?" She touches my shoulder. "Hey, look, I know I'm a little freaked out about this Dollmaker meeting, but you can tell me anything, I swear."

Her green eyes are so open. Her *heart* is so open. Always has been.

Welp, that's all the encouragement I needed. I fold my hands together like I'm about to recite a poem or attempt to take first place at a spelling bee.

"Soooo, I know I said I want to be a psychiatrist when I grow up, and I still totally do, but also, I think I'm the kind of person who wears a costume at night and smashes bad guys with a bat. I'm still figuring out exactly what this means for the rest of my life, but . . . are you cool with that?"

Ivy blinks up at me, trying to appear unfazed even though she is definitely a little bit fazed. "You mean like a superhero?"

"Mmm, give or take."

"Okay," she says, like that's it. It's been decided.

What the heck kind of answer is "okay"? It tells me absolutely nothing about what she's thinking, feeling. If she's planning on breaking up with me and turning me out of her estate. I wait on pins and needles, daggers and switchblades, for her to tell me something—anything—else.

But when she finally opens her mouth, she's all, "Yeah. Can you just—? I'll be right back."

AND SHE LEAVES.

Who just waltzes out after you tell them a big life thing like that? Oh crap, this is bad. Ivy has fled. Probably to the Tuscan villa. Should I collect my things? Wait for one of the staff to come escort me off the premises? Text her that I was just kidding?

I turn to Bernie (he told me he's happiest in the conservatory, and who am I to argue with a taxidermized beaver?). "What do you think? Is she leaving me for sure?"

He stares at me with those shiny, judgmental eyes.

"Well, you don't have to be rude about it," I snap, crossing my arms. I know when I've been insulted.

"Harley?" Ivy peeks back into the door of the greenhouse.

"Hey!" She's back! She has not, in fact, fled!

"Were you talking to somebody?" she asks.

"No!" I answer, cool as you please. "Just, like, thinking aloud."

Technically not the truth, but look, one big life reveal is enough for tonight. And speaking of reveals . . .

"Ives, is there a reason you're hiding behind the door?"

"Ye-es." She says it like it's two syllables, and her face and neck turn the color of cayenne peppers and tomatoes and rose petals.

When she's sweetly chagrined, it's just her cheeks. When she's well and truly mortified, her entire upper torso blushes.

"I need to show you something," she calls across the greenhouse.

"Okaaaayyyyy." I start walking over to her, when—

"Stop!"

I stop.

"Close your eyes!" she tells me. I (mostly) do. "And don't peek!"

(You can't say she doesn't know me.)

"One sec." I slide over to the shelving area where she keeps the bamboo stakes and tomato cages and jars of water charged under the full moon. I pick up one of the fabric strips she uses to attach delicate plants to their stakes. And I tie it around my eyes. "Okay? I promise I can't see anything." (Actually true.)

"Yup, just stay right there!"

I can hear her footsteps coming closer, closer. I know when she's right in front of me because I can smell peaches and cherries and grass. And because I can feel her somehow. Like electricity. The current strengthens as she moves her hands up toward my face. As her fingers brush against my hair.

She unties the blindfold.

And I open my eyes.

HOLY EFFING FIT CHECK.

Ivy bursts into giggles. "What did you just say?"

Oh, so that was out loud. Cool. Cool. It's honestly a wonder my brain hasn't exploded. She is wearing—whoa. Take a deep breath, Harley. Nope, not too deep. You'll pass out.

She is wearing leafy green fishnets and some mesmerizing piece of clothing that couldn't decide if it wanted to be a corset or a swimsuit or a cropped military jacket, so it decided to slay at being all three. Also the coolest eyeliner ever. And lip gloss that begs to be kissed. And high heels so red, they're almost maroon. And her hair is maroon, and her lips are maroon, and I want to do maroon things to her, so help me. I picture how it would all unfold—it comes to my mind in flashes. My hands in her hair, her nails down my back, her lips against mine. I can barely contain myself.

"You—you look—"

"Do you like it?" She does not hide her smile. Her queenly, triumphant smile. Oh, she knows. SHE KNOWS. She has every idea of exactly how good she looks in this costume or whatever the eff it is.

"YES." I'm no better than a man. I'm no better than a man. Holy smoke show, what the ever-loving glow-up. "Yes, are you kidding me? This is the best thing I've ever seen. When did you do this? How are you this hot? Also, sorry about the way I'm staring at you. Also, please tell me everything about why you did this."

Ivy blushes, the sweet kind this time. And she passes me a green leather-bound book that looks like a burn book had a baby with an ancient tome full of elf secrets.

"This is so cool-looking! What is it?" I hope it means we're going on a quest.

She bites her lip.

"It. Is. A forty-seven-point manifesto for how I'm going to save the environment, starting with Gotham City." She hovers nervously as I open it. She has handed me her entire heart with this book, I realize.

It makes me feel important. Special.

"I'm honored that you would share this with me." I start turning pages and find plans for public transportation incentives and stricter pollution policies for big businesses and creating an urban tree canopy and establishing a citywide composting program because food waste creates 8 percent of greenhouse gases. "Also, holy crap, Ives, this is amazing. You're a mastermind. You know that, right?"

She could not be more pleased. "Thank you."

The more I read, the more of a genius I realize my girlfriend is. She's so passionate. And driven. And organized. I wish I was like that.

"Is something wrong?" asks Ivy.

"Oh. No, this book is perfect, and you're perfect." I frown. "I just wish I had more of a concrete idea of what I want to do with my life now that I've decided to go full Harley."

"Aww." Ivy closes the book and takes my hands. "I'm sure you'll know once you have time to think about it."

It's kind of her to say. But . . .

"I don't know, does 'Be gay. Do crime' count as a life plan?"

"It totally counts as a life plan!" says the girl with the forty-seven-point manifesto.

And there's a part of me that still feels a little envious of my girlfriend. She knows exactly what she wants, and she's going after it with the gusto of a particularly invasive species of plant. I want to know what that feels like.

But underneath that, I'm so happy. I just confessed to her that I want to be a vigilante, and she came back wearing a full-on goddess of poison ivy costume.

We're in this together now, like two villainous little peas in a pod. Whatever happens, we'll always be in it together.

The Metamorphosis

Jett went first. She went into the surgical room and came back with one eye silver-gray and half the hair on the right side of her head shaved off. She said she had a prosthetic eye now. And some kind of special cochlear implant. That she could see like an owl or an eagle or a mantis shrimp. Hear like a wax moth. Watch a butterfly land on a flower two miles away and listen as its wings fluttered to a stop. See infrared and X-ray and who knows what else. She'd be able to walk tightropes in the dark now and sneak past whole teams of security at banks and museums. He had told her so. Is this what he was doing? Is this what making art meant? It honestly didn't seem so bad. I whispered to Londyn that we could get through the Metamorphosis if this sort of butterfly was the end result.

But then Angel. Angel was the first time I thought about escaping. He bolted/soldered/something-ed wings to her spine and told her to fly down from the roof of the Tower. He had us watch from the lawn below. It was supposed to be a triumph—when Angel soared down and landed in front of us. Instead, she fell. And she didn't get back up.

Next, Cecelia. I don't know what happened to her. But I know I could hear her screams from clear across the Tower, for hours that stretched into days. I asked The Dollmaker if I could help her. I'd gotten good at that here—tending to people's wounds. But he said she was too far gone. We still don't know what he did to make her scream like that. We just know she never came back.

With Londyn, it was like something out of a sci-fi movie. She came back with wings like a raven's. Feathers the color of midnight rain. Talons for fingernails. A completely different rib cage. *He says my name is Lenore now,* she told us.

And then the only girls left to turn into butterflies were Fallon and me.

CHAPTER 9

I WAKE UP THE NEXT MORNING BEFORE IVY'S ALARM GOES off. (Probably a first.) I check my phone and the mailbox and I go ask Mason, but so far "further instructions" have not arrived. So, I go to the kitchen and pace and make coffee and pace and check the mail one more time and pace and read an article about the science behind glitter and pace. I am no closer to having additional information from The Dollmaker about our meeting tonight, but I have gotten in 4,603 steps today and also I now know that glitter comes from New Jersey and that the making of it is more complicated than interstellar space travel. (Evaporate aluminum, emboss holographic patterns onto film, take sheets that are half the wavelength of light visible to humans, and stack them until you get 223 layers, that sort of thing.) Extremely useful information, if you ask me. Also, it's apparently all around us. In everything—including secret things that the article couldn't reveal. The whole taking-a-thousand-years-to-decompose issue is pretty bad, though, so I'm really glad I took Ivy's advice about biodegradable op—

"Whatcha doing?" asks Ivy, and I stop mid-pace with half a bite of breakfast sandwich hanging out of my mouth. I am fairly certain yesterday's eye makeup is smeared all under my eyes, and my hair is a nest of tangles.

Meanwhile, Ivy just woke up, and she has glossy red princess hair that looks like someone gently tousled it right before the wake-up scene in a teen movie. She's wearing green-and-blue-plaid Gotham U boxer shorts and a pale green crop top, and she looks so devastatingly beautiful, I honestly don't know how my brain functions around her.

I push the bite of breakfast sandwich into my mouth. Try to remember how to chew. "I'm pacing," I tell her.

And she knows me well enough not to ask why.

"Coffee?" I ask. I pour her a cup before the staff can, even though that kind of weirds them out. I don't know—she's my girlfriend, and I just like doing stuff for her. I like how girlfriend-ly it makes me feel.

We drink our coffee in the morning room (did you know rich people have a room called that because I didn't), and Ivy eats overnight oats, absently scrolling through her phone.

"Ohmygosh."

I tense. "What is it?"

"The Looking Glass Killer struck again. It's been ages, but someone just discovered one of his tea parties set up this morning in the middle of a subway car."

"Oh, good." I let out an audible sigh of relief, and Ivy raises her eyebrows. "I mean, not good as in 'good that some people got killed.' I just meant, like, I thought it was going to be something else with The Dollmaker."

Her eyes soften. "I'm sorry. I shouldn't even be bringing up violent things when you're in a situation like this."

"No, violence is okay. I am the queen of violence. Please distract me with your violence."

So, Ivy tells me everything she knows about this new set of murders, which is honestly not much seeing as how it just happened and the police are keeping it very hush-hush.

We finish our breakfast, and I pour another cup of coffee.

"Would you mind helping me feed some of the bigger plants in the conservatory this morning?" she asks.

"For sure!"

It'll help me take my mind off The Dollmaker and our meeting today, if it's even happening. But he's been too meticulous to back out the day of—the information about the meeting will come, I'm sure of it. It doesn't help to pace holes into the floor waiting for it. Plus, Ivy's man-eating plants are fascinating. When we get there, though, we've scarcely fed half a goat to a giant cobra plant before Mason enters with a package.

My breath hitches. I was expecting a letter. With information about tonight. That shouldn't require a box, right? I'm still reeling from him taking Stella yesterday. I don't know if I can handle another doll right now.

"Hey." Ivy touches my elbow. "I can open it for you if you want."

I nod gratefully.

Mason leaves the box with us—it's a bit different from the usual doll boxes, now that I'm thinking on it. This one is longer. Flatter. Like the kind you might get a sweater in as a gift. Ivy takes a deep breath and removes the lid.

"I think it's . . . clothes?"

I lean over the box. Inside is an explosion of red and black and lace and leather. I pick up the garment.

"It's a dress," I say.

Only that's a gross understatement. Technically, yes, this piece of clothing would be categorized as a short party dress, but it's the kind that would make you feel like you're wearing art. It's avant-garde and unique/daring/wildly creative and, I hate to admit it, beautiful. If I was ridiculously wealthy and going to commission a dress just for me, this is what it would look like. I hate that The Dollmaker knows me like that.

Ivy touches a piece of black lace with her fingers. "Do you think he made it?"

"Maybe. I mean, he made all those dolls."

She drops the lace like it's toxic.

It makes me realize that I should probably inspect the dress for sabotage, so I do, but I don't find anything odd or dangerous.

Now that I've removed the dress from the box, we can see that there is a piece of black cardstock underneath. An address and time are printed on it in silver text. Nothing else.

Ivy has her phone out immediately. "It's some club downtown, I think. Labyrinth. I don't know, Harley. I hate the idea of you walking in there—to *his* place, at his time, wearing his dress. It feels like he's got all the cards."

"So, you'll come with me. You can take on anybody."

Ivy doesn't say anything back, just bites the inside of her lips. She stews over things for hours as we feed the rest of her carnivorous babies (I swear I saw one of them lick its chops), as my meeting with The Dollmaker draws ever closer.

I run another test experiment for our kiss problem, but I'm so keyed up over what could happen tonight that I botch it. Like, notes-too-close-to-the-Bunsen-burner, fire-extinguisher levels of botching it. Ivy seems even more upset than before as she helps me clean up the charred wreckage that used to be my experiment.

"I'm really sorry," I say for the fourth time.

She crosses her arms tightly. "It's okay."

"I know your lab is important, and I'll take better care of it."

"It's not that."

"Then what is it?"

She shakes her head and walks over to the multipaned window and tilts her face up to the afternoon sunlight, almost like there's something in it that will fix her.

I touch her shoulder. "Ivy?"

And she crumples.

"I can't keep you safe tonight. *I can't even kiss you.*"

"Oh, Ivy." I wrap my arms around her, and she collapses onto the floor, and I collapse with her.

"I just feel so powerless right now." The thing that is killing her has bubbled to the surface, and now the floodgates are open. "I hate that I have to just let you walk in there. And I hate that we can't be close in the ways I want to be. And I just feel like I don't have any control over anything, and I don't know when that's ever going to change. You're, like, going into battle. Now should be the time when we share the passionate kiss that changes everything and guarantees your victory."

It breaks my heart to see how this is hurting her, even as I fall in love with her words. I love the way she talks about us. Like we're already a legend. Some great love story that's bigger than the whole sky. I hold her close and stroke her hair. "It's okay. It's going to be okay."

She shakes her head, her voice strident now. Desperate. "But is it? Is it really?"

"Yes." I say it like I've already seen a future where we're kissing in a park and I'm holding a ring box behind my back.

And then I have an epiphany.

"Oh my gosh."

Ivy jerks back. "What? Are you okay?"

I jump up and run over to my benchtop. "I'm having a eureka moment!"

I grab some prefilled test tubes and a fistful of cotton swabs. And I sprint back over to Ivy.

"I want you to think about Woodrue," I tell her.

She sighs. "We've already tried this."

"Not like this, we haven't." I get a swab ready. "Are you thinking of him?"

She sighs again, but she says yes and puckers her lips.

And instead, I run the cotton swab over her collarbone.

She jumps, surprised. "What are you—?"

But I'm already up and running back to my bench. "We only know your saliva has the toxin." It's all the explanation I give her because I am doing science like a mofo, and this might just work. It has to. We need a win, dammit.

Ivy actually gets up and helps me—my enthusiasm must be contagious. I hurry to finish the assay and run the analysis—and have Ivy double-check the analysis for me because (A) I'm delirious with excitement, and (B) I've never run the assay this fast before—and. Guess. Freaking. What.

"Ivy, your collarbone's not toxic." My face hurts, that's how much I'm smiling right now.

I can see the hope building within her. "So that means . . ."

"Yes." I literally cannot stop staring at her collarbone.

She goes silent and I go silent, only our breathing seems so, so loud. And I can feel my heart beating in my ears, or maybe it's hers. Maybe it's everything. I take a step closer, and she tilts her head to the side, just slightly, like she's offering her collarbone to me. And I lean down and press my lips against it.

Holy. Hell.

She shivers against my touch, and I nearly pass out. I have never felt this way about anyone else in my whole life. I want her, and I have her, and she wants me back, and there's too much. I feel entirely too much right now.

I never want it to stop.

"So, do you think it's just my lips that are producing the toxin, and the rest of my skin is safe?" Ivy asks when we've both recovered from the Greatest Collarbone Kiss of All Time.

"I don't know, but we can definitely test it." I'm smiling that goofy smile again. I just feel so hopeful. Like, now that we've figured out this one thing, it feels like all the other things are so much more within our grasp.

I press my lips against her collarbone once more, this time running my mouth down the length of it, waiting for her to shiver like before and feeling victorious when she does.

"But also, this collarbone!" I say, dizzy with how good I feel. "I freaking love this collarbone. It's, like, the most beautiful collarbone in the history of collarbones! I feel like it could sustain me for the rest of my days!"

Ivy has been smiling until now. So it surprises me to see her tear up. I pull away quickly.

"Oh no. What'd I do wrong? Was I too much? Sometimes I'm too much."

Ivy smiles and shakes her head. "You're exactly enough."

Magnificent

"We could kill him."

Londyn whispered it to me the morning after he took Fallon, right as the guards were changing their shifts.

Just as I opened my mouth to ask her how, The Dollmaker walked into the dining hall.

"Could you please pass the cantaloupe? Lenore?" I added at the end. He liked when we used our new names. And when we spoke politely.

He left as quickly as he came. He didn't notice my attempt at manners. But I noticed the blood on his sleeve.

I squeezed Londyn's leg under the table. "How?"

But we never got as far as the hows or the whens or even the whos, because by the end of lunchtime, he was yanking me away from the other girls. Did he know? Londyn and I waited until we were sure none of the guards or kitchen staff could hear, but I always suspected the tables were bugged.

His smile was too big for someone who'd just uncovered a murder plot, though. So big, it had me worried.

"I've done it." He grinned. "My most magnificent piece yet."

The worry grew.

He did this sometimes, when he and Mr. Tetch

argued. The Dollmaker needed someone to reassure him of his brilliance. Or maybe he just liked the control. I tried to remember if I had heard about any fighting recently. Maybe something a couple of days ago. Something about Mr. Tetch leaving the Tower again.

The Dollmaker unlocked a door. Ushered me into a dimly lit room. And I stared into the twilight—at the creature in the corner—and covered my mouth in horror.

It was Fallon, but it wasn't. A crimson-skinned demon of a child splashing in a kiddie pool. Wearing a shiny full-skirted dress the color of blood.

"Everly!" she gushed when she saw me.

"Hey, Fallon, you feeling okay?" I tried to smile at her. It wasn't her fault she was a monster now.

What did he do to her?

"Vampire squid and box jellyfish hybridization procedure," said The Dollmaker in a low voice, like he could read my mind. "Watch what she can do."

He crossed to a door in front of the kiddie pool.

"Fallon, would you like a treat?"

She squeaked and clapped her hands together. She did still have hands, at least. But something about her mouth was wrong. I couldn't tell what without moving closer, and I wasn't going to do that.

The Dollmaker unlocked the door, and a man

stumbled out of the closet. Dirty. Sinewy limbs. Red-rimmed eyes. Sunken cheeks. Torn clothes. The Dollmaker's type.

The man squinted at us and opened his mouth. "Hey, you said if I waited in here, you'd— Ohhhh."

A cloud of glowing dots swirled around him like a snow flurry, leading him toward the kiddie pool. Toward Fallon.

He reached out his hand to one of the lights, the way a child would to pop a bubble.

The Dollmaker rolled his eyes and put a small black thing (a recorder?) to his mouth. "Do it now, Fallon. We don't play with our food."

Fallon's eyes glinted. Her red dress lifted up. No, not a dress, I realized. It was *her*. It was part of her body.

Tentacles snaked out from underneath, pale blue and transparent, thin as spaghetti and longer than a car. They wrapped up the man as if to hug him.

I don't think I've ever seen a person in that much pain.

I ran out of the room and keeled over. Fought to keep my lunch down. My voice came out as a whisper. "Is that what you're going to do to me?"

But The Dollmaker just shook his head. "I have something different planned for you."

CHAPTER 10

THE OTHER GIRLS ARE MY AGE OR A LITTLE OLDER. ALL OF them in beautiful dresses and perfect makeup. The line is long, and it's late, and the city lights cut through the darkness like stars. No one is sleeping, though. It's too hot for that. The kind of sticky summer night that makes people restless. Reckless.

I touch the masks in my pocket, remembering what Ivy told me minutes earlier.

One for you. One for Stella. If you're not back in thirty minutes, I'm releasing plant toxins on everyone in that club.

I almost choked on my own spit because I thought she was suggesting we kill an entire club full of people, but it turns out they're knock-out toxins, not kill toxins, so we'll be slaying figuratively tonight and not literally.

I check that the masks aren't creating any unsightly bulges in my dress. (Luckily, avant-garde dresses are good for hiding things like pocketknives and glitterbombs and masks that filter out plant toxins.) The masks are Ivy's invention—smaller than usual, and collapsible, but they still take up a lot of room in my pockets. (Side note: I don't care if I'm being forced to wear this dress by some creeptastic self-styled artiste who's darkly obsessed with me—you better believe I squealed when I realized it had pockets.)

My phone buzzes.

> Ivy: You have got to stop fidgeting with your
> weapons and stuff or they are going to frisk you!

I attempt to glance over my shoulder at where Ivy is watching from a parking lot nearby. I can't see her, though.

I stand up straight and resist the urge to wrap my fingers around my pocketknife. Most of the people in line are glued to their phones. That, or talking. Ivy and I came to the address on the note card, but this isn't what I was expecting. All I can see so far is a spray-painted shack made of corrugated metal. It's not even as large as a shipping container. Certainly not big enough to hold all the people that have gone inside so far.

I lean toward the two girls in front of me. "What is this place, do you know?"

The girl with the blue body-con dress and raven hair turns. "It's a members-only club."

I nod. Yeah, that's what the internet said.

I eye the spray-painted designs on the metal building. "And you're a member?"

She laughs, and the gold bracelets jingle on her arms. "No. You have to be superrich. But sometimes they let other people in too."

Her friend (blond, dimples, heels that defy gravity) cuts in. "People who are young and pretty."

"Ohhhh." You know, now that she mentions it, they are both impossibly beautiful. And fit. And poised.

The girls look at me quizzically.

"I'm meeting a friend here," I say. Friend. Stalker. They're almost the same thing.

Their eyebrows rise at the same time. It's almost eerie.

"If they're a member, you're lucky," says the blond one.

I think of the boxes of dolls currently stacked in Ivy's closet and force a smile.

The girls turn back around and keep talking, but I'm not really hearing what they're saying. The closer we get to the front, the more antsy I get. The bouncer lets in a group of guys who can't stop laughing.

Closer.

The girl in front of me whispers something to her friend.

Closer.

A man in his forties flashes a black card and skips the line entirely.

And closer.

It's almost my turn now. The bouncer checks the IDs for the girls in front of me and lets them in.

Oh no. I'm not twenty-one yet. Why didn't I think of that earlier? My palms go sweaty. Have I really gotten this far only to be turned away?

But then I glance at the clipboard in the bouncer's hands, see a list of names. With a sudden burst of inspiration, I say, "Harley Quinn. I'm meeting someone."

I stand like a queen and pretend I don't care either way. That's rule number one for situations like this. If you act like you belong, everyone else will assume you do.

The bouncer's eyes flicker with recognition. He doesn't even have to consult his list.

"Miss Quinn," he says.

He lowers the velvet rope so I can pass.

"We've been expecting you."

Something Different

I'm the fourth Alice (Alice the Fourth?), only we're not allowed to call me that. Especially not in front of Mr. Tetch. He doesn't like to think about the other Alices. About what happened to them.

When I got here, the third Alice was still Alice the Third, and I was just a girl in too-short sweatpants, my brown hair pulled back in a ponytail. My hair was wrong, but my eyes were right. And my height. And something about my smile.

And so I became an Alice.

It was like the part of a modeling show where they make the girls over. Or that movie where the girl found out she was the princess of a tiny European country. Only not like that at all. This is the deeply harrowing horror movie version of that.

The Dollmaker reshaped my eyebrows and bleached/toned/straightened my hair until it shone like honey and sunshine.

Made my nose tilt up at the end.

The breast implants hurt. So did the part where he shaved down my jawbone.

But I heard Alice the Third had to have her clavicles sawed apart and put back together because Mr. Tetch thought her shoulders were too large. So I guess I should count my blessings.

The Dollmaker changes our outsides, which sometimes involves changing our insides, but Mr. Tetch is the one who changes our brains into something else.

CHAPTER 11

I ENTER THE SHACK TO FIND A LONG, DARK HALLWAY THAT leads down down down. I couldn't figure out how in the world all those people were cramming into this metal closet. It never occurred to me to imagine a secret passage leading underground. My feet don't want to take a single step farther, and I fight very hard against a mind that wants to conjure memories of Pop-Tart boxes in tiny bathrooms. *He's gone*, I tell myself. *He can't hurt you anymore.* The raven-haired girl in front of me mistakes my fear for awe.

"It used to be a bunker, but they turned it into a club," she whispers before she traipses off.

I feel like this would probably be pretty cool if (A) I wasn't on my way to a meeting with The Dollmaker, and (B) the enclosed, dark hallway didn't trigger my claustrophobia and make me feel like I'm going to die. I manage to get to the end of the tunnel, though, and eventually it does open up into an opulent club that feels very "dark academia meets strange colorful art installation." Dark walls and shelves of ancient books and marble statues with neon-feathered angel wings.

I search the faces of the patrons, mostly rich-looking men talking to beautiful women. Any of these men could be The Dollmaker.

I scan the room again and again. And then I do a double take. There's a girl at the bar who looks just like Bianca. At first glance, anyway. It can't be her, I realize with no small amount of disappointment. This girl has much bigger muscles (which, honestly, I didn't think was possible). She's taller too.

I shake my head and try to ignore the pang in my chest. I'm probably just seeing things because I miss Bianca. I resist the urge to pull out my phone and sad-scroll through the Reckoning Secure Chat. I have things to do here. Important things. Dangerous things.

A server offers me an hors d'oeuvre from a silver tray. Snack things?

"No, thank you," I say. Snacks are my love language, but I have to focus.

But the server is insistent.

"I think you'll like the Wagyu beef tartare," he says meaningfully.

Then, he blocks my path, like, *You are taking a damn tartare.*

"All right, all right, I'll try one." I inspect the tray. I think the beef tartares are the ones that look like a cylinder of cat food with a tiny egg yolk on top. Rich-people food is so weird.

But underneath one of the beef tartare appetizers, I

notice something. A message written on a napkin. In scrolling handwriting I can't help but recognize.

Lower level.

I pick up the appetizer. My heart beats faster.

None of the men in the booths lining the wall are sitting alone, staring at me in a singular and menacing way while rubbing their hands together. (What? That's what bad guys do.) I pop the Wagyu beef tartare in my mouth, and luckily it does not taste like cat food because I have a lot going on at the moment.

I weave across Labyrinth's dance floor to a spiral staircase and make my way downstairs. And when I do, I realize the lower level isn't just some one-room VIP lounge. There's a whole maze of hallways and rooms down here. And in front of me? A huge white screen that reflects the viewer, reflects *me*, in my red-and-black stomp-the-runway-at-a-midnight-fashion-show dress. Letters fall down the screen like leaves. It's strange, the way the installation makes you part of the art like that.

I stand there, transfixed for a moment, watching the letters fall to the ground. Puzzling as an *A-L-D* lands on my head and stays there for a few seconds before vanishing. The letters fall on my head again, another *A-L-D*. But that's too big a coincidence. They have to mean something. A girl passes me to the left, and I see an *M* teeter on her shoulder on the way to the floor.

Oh!!

I hold out my arms, stretching them as far as they'll go. The letters fall again, in no particular order, but I hold steady, stretching, reaching, waiting for them to make sense.

EMERALD STUDY

Aha! I feel like Sherlock Holmes or Nancy Drew or Velma from *Scooby-Doo*. (Side note: I feel like the fact that I had crushes on not one but *two* girl detectives growing up explains a lot about why I decided that sneaking around the subbasement level of some club was a much better idea than just handing the note over to the police.) I pace the hallways, searching for the study. There are rooms that look like little libraries, rooms for playing darts, rooms with cigars and brandy. Bachelor parties and rich young businessmen playing pool. So maybe not everything happening here is nefarious?

I stalk the hallways faster, growing more agitated the longer it takes. One of the libraries I pass has a green sofa, but really, it's more of a teal. Next to it, a door is cracked open, giving me the barest glimpse of the girl inside. It's the girl who looks like Bianca!

No, it *is* Bianca.

But that's impossible. This girl is huge.

Her eyes widen when she spots me, and I know I'm right. "Bianca!" I call out.

It's her, it's really her, and she looks like she's okay, not at all like how someone who recently had an experimental surgery would look. I try to peer around the door—I think she's alone in there? She crosses the room in three short strides. Moves to shut the door fully closed. I put my palm out to block it.

"Bianca, it's me! Harleen."

For a second, I doubt myself, thinking this is just Bianca's very jacked doppelgänger.

"I think you must have me confused with someone else," says the doppelgänger.

But she mouths the words *Stop it* as she closes the door before I can step into the room.

I KNEW IT! I FREAKING KNEW IT WAS HER.

What in the world is she doing here, and why hasn't she replied to my Reckoning Secure Chat messages, and how come her muscles have muscles on top of muscles?! I don't know what to think, and there's a part of me that wants to pound on the door and demand that she answer my questions while also tackle-hugging her and telling her I'm so glad her back is okay, but also I can't forget why I'm here.

So, as intriguing as this mystery is, I think about my meeting with The Dollmaker, and I think about Stella and whether she's trapped somewhere in this building. I continue down the hallway, searching, searching.

And then I see it.

A room decorated in the richest shades of green. Sage and moss and seaweed and shamrock. A green glass table lamp casts sickly light on a matcha-colored bookshelf. On a couch the color of snakes.

Across the room, a thin-legged desk that shines like jade beckons me closer. There's a gold key in one of the drawers. Am I supposed to open it? But even as I'm padding across the lush green rug, I get this eerie, finger-tracing-down-your-spine feeling like someone is watching me. And I turn.

Not someone. Some*thing*. In the light of a modern gold multiarmed floor lamp that makes me think of a praying mantis, I see her. On the love seat behind me, where I wouldn't have noticed it until I had already entered the room, sits a doll, and this time it's not Stella or a girl from a poster. This doll has one red-tipped pigtail and one blue. She wears ripped jeans and a wicked smile. Porcelain skin and master plans. You can see them lurking behind her eyes. How did he manage to get my eyes so right? It's unnerving. Like looking into a tiny sentient mirror that can read all your thoughts and use them against you.

She's not changed, though, not modified. Which, now that I think about it, why isn't she? Because I'm not (yet)? Because he's still deciding what he wants to do to me? I shiver. The potential, the wondering, is almost scarier.

The doll's crooked gaze draws me in like a beacon, and I take one step closer, or two—I don't even know that I'm in control of my own legs anymore. It occurs to me that the love seat she's nestled on is grotesque. The green of bile and swamps and pure spite. The leather it's made of looks pocked and rippled. I get the freakiest feeling, like sitting on that couch would feel like someone made upholstery out of Killer Croc. Attached to the doll's wrist by a celadon ribbon is a dainty white card. No, not white. Something richer. Ivory or linen or bone. I take the card with shaking fingers and flip it over.

Soon.

A Boy in the Tower

He's been here eleven days.

His name is Noah. Sixteen. Brown eyes. Tan skin. Dimples when he smiles. Dimples even when he doesn't.

He used to live on a reservation in Minnesota, and then he used to live in the Bowery when he moved to Gotham City with his dad, and now he lives in the boys' dorm all by himself because he's the only boy.

He sits by me at every meal.

He whispers cheesy jokes to me in the hallways.

He finds excuses to come to the Alice classroom so he can ask me, *How long have you been here?* and *Why are all the windows painted black?* and *What's your favorite kind of pie?* and *What do you want to do when you grow up?* and *Do you feel compelled to finish every book you start?* and *When we get out of here, do you want to go on a road trip together, and where?* I answer all his questions because I like pretending. He'll find out soon enough that we don't get to grow up.

When he gets hurt, I fix him with bandages and gauze, and I touch his skin for longer than I need to, and he forgets to breathe.

I think he is the most beautiful boy I've ever seen.

I think if I could kiss him, we'd both disappear out of here like a fairy tale.

I think The Dollmaker saw us talking.

CHAPTER 12

A THROAT CLEARS BEHIND ME, AND I TURN AROUND sharply, body falling into a fighting stance, hands clenching into fists. Like I'm expecting to find The Dollmaker standing there in the Emerald Study with a meat cleaver and a rag soaked with chloroform.

The room is empty. But I can't shake the feeling that someone is watching me.

I turn around and pick up the doll, and when I do, a rumbling voice says, "Have a seat."

I turn again, startled, searching for the source of the voice, but it must have come from a speaker. The room remains empty. At least, I think it is. I snatch a letter opener from the desk and search behind the couch, in the little closet.

"I'm not in there," says the voice. And I expected it to be raspy or piercing. A cartoon movie villain sort of voice. But it isn't. It's low and warm. A hero voice. But unsettling all the same.

This time I could swear it came from the bookshelf.

Fine. If this is the way he wants to do this, fine.

"Where is Stella? Is she okay?" I do not put down the letter opener. I like the way it feels powerful in my hand. I would fight everyone in this club to get her back.

He answers me again. Again, over a speaker (I'm assuming). Only this time it comes from somewhere near the desk. I'm surrounded. He wants me to feel like prey.

"Stella is fine," he assures me. "For now."

I roll my shoulders. He better be glad he's not standing in front of me.

I turn in a half circle, trying to find the camera he's watching me with. Wanting to stare him directly in the eyes when I say this next part. "What do you want with me?"

I don't scream it, but there is violence in my voice just the same.

"It's not about what I want with you." His tone is softer now, almost hurt. "It's about what I can offer you."

My mouth falls open, but my brain isn't ready with the clapback.

He continues in that same even tone. "You don't have powers like your friend. Wouldn't you like to?"

I suck in a breath. He knows about Ivy. I guess it shouldn't be that shocking. He knows the precise shade of my hair. Is intimately acquainted with the gleam that lives in my eyes.

"You can have that seat, you know," says the voice, this time from the direction of the closet.

I narrow my eyes. "I'd rather stand."

"Suit yourself," he says, like it doesn't matter to him either way. "Do you like the present I made you?"

I'm reminded that I'm still holding the doll, the one that

looks like she's trying to steal my soul, or like maybe she already has.

"She's different from the others," I say. But I don't ask why. I sense he wants to tell me, and I'd rather not give him that bit of satisfaction.

"She is."

Ugh. But I can play this game. "Run out of creepy ideas? Can't decide if you'd rather staple wings to my back or fuse me with a honey badger?"

I smirk. He doesn't answer for so long I worry I've lost him.

And then the door to the Emerald Study slams shut, despite the fact that there's no one there.

"Hey!"

I run and try the handle, but it doesn't budge. I'm locked in.

"Careful, Harley."

I note that he doesn't call me Harleen. I knew from his letters that he wouldn't. That he had somehow figured out I go by my nickname. My new name. There's still something unnerving about hearing it in person, this name that only my closest and dearest have begun to call me.

I take deep breaths and try not to lash back at him. I don't search the room for an escape, I don't want him to know that I'm looking, but my eyes test every corner and wall and window.

"I'm hurt that you don't know me better by now," says the voice. "I care deeply about each one of my pieces. This isn't for sport. I'm not some kind of common stalker or serial killer. I'm creating something new here. And rebirth is a violent thing. Violent, but beautiful."

There's a dark pause.

"I can make you beautiful."

I refrain from telling him I'm already the whole damn meal.

"You don't agree," he says.

Again, I remain silent.

He sighs like it's terribly exhausting that I haven't come over to his side yet. "Listen, I want you to do this of your own free will, but if I have to, I'll perform Stella's entire Metamorphosis without anesthetic. I could start now. I wonder how much of it you'd be able to stomach listening to."

I grip the letter opener even tighter. "You won't touch a hair on her head."

"I would and I will. I'll send you the scraps I don't need in a box if that's what it takes. And if that doesn't work, I'll use someone more important."

He doesn't mean—

"That couch—it's a beautiful shade of green, isn't it? Almost the exact color of English ivy."

"KEEP HER NAME OUT OF YOUR MOUTH."

"Gladly. As long as you keep up your end of our deal."

"We haven't made any deals."

"Then have a seat, and we will."

I continue to stand.

"*Sit down*, Harley." And I hear this noise in the background, a whimper. Stella?

I sit.

"Thank you," he says, his voice calm again. "And I'm sorry for that unpleasantness. I want this to be a collaborative process. A creative partnership. But I need you to meet me halfway."

"What is it you want from me? Do you want me to go

with you?" I fight so hard to keep it together. I don't want him to know I'm fraying at the edges. That he got to me the second he mentioned Ivy.

"Not today. Today all I want is to talk."

Then talk. But I don't say that. "All right."

There's quiet, like maybe he's trying to put his thoughts together. Or maybe the girls he's taken have broken out and clubbed him over the head? One can only hope.

In the silence, I can hear the noise of the club filtering down the hallway. And something else, almost like the sounds of a struggle. I tilt my head, listening. It feels like it's coming from the direction of the room where I saw Bianca.

But then his voice breaks in again, and I can't hear anything but him, all around me, consuming every molecule of oxygen in the room without even being physically present.

"I want you to be my muse. Hell, you already are. You don't know the things you've inspired me to do. You make me dream colors that never existed. You make me have ideas that feel like plugging a live wire directly into my brain. But the point is—I want you to *want* to be my muse."

"And what would I get out of that arrangement?" I say. Smoothly, carefully. A knife hidden in a silk pillowcase.

"Whatever you want." He's desperate now. "Don't you understand? You say Icarus, and I'll make the wings. Medusa, and I'll start researching venomous snakes. I've drawn hundreds of sketches. Thousands, maybe. My hands are blistered. I can't keep my eyes open during the day, and I can't close them at night. And I realized—it's because you're not just some art piece. It won't be right until you're a part of the process. So I need you to tell me. . . . What is it you want?"

"I want Stella back."

"That's not what I mean. Don't go simple on me. I know

you. I don't have to ask you if you've ever dreamed of being able to light a building on fire with your eyes or to shoot razor blades out of your fingernails. I know you have. So, tell me what power you crave the most. Tell me the darkest desires of your heart. And I'll sculpt them into reality."

I take a deep breath. For a second, I get caught up, imagining. There are times when I've been practicing with Ivy, helping her harness her powers, that I've thought about— dreamed about—things like having superstrength or being able to fly or teleport or become invisible or— But, no. This isn't the way. I shouldn't—

"You're thinking about it. I can see you." I try not to flinch. "Tell me," he says desperately.

Power. I want power.

But before I can say it, there's a scream from down the hallway. This time I'm certain it's Bianca's.

So I leap up from the couch, and I smash through the Emerald Study door.

The Calming

I stand on a pedestal, like a mannequin at the mall, wearing my new clothes—a blue dress and a white apron. My newly blond hair is pulled back in a black headband. I have been instructed by Anton not to speak under any circumstances. That he can't be held responsible for what might happen to me if I do.

I don't know Mr. Tetch very well. I've mostly heard things from Alice the Third.

Anton looks me over. Pulls a thread from my dress. Twirls a cotton swab under my left eye.

"Stand a bit straighter. Shoulders back."

I comply.

"And you remember not to speak?" He narrows his eyes, even though we've been through this.

"Yes, Dollmaker." It's what he likes to be called.

I wonder why we are doing this in the surgical room, but I know better than to ask.

And then he nods and opens the door, and I see *him*.

Jervis Tetch is shorter than I would have expected, now that I'm seeing him up close and not from across the Tower. He has a brown handlebar mustache, and he wears a green plaid suit with a red cravat and a funny, old-fashioned top hat that I hear is the source of his other name, The Mad Hatter. Not that I'm looking at him. Much. Only when I can sneak a glance. I've been told to stare directly at the clock in front of me.

Mr. Tetch's eyes rake over me, scrutinizing the details of my body, having me open my mouth so he can check my teeth like I'm a horse up for auction.

"Smile for me," he says in a thin voice.

I glance nervously at The Dollmaker, but he nods, so I pull my lips upward in what I hope passes as a natural smile.

"For me," he says, and I realize I am still looking and smiling at the clock.

My heart beats faster, but I fix my gaze on his and take a deep breath and smile again. I let my eyelids flutter shut delicately, and I don't know if that was the right thing to do—I'll have to ask Alice the Third what the right things to do are—but maybe it was okay because when my eyes open, he is smiling back at me.

"Her hair wants cutting. But she'll do," he says. And he immediately goes to the sink and begins scrubbing his hands without a second look in my direction.

The Dollmaker approaches my pedestal. "Good," he whispers, leading me by the arm to the surgical table and giving me a hospital gown. "You can put it on over your clothes. This will be a simple procedure." I wonder what it is that's wrong with me. Was it my jaw again? The Dollmaker talked a lot about how strong my jaw was. About the need to make it dainty. But then I didn't hear Mr. Tetch say anything about it.

"I hope this will curb your desire to make any

nighttime excursions," The Dollmaker says to Mr. Tetch in a low voice.

Mr. Tetch bristles. "I'm not one of your prisoners here. I can leave anytime I want."

"Of course you can. It's not about you leaving. It's about what you bring back." He walks away like that's the end of the conversation, though it certainly doesn't look over to Mr. Tetch.

The Dollmaker helps me onto the surgical table and pulls back the curtain. Mr. Tetch wears a gown over his plaid suit. A surgical mask. Gloves. It occurs to me to notice the scalpels and sutures and other odd medical tools. One of them looks kind of like a metal straw. Next to it is a tiny white piece of plastic. Like a doll accessory. A playing card the size of a pencil eraser.

Mr. Tetch sits in front of me. This is different from the other surgeries. Usually they are done by The Dollmaker, and usually this is the part where he gives me anesthetic.

Instead, Mr. Tetch pulls out a golden pocket watch on a chain and says, "Relax."

I remember the clock ticking, ticking, and his eyes, his pupils swallowing me whole. Those pupils were the very last thing I saw before I woke up. Before I woke up different.

CHAPTER 13

I RACE DOWN THE HALLWAY. KICK OPEN THE DOOR TO Bianca's room. That scream was definitely hers. Inside, Bianca fights two guys simultaneously while three others lie on the floor, injured and moaning.

We need an exit route.

There's a stained glass window opposite me. Thank goodness Bianca was in an exterior room.

I grab the end table next to me, even though it probably costs more than a beater car, and I throw it through the window. The shattering sound is gorgeous; the stained glass becomes a broken rainbow as it falls to the floor. And behind it . . . cement. And a light bulb. BECAUSE WE ARE UNDERGROUND.

"Oh crap." That didn't turn out how I'd hoped.

Bianca rolls her eyes.

In response, I backflip across the room and punch out a goon who has pulled himself up by a bookshelf and is thinking about sneaking up behind Bianca. I pull the letter opener out of my pocket and fling it across the room at another one, pinning him to the wood-paneled wall by his jacket.

"You're *welcome*." I shoot a pointed glance at Bianca, but she does not look nearly as grateful as you'd think.

"I wouldn't even be fighting these guys if you hadn't blown my cover."

She picks up the guy who's trying to attack her and throws him clear across the room, splintering a coffee table like it's one of those little balsa wood model airplanes. Damn. She was always strong, but this feels like a whole other level. A superhuman level? The thought just pops into my head. I don't know where she'd get that kind of power, though.

Despite the annoyed-as-hell look on her face, Bianca doesn't hesitate to fight back-to-back with me. We punch/kick/smash our way out of the room. Fight past some men and women in the hallway too. But when we get to the stairway to the main room, it's silent as the grave. Bianca exchanges glances with me, clearly as uneasy as I feel. I turn to her to formulate a plan of attack, but she's already taken the spiral staircase in two giant leaps for womankind and landed cleanly on the floor above. Okaaay. I follow her using a combination of parkour and gymnastics because I'm not about to let her show me up.

I land next to Bianca to find that every last person is keeled over in their chairs or flopped on the floor.

Ivy must have released the toxins already.

Bianca stands there, stunned.

"Here!" I toss her a mask and hurry to put on my own.

Ivy stands up from behind a bar.

"Oh thank goodness," she says, pushing her red hair out of her face. She doesn't wear a mask. Doesn't need one.

I turn to say something to Bianca, introduce her to Ivy, explain what's happening, I don't know. But Ivy's already running for the long hallway that serves as an entrance.

She glances back at us, her eyes intense. "C'mon."

Bianca and I follow.

She turns to me as we run. "So, she's the one who killed all these people?"

"They're just asleep," Ivy calls over her shoulder. "I disabled the bouncer with some nearby weeds and then dusted everybody like pollen in the springtime. They'll be fine in a few hours."

Bianca seems relieved but only a little.

"What about Stella? If everyone's asleep, we can go back and—"

Bianca shakes her head. "That's a negative. Someone must have gotten off a 911 call before they passed out. The police are coming."

My head practically turns around like an owl's.

"How do you know that?"

Bianca taps an earpiece in her left ear. I wonder who's providing her with the intel. Jasmin? If anyone I know is capable of getting that kind of information, it's her. I think about my unanswered messages in the Reckoning Secure Chat, and my heart gives a squeeze, even though we have entire whale sharks to fry here.

When we reach the surface, Ivy runs straight for her car.

I hang back. I don't want to leave Bianca now that I've only just found her. She hangs back too, and it gives me the hope I need.

"Bianca?"

"It's Vengeance." She winces. "I go by Vengeance now."

Vengeance. I guess it fits her. But. "Wow, that's intense."

She shrugs. "Yeah, well, that's my dad for you."

"And your dad is . . ."

She glances around like she'll find someone else listening. "Bane."

"Holy crap, Bane?! Like, Bane-Bane. *That* Bane?"

"Harley!" yells Ivy from the parking deck, but this is entirely too juicy for me to walk away from.

"Has Bane always been your dad?" I blurt out.

She makes this "ach" sort of sound, offended.

"Sorry! I didn't mean it like that! I just meant, like, you never mentioned him before, and people don't always know who their dads are. Like, maybe you just took a DNA test and found out he's 100 percent that Bane. And—"

"*Harley!*" Ivy yells again, thus saving me from my own mouth.

"Again, sorry, it's just surprising to find out one of your best friends' dads is a world-famous Super-Villain. And Bane of all people! How come you never told us?!"

"Well, I told you I'm from Santa Prisca and I had a rough upbringing."

"Mmm . . ."

"And that I was in prison as a child."

"But—"

"And I'm reallyreallyreally muscular, and I have this pump." She pulls up her shirt to reveal part of her stomach, and I see a device that I always assumed was an insulin pump.

"Well—"

"And it was my idea to name our girl gang the Reckoning, and my initials literally spell BANE."

"Okay! Okay! The pieces were all there." I jump up and down as I say it, and a hint of a smile appears on her mouth. I saw it before when I called her one of my best friends. Which means there's still a chance. After everything we've been through, all the ways I've failed her, there's still hope that we'll find our way back to each other.

"Harleen," she says.

"Oh! I go by Harley now!" Speaking of awesome new names.

"Harley! Freaking! Quinn! I need you to get in this car right now!" Ivy drives up alongside me, and she is not playing around. I suppose I really should hurry the eff up—the police are coming and all—but gah, there's Bianca, I mean, Vengeance.

"It really does suit you," I tell her as I get into Ivy's car.

And we know each other so well that she understands I mean her new name without me having to explain it.

"Just a second," calls Vengeance as she straddles her motorcycle. "I need you to know why I was here. I'm working for Talia now, and I was looking for information."

I feel a pang in my chest at her being Talia's sidekick. That could have been me. But there's no time to think about it because Vengeance is saying, "Harley?"

And something about her voice makes me freeze. The police sirens are blaring down the street, and Ivy starts to drive away, but all I can see is the girl who used to be my friend as she says, "They've got Jasmin."

Waking Up Different

My eyes flutter open. At first, I'm groggy and confused. Wondering how I ended up in a hospital bed. But then I see him and nothing else matters.

"Jervis!" I exclaim.

I don't know how long it's been since I've seen him, but it feels like ages, and he smiles at me, and I'm the luckiest girl in the world. I throw my arms around him and squeeze him close. But I have to pull back after just a second because if I'm hugging him, I can't be staring into his eyes.

"Alice," he says, brushing a strand of hair from my face. "Are you feeling all right?"

I clasp my hands together, blissful. "Oh, I'm wonderful, Jervis. Now that you're here."

His smile practically splits his face open. "I'm so glad to hear that, Alice."

He stands. "I want you to stay here with The Dollmaker. I have to go to work."

My face falls. "You don't want me to go with you?"

"Soon, sunshine." And then under his voice to The Dollmaker, "She'll need voice lessons. She's very good, though. You've really outdone yourself."

I don't know what any of that means, but The Dollmaker seems proud. Except . . .

"I hate making the same thing. It's so boring," he says, after Jervis (my Jervis!) leaves. "We'll start lessons in the morning."

I don't know what *lessons* means either, but it was Jervis's idea, so it must be a good one.

"I can't wait," I say brightly.

But when I'm eating dinner that evening (at a new table? A part of me feels like this isn't my usual table, even though my legs told me to sit here), I wonder if I really do want to do my lessons, whatever those lessons are.

It occurs to me during exercise time that maybe I didn't want to tell off that boy, Noah, who came up to me behind the gardenias and asked me what was wrong and tried to grab my hand. Maybe I didn't want to hug The Mad Hatter on that hospital bed either. Maybe my arms made me do it. But, of course, that's silly. Your arms can't make you hug someone.

And that night at bedtime, when Fallon runs up to me in the hallway outside the bathrooms and hugs me good night, she calls me Everly, and for a second, that really does feel like the right name. Curiouser and curiouser. But then Alice the Third glares at her, and Londyn hushes Fallon and pulls her away, and I think, *Of course my name is Alice too. Alice is the most perfect name in the whole wide world.*

CHAPTER 14

I FURIOUSLY TEXT VENGEANCE AS IVY DRIVES US HOME AS fast as she can without drawing police attention.

> Harley: What do you mean he's got Jasmin?!

> Harley: When did this happen???

Vengeance doesn't answer, but then, she *is* driving a motorcycle right now.

Ivy's convertible screeches through the city, stars overhead, hot summer night surrounding us, police maybe possibly searching for us right this minute. If I hadn't just learned that one of my dearest friends was taken by The Dollmaker, this would definitely be one of the top ten most romantic nights of my life.

She squeezes my hand. "You okay?"

Even though she's never met Jasmin, I've talked about her—about all the Reckoning girls—enough that it almost feels like she knows them.

I try to sort my feelings like so many playing cards. "It was bad enough that he had Stella, ya know? But Jasmin too? I feel like I'll never have the upper hand with this guy. Like he'll always be ten steps ahead of me and there's no way of winning."

Ivy nods, eyes on the road.

"How did it go with him, by the way? Are you okay? Your, uh, arm is bleeding."

Is it? I glance down, and huh, sure enough, a trickle of blood leaks from my bicep, dark in color now, nearly dry.

"I must've scratched myself fighting off those guys with Vengeance."

"Guys?" Ivy asks, an edge in her voice, like, just give her a reason. Give her a reason to turn this car around and go back and kill them all because she will do it and plant rosebushes on their graves.

I explain what happened with the guys. And with The Dollmaker. How I didn't actually see him. How I didn't get nearly enough clues out of him. I try to explain the hows and whys of Vengeance being there, but I realize I don't know the answer to that myself.

On the plus side? Going over everything with Ivy makes me feel less freaked out about Stella and Jasmin. Heck, that was probably the point of all her gentle questions.

We manage to get home without any run-ins with the police. But when I check my phone to see if Vengeance texted me back yet, the story is all over the news.

"'Bioterrorists broke into an exclusive club downtown. Dozens were found unconscious, and some beaten, but no deaths have been reported at this time,'" I read aloud to Ivy.

She paces like she's trying to wear a path through the

herringbone tiles of her bathroom floor. "Oh, we're in trouble. We're in trouble."

"It's gonna be okay." I try to put my hands on her shoulders, but she's really all in on this pacing business.

There's a knock at the front door—big knock, menacing knock—and we jump. Ivy's front door has one of those huge fancy door knockers, and the sound of it echoes clear through the house, even to Ivy's room on the second floor.

We run out to the hallway, to the balcony that overlooks the entrance hall. My phone buzzes in my pocket as we reach the banister. A text from Vengeance, though she's still in my phone as Bianca.

> Bianca: The police are coming. Pretend you're not home.

I turn my phone to show Ivy. She clears her throat and catches Mason's eye as he walks across the gleaming floors to the door. A slight shake of her head is all it takes. He nods in affirmation, and we retreat into the shadows of the hallway. Is that enough, though? Should we be rappelling out the window on a rope made of bedsheets? Hiding in Ivy's closet? Meh, closets aren't really for me, but I do wrap my fingers around a glitterbomb I had stashed in the pocket of my dress. Just to be safe.

The door creaks open downstairs. Ivy and I stare at each other, hearts pounding. Waiting.

A gruff voice splits the silence. "Hello, I'm Sergeant Stark with the GCPD. I'm here to speak with a Pamela Isley."

I suck in a breath. I'm not feeling good about this.

"Miss Isley isn't home right now," says Mason in this nonchalant voice like he's turning away a vacuum salesman.

I hold my breath. Will they believe it? Will it work? Or will they push past him and search the house—rush the stairs—find us lurking in the hallway?

"How about a Miss Quinzel? Is she here? You know anything about her?"

We lean forward, straining to hear. There are muffled sounds, not quite a scuffle. (Or maybe a mild one?)

"Do you have a warrant to search Hawthorne?"

"What?" asks the officer.

"Hawthorne," says Mason in the richest, snootiest voice I have ever heard him use, "is the name of this estate. If you don't have a warrant, I'm afraid I'll have to ask you to leave."

I hear a "We'll be back" along with some muffled swears. Hell yeah, Mason!! I do a victory celebration in the hallway, complete with this dance move from a long time ago called the running man. Meanwhile, Ivy is shaking her head at me while trying not to hyperventilate. Different people handle stress differently.

Mason is coming up the stairs now.

"My man!" I slap him a high five (he is surprisingly spry with the high fives given that he's a million years old). His salt-and-pepper eyebrows knit together with concern.

"Is everything all right, Miss Isley?"

Ivy watches the lights of the police cars retreat down the driveway. "Yes," she says with a sigh that is bone-deep. "For now."

He nods. "I'll ask the kitchen to make chocolate chip cookies."

I mean, is this guy good in a crisis or what? He disappears to make cookies happen (cookies so delicious they likely contain dark magic, just FYI). The adrenaline starts to wear off, and for half a second we can just breathe.

Until I get a phone call from Montoya.

My phone vibrates in my hands—*Renee Montoya* popping up on the screen. Must be her direct line.

I toss my phone to my other hand like I'm playing hot potato. "I don't know, do I answer it?"

Ivy panics. "No! Maybe? I don't know either!"

"I think I should answer it. She's always been good to me in the past."

"Okay. Okay-okay-okay."

"Okay." I take a deep breath and slide my phone to answer. "Hello?"

Officer Montoya's voice comes through on speakerphone, clear, firm, gentle. "Hey, Harleen. Sorry for calling so late. How are you doing?"

(Do not be fooled by the gentle part.)

"Oh, ya know, I'm okay."

"Where are you staying these days? The school said they didn't have you on record for this summer."

"Um, around."

"Uh-huh. I'm sorry that we missed your friend Pamela when the officers came by earlier. They said she . . . wasn't home?"

I make a face at Ivy. Montoya knows. She knows that we were here and we were hiding.

"Yeah, sorry about that." I try to say it brightly, all honesty and lightness. (I fail miserably.)

"I want to help you, Harleen. But I need you to come downtown in the morning and answer some questions about the incident at the club."

My eyes go wide. So do Ivy's. "I don't know what you mean."

"We have security camera footage of you entering at 10:39 p.m. And Miss Isley a little after that."

I cringe. "Right."

"It doesn't look good for you, and if you don't come down and tell me your side of the story, then everyone is going to watch that video and believe the worst."

Should I trust her? I look at Ivy, hoping I'll find the answer in her eyes. There's a whole-ass club full of passed-out people and a futile police search for missing girls and a criminal mastermind/tortured artist who will find me no matter where I hide, and can Montoya really get me out of all of that? Can she really help me?

I stare at my phone and take a deep breath. "I'll come down in the morning to answer the questions."

Then I hang up the phone and look at Ivy.

"We need to pack. Tonight."

The Alices

There are five of us now, our beds in two straight lines, four and four, just in case The Dollmaker finds others.

When I first became an Alice, there were only three of us. Me and Shy Alice and Alice the Third. Now there's Funny Alice and Pretty Alice too.

We sleep in the same room. We eat our oatmeal and eggs and strawberries. Some of us get honey in our oatmeal and cheese on our eggs, and some of us get egg whites only. It's important that we all be exactly the same size.

We whisper to each other when the guards leave the room.

Alice the Third gets to wear dresses of the finest silk.

Alice the Third gets to eat tea cakes and petits fours and cucumber sandwiches.

Alice the Third gets to go to tea parties every day.

In school, we sit in a classroom with blacked-out windows and watch videos of the first Alice. We don't ask where she is now. Or Alice the Second either. A part of us knows.

We mold our lips and throats around our words until we speak the way she speaks. Our spines and shoulders until we walk the way she walks. The Dollmaker calls this the Engraving.

CHAPTER 15

IVY AND I ARE FRANTICALLY PACKING. AND TRYING TO FIG-
ure out a plan for what to do next. And packing. Occasionally I fire off a text to Bianca/Vengeance.

Harley: How did you know about the police?

I pack a cardboard box with weapons. "Ives, do you think
thirty glitterbombs is enough?" I yell.

Ivy pokes her head out of the bathroom. "Enough for
what?!"

"Good point! I'm bringing fifty!" I call back.

"You are bananas. Also, I just packed all the stuff for our
skin routines, so don't worry."

"Awesome!" I do not tell her that I used to fall asleep
with my makeup on before I met her.

Bianca: Did you forget who I'm working with?

Right. Talia. She seems like the kind of person who'd have
live access to police scanners. I bite my lip, and for a second,

I allow myself to imagine what it would be like to work with someone who has that level of resources. To work for Talia. She wanted me to, practically begged me to join her. What if I *had* grabbed her hand and followed her into her helicopter that day? I don't always agree with her methods, but there's something intoxicating about being tapped as someone's protégée. It makes you feel special, important. Wanted. If I had gone with Talia, would I have a clearer idea of how to be that side of myself? Vengeance sure seems to know. *Everyone knows what they want to do with their life except you*, whispers the voice in my head.

Vengeance texts again, and I shake away the old ghosts. Talia and I were too different. It never would have worked.

> Bianca: I shouldn't be telling you this, but I guess you did keep me from passing out back there.
>
> Bianca: Talia thinks he's planning something big. She's heard rumors about a launch or an event of some kind. I was supposed to be looking for information on it.
>
> Bianca: I found these tonight.

I wait, uneasy, to see what will come through. Dolls? People in cages? Something worse?

But it's just photos of some forms. I don't really have time to look at them because a flurry of new texts come through.

> Bianca: Jasmin went looking for them. After I got hurt and you had your accident.
>
> Bianca: I'm sorry about that, by the way.

Bianca: She managed to get location data on the girls' phones by hacking the phone companies. He discards their phones eventually, but Jasmin was able to map the points of last contact and make a perimeter of which warehouses and abandoned buildings were in the area. She was checking off the buildings one by one, searching for The Dollmaker.

Bianca: And I guess she found him.

Bianca: He's doing these horrible experiments on girls, Harleen.

Bianca: And his collaborator, Jervis Tetch, is even worse.

I feel sick to my stomach reading the message. I wonder if somewhere in the city The Dollmaker is carving up a Jasmin doll. What are they doing to her? What have they already done? He hasn't sent me a doll of her, though. I'd know it if one of those dolls was Jasmin—no matter what he did to her. Does that mean he hasn't started on her yet? Or just that he hasn't finished? And did he really take her because she found him, or is it targeted at me somehow? But then, wouldn't he have taunted me with her and sent a doll even if it was just a blueprint? A more devastating thought—what if the fact that I haven't gotten a doll means she didn't survive the process?

I keep running it over and over in my head, like a song that you can't turn off, as we load up Ivy's car. I stuff my golden baseball bat in Ivy's trunk and put the wooden one in the passenger seat. YOU NEVER KNOW. I also try to convince Ivy that we can't take ALL the plants. She says a tearful goodbye to each of them like they're her children. No joke, we're in the greenhouse for a good half hour. I freaking love this girl.

But I love plants only so much, so after the fifteenth orchid, I pull up the pics that Vengeance texted and finally have a look. What I see nearly makes me drop my phone.

I zoom in on the text to be sure of what I'm seeing.

And I realize in horror that they aren't tax forms or insurance papers or applications for club membership. They're order forms. They're order forms for people.

Lapses

It's harder to think your own thoughts, after. Your brain only wants to think Alice's thoughts. The ones that The Mad Hatter put there.

But sometimes, sometimes, late at night or when you're feeling especially tired or mad or confused, you'll get a moment, like the door opening at the end of a hallway, except the hallway is in your mind. And if you go through the door, then for a minute, or seven minutes, or twenty-eight— you get to be you. Just you. And it feels like putting down a heavy bag at the end of a long day.

You have to just enjoy it. For however long it lasts.

CHAPTER 16

WE SCREAM THROUGH THE NIGHT IN IVY'S PINK CONVERT-ible. Gotham City rises up around us—walls and lights and noise. We cut through it all.

Harder to cut through? The order forms I've just seen. I feel like I could go to sleep, and they'd still be there. Squatting rent-free in my mind. Burned onto the insides of my eyelids. Vengeance says the orders are coming from some very powerful men—Talia doesn't know every player involved, but there are at least two crime lords and a politician doing the asking. And others going to what Talia thinks is likely an auction. The Dollmaker may see the girls as "dolls" and "pieces." But he's advertising them as perfectly brainwashed, designed-to-your-specifications sidekicks.

"Who the eff cares about a shoe size?!" I blurt out.

Because out of everything on those forms—powers and abilities (forged through horrific experiments), temperament (because that's totally something men should be able to tinker with in women, like changing a channel), height and weight (ughhhhhhh)—the shoe size is the thing that really got me.

Ivy glares at the stoplight ahead like it's her personal nemesis. "Men. Men is who. It's not all that different from the bullshit qualifications they list on dating apps."

I just about fall out of my seat. "You've been on a dating app?"

She snorts. "Attempting to make connections with people on purpose? No. But enough of my mom's friends are on them for me to know they're a toxic wasteland."

"Oh."

"Don't worry. There's no one I'd rather Thelma-and-Louise it with than you."

I'm embarrassed about how happy this makes me. It's probably just because I really like being compared to Thelma and Louise. Yep, that's it.

I scroll through the forms again. "It's so messed up. It's like picking a Build-A-Stuffie or a USA Girl Doll, except it's sidekicks, and it's deeply disturbing."

I imagine one of the forms but applied to Stella or Jasmin, and I have to take out my pocketknife because carving things into my baseball bat is probably better than smashing off Ivy's side mirror.

I get to work on a letter G, scraping it into the bat. I can go over it in some red ink later to really make it pop.

Ivy's gaze slides from the road to my hands. "You okay there?"

"Just thinking about Stella and Jasmin," I say. And if it hurts to think it, it kills to say it.

"I'm sorry," says Ivy, and her voice feels like a hug.

I start carving an O.

"So, what's our next move? Also, where am I driving us?"

I look up and realize we're pretty far from Ivy's house now, right in the heart of the city.

"I don't know," I say, finishing up the first O and moving on to a second. "In the movies, they always hide out in the mountains or the desert or something."

Ivy gnaws on her lower lip. "We have a house upstate? It's about a four-hour drive, but—"

She cuts off, sucking in her breath abruptly as a police car passes us. I resist the urge to do something suspicious like duck. My hand remains frozen over the letter D.

But the squad car makes a left at the Wayne Industries building, and we can breathe again.

"We can't leave the city. We need to be here. To do stuff." I stare out the window at the signs for BREAKFAST 24 HOURS and ZIPPY'S PACKAGE STORE and LIVE NUDE GIRLS and a tiny pop-up museum in a freight elevator shaft like I'll find the answers written there. "Maybe we could stay with a friend."

"All my friends are in this car." Ivy's voice is on the border of dryness and sarcasm, but I know better.

I stop carving an N and put my hand on her leg. I hate that the world has been like that for her.

"Ivy, did something in particular happen?"

She doesn't answer for a long time.

"It was at a middle school sleepover," she finally says. "I suspect I only got invited because my mom pulled some strings, and I was supposed to be hanging out with the rest of the girls, but then the birthday girl's brother came by and asked if anyone wanted to go hiking with him. They lived next to a nature preserve, Harley. *With a waterfall.*"

"Oh wow, you didn't stand a chance."

"Nope."

"Was the waterfall worth it?"

A small smile forms on her lips. "It was amazing. Owen and I talked about movies and school and how we both secretly dreamed of trying to live off the grid someday. I felt like I had maybe made my first real friend."

"But?"

"You could feel that coming, huh?"

I nod.

"When I got back to the sleepover, things felt off. The girls were having a picnic, and when I sat down at the edge of the blanket, they all subtly shifted away from me and toward this really popular girl, Lizabeth."

"Eesh."

"And she was all, 'Let's play a game,' and something about her tone made me want to run, but I didn't, and then she plucked a daisy out of a nearby planter and said we were going to find out if Owen loved me or if he loved her." Ivy talks faster now, like a train that just wants to barrel its way to the end of the story and get it over with. "And I guess I was flinching every time she pulled a petal because she was all, 'Gosh, this really seems to be bugging you. You must like Owen a lot.' And I was all, 'I just don't like when people pick flowers like that. If we're going to use up nature, it should be for a really good reason.' And she looked me right in the eye as she grabbed a whole bunch of flowers, ripping their stems right out of the ground . . ."

I wait, breath held.

". . . so I tackled her."

Not where I thought this was going. "Are you serious?!" I try not to sound too gleeful, but hi, this is me we're talking about.

Ivy cracks a smile. "Oh, yes. And I punched her too. Repeatedly."

"Take that, Lizabeth!" I yell, punching my fist in the air. "What happened next? Did you get ejected?"

Ivy looks so sad that I wish I had just closed my mouth and not asked any stupid questions.

"My mom made me stay," she says through clenched teeth. "She made me apologize because she was hoping Lizabeth's mom would put her on the board of some gala."

"Oh, Ivy."

"I begged her to take me home, but she told me I wouldn't get my greenhouse if I wasn't nice. Said she'd be checking with the birthday girl's mom. So I soldiered through the rest of the party and went to sleep thinking the worst was over. But when I woke up, my sleeping bag was full of dead flowers."

"What the actual eff? I will kill them. Tell me their names, and I will kill every last one of those girls. With dynamite."

But Ivy just shakes her head. "It's okay. I'm over it now."

I don't see how she's being this calm. "What did you do?"

"What could I do? I wanted that greenhouse." Her eyes are on the road, but they're glassy now. "So I rolled up my sleeping bag with the flowers inside and I thanked them so much for a lovely party, and after I got home, I screamed at the moon and processed the seeds from the flowers so I could plant them. But I never let my mom talk me into another sleepover or playdate after that. It's been hard for me to trust people ever since."

"I'm so sorry, Ivy." I put my hand on her shoulder.

"It was a long time ago," she replies. But the bitterness in her voice feels fresh.

I want to tell her not everyone is like that. That I've had

real friends, good ones, and she could have that too. She deserves that. But there's something about the way her arms are tensed as she holds the steering wheel that says now is not the time. So, I stay quiet.

And then it hits me.

"I might know someone we can stay with."

I quickly give Ivy directions, and she has to change a bunch of lanes and pull an almost-U-ie, and I nearly carve half a letter into my hand. Oops.

"Are you sure it's a good idea to be using a pocketknife to carve things while in a moving vehicle?"

"Sure, it's safe!"

"Says the girl who almost took off her own thumb."

I laugh and keep carving.

We do need a plan, though. And I know Ivy meant in the immediate sense, but I can't help thinking about it in the global sense too. Ivy has her whole life figured out, complete with a manifesto full of smart goals. And I'm carving the words GOOD NIGHT into a baseball bat like some kind of Neanderthal.

I think about Stella and Jasmin and all of the other girls who have been taken. Is that my life's mission? Making sure terrible things don't happen to women? Blowing up anyone involved and smashing their stuff to smithereens? I do really like smashing.

Why can I fight everyone's monsters except mine?

The words just pop into my head out of nowhere. It was something I used to say to myself. When I was tearing up campus misogyny in a vigilante girl gang but I was too scared to face my own dad. When I was trying to remember who I was and who was haunting Arkham Asylum after my brush with amnesia but The Scarecrow was turning my days into living nightmares.

I guess I did fight my monsters. Stood up to my dad. Battled The Scarecrow. They're both gone now. One dead, the other in jail. But sometimes it's hard to know what to do with yourself after the immediate threats are gone and the urgent life needs have been solved. Like when some well-meaning counselor asks a kid in the East End to tell them their hopes and dreams and career plans, and it's like, *Lady, they're just hoping to have enough food to eat tonight and a safe place to sleep.* I've never really been the type of person to have the space to figure this stuff out. Until Ivy.

I stare at her with soft eyes, grateful eyes. She grips the steering wheel with hands that can make entire forests grow from a single seed. What does it feel like to be that powerful? And that good? Because all she wants to do is help a planet that everyone else is wadding up like a piece of scratch paper and throwing in the garbage. I watch as the lights of the city converge in her hair, making it seem like she's wearing a crown or a veil, bejeweled. Gosh, she's beautiful.

She catches me staring at her. "You okay?"

"Yeah," I say, all gentle-like. "I'm just really glad you're my girlfriend."

"Me too," she says.

And then she guns it, and the engine roars like a siren or a lion or some kind of fantastic beast, and we burn up the highway at a hundred miles an hour, and I put my hands in the air like I'm on a roller coaster as our hair streams be-hind us.

The police couldn't catch us even if they tried.

Lapse Notes

We overheard Alice the Third talk about The Mad Hatter today. Based on that and our training, some theories about the first Alice:

1. She was a girl that he loved. A girlfriend? Maybe. Or unrequited? Probably.
2. And he followed her. Stalked her. He must have. Otherwise, where did he get the videos of her?
3. She's not alive anymore. Why?

CHAPTER 17

I DIRECT IVY TO THE SUBURBS OF GOTHAM CITY, ON THE north side by the bay. You can smell the salt in the air as we pass a thick wooden sign carved with a name like Saddleford or Maplehurst or whatever they're calling upper-middle-class neighborhoods these days.

"Who did you say you know here?" asks Ivy, taking in the monstrous houses with their three-car garages and bespoke pergolas and perfectly landscaped yards.

I shoot her a look. "Um. Like a lot of people. I'm super fancy that way. Also, one of my sorority sisters lives here." I go digging around in the back seat. "Do you think this counts as a road trip? Because if so, I'd like to cross it off the bucket list."

Ivy concurs, and I run a black marker over item number seven. I freaking love the feeling of crossing something off a list.

Harlivy Summer Bucket List

1) Adopt a pet
2) Go to Pride

3) Find a cure so we can kiss for approximately forever
4) Find the girls. Defeat the bad guys. Save the world.
5) Liberate the hyenas at the Gotham City Zoo
6) Mani-pedis
7) ~~Road trip!!!~~

"One down! Six to go!" I yell.

Ivy pulls her convertible up the steep hill that is the driveway of 138 Crestwood Avenue. The house hovers over us, all brick and Austin stone and everything painted modern white with black accents like every other unique house in the neighborhood. It's just before dawn, but I can already see people moving inside the house. (Sophie is one of those wake-with-the-sun-and-go-jogging people. So is her dad. Whenever she's at home, it's their daily ritual. I would vomit if I wasn't so busy being astronomically jealous.)

I hop out of Ivy's convertible without opening the door because I always loved it when people did that in the movies.

"Hot," says Ivy, and she giggles.

And honestly? That's it for me. We're endgame.

Most people would not be flirting and giggling when the police are combing the city for them, but Ivy's not most people, and neither am I, and all I want to do is be not-most-people together for the rest of our lives.

I can feel my heart swelling like a helium balloon inside my chest, and I'm filled with this overwhelming desire to press her against her car and kiss her collarbones and whisper sweet nothing after sweet nothing into her ear, but also police chase and safe house and all that. So, I skip across the pavers, holding Ivy's hand, which is really not all that easy a thing to do while skipping (a testament to my love if there ever was one). Then I knock on the white door with the rectangular windows.

Sophie answers! She looks puzzled at how early it is, but still. I take this as a very good sign and plow ahead.

"Hi! Can we crash here for a little while? Just until some stuff with the police blows over."

Sophie's eyes bulge. "I'm already hiding a giant shark-person in my pool house for you."

Realization flashes on Ivy's face. "Ohmygosh, you're Sophie."

Oops. Guess I could have mentioned that before we knocked.

But it's perfect. Because Sophie is all, "Harley talks about me?"

And Ivy is all, "Of course. You're one of her best friends."

And then Sophie smiles this pleased smile and says she'll let her parents know she has friends visiting.

I'm reminded of something she said to me during the school year, when I first found out she was my Big Sis. We were bonding over how much we missed Kylie, and Sophie sounded almost jealous.

It seemed like she had a special kind of friendship with you. And the other girls y'all hung out with too, but especially you. It was like you and Kylie had secrets that we would never have.

Sophie didn't know it, but she was talking about the Reckoning. And I know we're not the Reckoning anymore, but it occurs to me that maybe it means something to Sophie to be part of this. Whether it connects her to Kylie or to me, I'm not sure, but I'm happy to do it.

I give her a huge hug. "Thank you so much! Also, we were going to have a strategy session later. Wanna help?"

Her smile tells me everything I need to know. "Yeah, that'd be cool."

She runs inside to ask her parents, and Ivy touches my elbow.

"You're amazing. I don't know how you do that."

"What?" Be obnoxiously bubbly? Low-key force people to help me with stuff?

"Make people feel special. Be friends with people." Ivy's eyes flick to the ground, and oh. You know you're in love when someone else's heart takes the punch, but yours feels the sting.

"You could do it too."

Ivy shakes her head. I hate that for her. She's such a great person when you get to know her. So many people are. Why don't other people take the time to try? But in some ways, it makes me feel more special for being one of the people who did take the time. Who noticed what was clearly right there.

"Well, if you were ever going to give making new friends a chance," I say gently, "these would be the people to do it with."

She forces a smile for my benefit. "Maybe."

Sophie comes back, and obviously we're allowed to sleep over, so we hide Ivy's car in Sophie's parents' garage and take our bags inside and then go directly to the pool house because KING SHARK IS HERE!!

"I haven't seen you in forever! How are you?!" I squeal.

King Shark's mouth spreads into a toothy grin, which, if I didn't know him, would be absolutely terrifying, but it's cool. People are friends, not food.

"Also, how do you feel about hugs? I feel like I don't know the answer. How have we never talked about this?"

"Very pro," he says. Which, of course. Which, obviously. He's a cinnamon roll with razor-sharp teeth. A rescuer of ladybugs who could bite you in half. A compassionate sweetheart in the body of a killing machine. I AM OBSESSED.

"As long as I can see them coming, it's fine. Especially big hugs. Tactile pressure is really good for my sensory stuff," he adds.

"That makes total sense." I leap up at him (he IS seven feet tall) and hug him around the neck, my fingers just touching in the back. Have you ever hugged a shark? It. Is. Awesome. Like hugging one of those giant squishy stuffed animal things but with rougher skin.

"Sophie's been so nice to me. Her parents too," he says, and I try not to balk because I didn't realize that (A) Sophie had told her parents, and (B) they were cool with it. "Her dad built a special shark-sized sensory swing for me. And I get to go swimming every day."

"He helps me practice my cheerleading stunts too," says Sophie. "Apparently, sharks make really good bases."

"Aw, I love that for y'all."

I look at King Shark, really look at him. His toothy grin. His bright eyes. His (incredibly detailed) daily schedule tacked to the wall. This is the most I've ever heard him talk in my entire life. I didn't even know he was capable of talking this much. His Arkham file seemed to suggest that he was largely nonverbal, but what if some of that was due to his environment? And what if it caused them to misdiagnose the severity of his autism? He was fifteen and in a prison for grown-ass adults. And not just any adults—the most hardened, most diabolical Super-Villains in all of Gotham City. I can't help but notice how different King Shark looks outside of Arkham. How happy. I think about the day we first met—when he was collecting ladybugs inside the asylum so he could release them into the wild. Or the day Talia escaped and took The Riddler, The Joker, and Two-Face with her. King Shark was there too—was one of the inmates Dr. Crane implanted with a mind-control chip. There are pieces of that day that are and always will be hazy for me (falling into a pit of toxic waste will do that to you), but I still remember Talia removing that chip from King Shark.

I don't remember what happened to him after, though. Maybe I was drowning in chemicals by then. I guess he escaped somehow, and I thought that was that. I'd never see him again. (Honestly, it was pretty tragic.) But two months later, he popped up outside my dorm room window. He had been living on the streets. He was desperate. So I introduced him to Soph, and the rest is history.

And speaking of Soph . . .

"Hey, Harls, can I talk to you for a minute?" She jerks her head in the direction of the house.

"Sure thing."

I turn around. King Shark is pretending to read an entomology poster on the wall while Ivy stands stiffly, arms crossed, looking at her mint-green running shoes. You know, I really think the two of them are meant to have a great friendship that spans the ages.

So I very discreetly and nonchalantly push Ivy at the giant man-shark who nearly reaches the ceiling of the pool house and shout, "Be right back! Talk amongst yourselves!"

Soph and I go inside, and I say hello to her dad, and he asks me if my girlfriend and I like waffles and sundried tomato frittata. (Yes.) Then Sophie tells him she wants to show me this super-adorable Alpha Kappa Nu travel mug she bought, and we run upstairs to her room so she can do anything but.

"What's up?" I say.

Soph is making her something-is-up face.

"You know I love King Shark. He's basically my brother now."

"But?"

"He can't just live in our pool house forever."

"Right, I'm sorry." I should have thought of that before now. How hiding him is such a big ask, and he's probably wearing out his shark-y welcome. I should have checked in more. But then Soph is all, "He deserves more out of life than that. I think we need to figure something out."

"Yeah," I say. Wow, that is not where I thought this was going at all.

"Like, a way to get him pardoned or something," she continues. "Kylie's mom is a lawyer. I thought maybe she could help. Would you be okay with that?"

"Of course! I think that's an amazing idea." Like, seriously, why didn't I think of that? "Let me know if you need any help with anything."

"Awesome. I really want to talk to King Shark about it more first, but I think this could be really good. I'm glad you're on board."

"Breakfast will be ready in five," Soph's dad calls from downstairs.

"I'm gonna go wake my mom up," she says. "If we let her, she sleeps till *nine o'clock*."

I snicker. "The horror."

"Can you go get Ivy and King Shark?"

"Sure."

I head outside and tiptoe down the stone stairs in Soph's backyard. They're talking by the pool, King Shark dipping his legs and Ivy sitting cross-legged, the moon still out overhead in the pink daylight. The moment seems so perfect, like it's encased in a bubble, like it's going to be a core memory for both of them, that I don't want to interrupt it.

(Instead, I just accidentally listen in like a creeper.)

"People can be scary. And cruel," says Ivy, reaching out to pat his hulking shoulder and then second-guessing and tucking her hand under her leg.

He nods fervently. "I think that's why I like animals so much. A ladybug would never hurt anyone. It won't look at me and think I'm a monster on the inside either."

Ivy startles. "You're not a monster." I can see her heart squeeze on his behalf. "But I know what you mean. I feel the same way about plants. They'll never betray you. They'll never hurt you. They just return the love you put into them."

DOES ANYONE ELSE FEEL LIKE THEY ARE MADE OF SPARKLERS RIGHT NOW?

She reaches out her hand again, and this time she doesn't falter. She pats his shoulder, and he smiles back at her like his entire face is made of sunlight. A realization: I think King Shark's love language might be touch. A second: and everyone is afraid to touch him.

Not Ivy, though. Not my girlfriend. She pours love into man-eating plants with poisonous fangs, and she is one of those people who take the time to try. I head back inside because there is no way I'm interrupting that. But when I get to the top of the stairs, I can't resist one last look.

It's almost surreal, this cinnamon-haired wood sprite

sharing a moment with a giant shark-man under a daytime moon. Like snow on the beach or something.

King Shark and Ivy come inside just as Soph and I are sitting down at the table with her dad. He serves us all frittata and waffles (a triple stack for King Shark), and then Soph's mom appears in her poppy-patterned bathrobe, rubbing her eyes.

"I need—"

"Coffee," finishes Soph's dad, pressing a cup into her hands.

"Mmmm." She gulps down half the cup and kisses him and takes another gulp. "Have I told you how much I love you?"

She takes a seat right next to him, and they hold hands practically the entire meal. And everything is "Can you please pass the butter?" and "What are you up to today?" and "King Shark, would you mind changing the light bulbs in the chandelier? You're the only one who's tall enough."

King Shark grins. "Sure thing, June."

I shoot Ivy a glance, like, *Can you imagine growing up this way?*

And she shoots one back, like, *I know, I'm jealous too.*

Literally, it's like one of those black-and-white shows from the sixties where everything is permanently happy and sunshiny. (Minus the sexism and racism.) Only instead of identical cousins or talking horses or nose-wiggling witches, PLOT TWIST, THE BROTHER IS A SHARK.

King Shark cuts a perfectly triangular bite of his waffle stack, and then he eats it, chewing slowly and taking one sip of milk and one sip of juice and one blueberry from the little bowl to the side of his plate to finish everything off. He repeats the pattern, just like that first day I saw him at

Arkham, only today there is no one to interrupt his quiet ritual. No one messing with him for sport. It honestly never clicked for me that Sophie's dad being an occupational therapist for kids would be a great thing for King Shark, but wow. He's really thriving here.

After breakfast, Ivy and I crash in Soph's room because we haven't slept in twenty-four hours, and Sophie and King Shark go about their day. Ivy is gone when I wake up, so I go downstairs to look for her. She's not there either, so I head outside.

"Ives?"

"Over here!" she calls from a picnic table nestled under a dogwood tree.

"Whatcha doin'?" I ask, even though she clearly has her Earth Goddess Manifesto in front of her.

"Just writing down some ideas."

"Cool." I try to inject some brightness into my voice because it *is* cool, and I am genuinely happy for her and proud of her and all the good things.

"Actually," Ivy says with a blush that creeps up her neck, "I got you something."

"You got me a present?! Wait, how did you get me a present when we're on the run from the law?"

"Okay, so, Sophie may have done the actual getting, but I wanted you to have this." She passes me a shopping bag, and I dig in like a five-year-old because I am a firm believer that that is the only correct way to open presents.

Inside the bag is a beautiful red journal and a pack of glitter gel pens.

"I kept thinking about that look on your face when you were flipping through my manifesto."

"Oh, no, Ivy, I didn't mean—"

But she just smiles. "It's okay. I just wanted you to know that even if you don't have everything figured out today, I know you're going to get there. I believe in you."

I don't think I've ever had anyone tell me that. I blink as fast as I can and focus on flipping through the journal instead of full-on ugly crying.

"This is an expensive-looking journal," I say.

"Well, your ideas are important. I wanted you to feel that when you wrote."

I grin. "And the glitter pens?"

"But I also wanted you to feel like you." Ivy gets up and squeezes my shoulder. "Even if you don't feel like you have ideas, just try to write something. Anything. For thirty minutes a day. You'll be surprised by what ends up on the page, I promise."

I thank her and wish I had better words, and she gives me one more squeeze and leaves me to my journal. I open it, but as soon as she's gone, the blank pages taunt me. I remind myself of what Ivy said—just thirty minutes. I can do that. Isn't that how I write rough drafts of papers? By setting a timer and pretending I have to have a completed draft at the end of twenty-five minutes, thirty minutes, an hour. Something about timing it kicks my ADHD brain into deadline mode.

So, I pull out my phone and set a timer for thirty minutes and choose a glitter gel pen from the pack (purple) and just start scribbling.

~~What I Want to Do in the World~~

Nah. Cross it out.

149

~~List of Places in Gotham City I Want to Explode with Dynamite~~

Nope. Not that either.

~~Harley's Big Goals and Life Dreams~~

~~How to Be Gay and Do Crime~~

~~Dear reader,~~
~~Here are all my best tips on how to be an anti-hero:~~

UGHHH. Why is this so hard?! But I force myself to keep going, no matter how stupid I feel, and eventually my inner critic disappears.

> I care about helping women and girls. That's the bottom line, and I know I'll be able to do that by going to med school and becoming a psychiatrist, but it doesn't feel like enough. Nothing feels like enough. I'm so damn tired of waiting on the world to change. I'd rather change it myself.
> So, okay. That's where the vigilante part comes in. But what does that mean exactly? And why am I having such a hard time figuring it out? I keep trying to picture myself being a vigilante, like, specifically what I would do, and that's where it all falls apart. I don't get it. I can picture myself last year. With the Reckoning.
> Wait a minute.

Maybe that's the problem. I keep trying to picture myself alone. Maybe the whole point is that if I want this to be as big as my delusions of grandeur are telling me, I have to have other people in on it with me. We have to be fighting for the same things. Together.

And maybe that's why I've been so stuck. Because I'm desperate to have something like the Reckoning again, and if I think about it for too long, I have to put my fault in us disbanding under a microscope and examine it, and maybe I haven't been ready to do that yet.

Maybe not until now.

I set down my purple glitter pen and release the biggest sigh ever. Wow. Ivy wasn't kidding. This really did wonders for me. I still don't have a forty-seven-step plan, but I definitely feel like I've gotten somewhere.

I find Ivy helping with dinner because we slept straight through lunch. And I try to keep this hurricane building inside me quiet. All through setting the table. All through the eggplant lasagna. But after we clear the table, I have to pull Ivy aside because I'm about to burst.

"Can I talk to you for a second?"

"Of course," she says, eyes searching me like they're trying to figure out if something is wrong.

I go outside and sit on the diving board, and Ivy follows.

I take a deep breath. "Ivy, that journal you gave me—it's amazing. It's, like, really, really helping me, and it's not just the journal. It's what you said too. I've never had anyone say things like that to me before." That they knew I could do it. That they believed in me. "And I just wanted to say—" My mouth goes to form the words *thank you*, but something else comes out instead. "I love you."

Ivy has just choked on her own breath. That's what it looks like, at least. But her green eyes are filled with warmth and the beginning of tears, and her hands shake a little as she laces her fingers through mine.

"I love you too."

I feel like I'm made of sunshine, and I feel like I could do anything, and I feel like I am the luckiest girl in the whole entire world. *She loves me too.*

I throw my arms around her and hug her until the stars come out.

Later that evening, Ivy, King Shark, Sophie, and I decide to roll out sleeping bags and have a sleepover in the pool house. We paint our nails (mani-pedis—double check), and I make a mental note to cross it off the bucket list later. We eat peach rings. We make popcorn and throw it at the screen while watching iconic teen movies from the nineties. Also—we try to formulate a plan.

Step one involves Ivy and me doing one of those fun, change-your-appearance-because-you're-on-the-run make-overs. I cut a few inches off my hair with kitchen shears and then dye the new tips in King Shark's sink.

"What do you think?" I clap my hands together gleefully. "Can you barely recognize me?"

Ivy blinks. "Um. You just changed your dip dye from dark blue and red to aqua and pink."

"Exactly! What are you gonna do?"

"Oh, um." Ivy scuffs her shoe against the cement floor of the pool house. "I figured if we need to go out in public, I'd, like, play into the masc side of my style."

"Cool," I say in my best supportive-girlfriend voice, even though I'm having trouble visualizing exactly what the end result will be because I've never seen her dress in a way that I think of as masc. (Does she mean like when she wears overalls during finals week?)

Ivy goes in the bathroom and shuts the door. I hear water running and clothes rustling and one unintelligible squeak.

"You okay?"

"Yup." She opens the door. "I used to dress like this a lot more, and I think I miss it," she says quietly.

"Whoa," says Sophie.

Whoa is right. Ivy is wearing a green vest with no shirt and men's jeans, and she has her hair tucked back in a hat—a backward effing hat—so her red bangs are all short and boyish in the front.

"HOW ARE YOU TWO HOT PEOPLE IN ONE?!"

Ivy blushes. "Does our plan have a step two?"

Step two mostly involves us staring at each other with dopey expressions on our faces while poring over a map of Gotham City. (Do we have any plans laid out on this map? No. No, we don't. But having the map gives us a sense of purpose.)

"We need to draw The Dollmaker out so we can follow him back to his lair and find the girls," I say for what has to be the fiftieth time.

"Yeah, but again, how do we communicate with him? You've never been the one to contact him before," says Ivy. "He always seems to know where you are and get in touch with you."

Soph nods. "Especially now that you and Ivy are on the run. I don't know how we're going to do this."

"Paint a billboard?"

"Post something on social media?"

"Place a secret message in the personal ads?"

I glance at the pile of junk we brought in from Ivy's car. On top of a bag of brass knuckles and potted ferns rests our Harlivy Summer Bucket List. I turn back to my friends and unleash the wickedest grin known to man.

"I think I've got an idea."

The Final Day of the Reign of Alice the Third

She's nervous when she wakes up. Dark circles under her eyes. Dark thoughts pressing down on her.

I help her get ready because she seems so shaken. Poor thing, she's in no state to see Jervis. I wish I could go instead. He takes such good care of us, and he works so hard. He shouldn't have to deal with this too.

I press concealer under Alice's eyes. An Alice should always look young and beautiful and healthy and well rested. It's the least we can do when we want for nothing. I apply the concealer to the bruises on her arms too. They almost look like finger marks, which is funny because I know for a fact she fell down the stairs in the rose garden yesterday.

"You have to become very good with makeup," Alice tells me with dead eyes. "The Mad Hatter doesn't like to see his Alices with bruises. Even if he's the one who gives them."

For a moment, I am fearful. There's this part of me that wants to run away from here so fast. But it disappears just as quickly, and I feel silly for letting my imagination get the best of me.

"Don't let's be silly, Alice. Jervis loves us. He'd never do anything to hurt us."

I've only ever talked to Jervis the one time, but I know this to be true with every fiber of my being.

Alice doesn't answer me. Just clenches her jaw and fastens her black patent leather shoes for the tea party. I'm not sure why she tucks the cuticle scissors in her purse. I guess it *is* important to have pretty nails at all times, though.

Before she leaves for the party, she does another strange thing. She stands in front of me and hugs me, and she whispers in my ear, "Be careful."

It's the last time I ever see her.

CHAPTER 18

SOMETIMES WHEN YOU'RE ON A COVERT MISSION, YOU have to stop and pet the goats. This is not some stop-and-smell-the-roses metaphor. It's a fact. And no, I don't mean G.O.A.T.s, though the pygmy goats at the Gotham Zoo *are* pretty great.

"I've missed you so much," I tell the one with all the relationship drama as I scratch him behind his ears. "How are things?"

As I greet the rest of my goat friends one by one, Ivy waits patiently, aka taps her index finger against the railing rapid-fire while anxiously looking around for police/surveillance cameras/security guards. I'm less worried, mostly because I know we can take anything anyone throws at us.

So, I skip through the zoo in my pink-and-blue-striped pants and my leather jacket with the diamond pattern and the rainbow fringe, and Ivy strides along next to me in her villain-era plant-mommy fit, and I feel like we are the queens of Gotham City, or at the very least the queens of the

Gotham Zoo. I give a royal wave to the red pandas and tell the sea lions how absolutely gorgeous they are—and, awww. The sea lions. Their exhibit is where we used to have our Reckoning meetings sometimes. Back when I was just a gap-year student and Bernice hadn't gone to prison. Back when Kylie was still alive.

I twirl my golden bat like a baton and pretend to fight hired goons that aren't really there.

Ivy raises her eyebrows at my latest smashing victim. "Did that sign about llamas personally offend you?"

I take in the splintered remains of the wooden sign. "Um, no."

"We have to be careful. Someone might hear us."

"C'mon, Ives! You're the most powerful woman in this whole city."

Her shoulders hunch. "I don't have enough control over it yet. And I don't like hurting people."

I remember when we snuck into the morgue last year. When we discovered that Ivy's girlfriend was dead, and not from injections from Dr. Woodrue but from a poisoned kiss.

I'm a monster. He turned me into a monster.

"You're wonderful," I tell her, squeezing her against me as we walk. (Which, just FYI, is not an ideal way to walk if you're into things like not falling over.) "You're the best person I know, and the fact that you're so worried about hurting people only proves that."

"I guess," says Ivy. "But still. Maybe we could be a little less conspicuous. Just a smidge."

I think by "we," she really means "me." And it's a fair point. I guess it's not necessary for me to smash signs. Or have a therapy session with every goat. Or sneak into the giraffe enclosure to see what color their tongues are— Oh! Cotton candy!!

I nudge her. "Ives, you know what would cheer you up right now?"

"Policy changes at the state and national levels?"

"COTTON CANDY!!!"

I jump up and down. It is physiologically impossible not to jump up and down when you yell the words *cotton candy*.

Ivy smiles. "I do actually like cotton candy."

I know this about her. Ivy Fact 247: even though she's all Mother Earth/eat the rainbow/veggies are my love language, she has a soft spot for cotton candy.

I break into the cotton candy stand, cool as you please, and then I decree that sad, stale, day-old cotton candy is nowhere near good enough for the girl of my dreams, and then Ivy blushes when I say the "girl of my dreams" part, and I am inspired to turn on all the machines (So. Many. Shiny. Machines. So. Much. Spun. Sugar.) and make her a creation all my own.

I pour the colorful sugar into the melter at the center of the machine. I hope this works—I think it's melting? I turn on the motor. Oh! There it goes. The sugar webs start shooting out through all these tiny holes and collecting on the sides of the round metal container. I remember Shiloh sharing a video with me a couple weeks ago—it showed how to make ridiculous 3D artwork out of cotton candy.

I'm no expert, but I'll take a whack at it. I do my best to make the cotton candy into a tricolored sculpture of a unicorn holding a bouquet of (potted) Venus flytraps. The result is vaguely horrifying. (What? I said I wasn't an expert.)

I present my "masterpiece" to my girlfriend. It tastes

delicious, I'll have you know. Cotton candy is like pancakes; it's fundamentally tasty and therefore hard to screw up.

Ivy takes a bite. "This is pretty great. Thanks, Harley."

And I don't know if she means the cheering her up or the cotton candy itself, but it doesn't matter. When we get married, I'm having a cotton candy machine at our wedding.

I make a few more cotton candy sculptures for whoever finds them tomorrow: Mr. Freeze wearing a bathing suit, a heart with the words *Love Is Love* across it, and Gotham City's mayor styled as an old-timey thief holding bags of money.

Now it's time for why we're really here.

Stealing hyenas.

The chain-link fence surrounding the hyena enclosure was made to be broken. I wind my fingers through it as I stare at them in all of their majesty.

"They're beautiful," I breathe.

I introduce myself to all three very good boys and girl, letting them sniff the back of my hand and feeding them scraps of Mrs. Isley's specially sourced Wagyu beef jerky that Ivy thought was a critical item to pack in her getaway bag.

"You know that stuff is twenty dollars an ounce?" she says with a smirk, probably imagining her mother finding it gone.

"And these sweet angels are worth every penny," I say in my best baby-talk voice. The hyenas love that. "Did you know their jaws are stronger than a lion's and they can snap a bone in half?" I sigh.

"Sounds . . . adorable."

It doesn't take long before Ivy is as smitten as I am, which is good because I'm planning on storing these baddies at her house.

The hyena in front of me (the one with a ripped ear who really looks like a Bruce) rolls over and lets me rub his belly.

"Babies! Couldn't I just keep one? Maybe this one?"

Ivy hits me with a side-eye. "That thing is going to eat your face. . . ."

But she's close to caving. I can feel it. "I know we were going to let them go. But . . . ?"

I rub Bruce's belly and give her my best puppy-dog eyes.

She sighs. "We do have an empty set of stables at Hawthorne right now."

"Yay!!!!!" I literally shout with glee. "Plus, this totally checks off 'Liberate the hyenas at the Gotham City Zoo' AND 'Adopt a pet' simultaneously."

Step 1: Charm hyenas (also, Ivy)—done.
Step 2: Put leashes on the hyenas and replace them with stuffed animal replicas.

This step is proving to be a little more difficult, mostly because hyenas are like me and their hearts can't be tamed. But eventually I convince them all that leashes are a very good idea and they come with more beef jerky, and we're good to go. Then, Ivy pulls the stuffed animal hyenas from her bag. (We bought them online, and they're terrible, but our resident stuffed animal maker is in prison, so what are you gonna do?) She does her best to position them in realistic poses around the hyena enclosure.

"I appreciate your attention to detail," I say, and she

laughs, further cementing that we are on the funnest mission ever.

Bernice really would hate these stuffed animals, though. The eyes have no light in them, and they're cutesy in a totally cloying and not at all kawaii way. Last I heard, Bernice was going through an appeals process. I remember Kylie's mom saying her chances looked promising.

"You put a note in each one telling The Dollmaker where to rendezvous for your next meeting, right?" asks Ivy as she walks over from placing the last stuffed animal.

"Yep," I say, but I feel suddenly unnerved for the first time on this mission. It's because she said his name, I know it. There's something about it that puts a chill in you. Like if you said it three times to your mirror in a dark bathroom, he'd leap out and strangle you. I think about the notes and exactly what I wrote in them. I told The Dollmaker that I was willing to trade myself for Stella, but there is no way I'm telling Ivy or anyone else that. They'd never let me go through with the meeting.

"I'm just trying to be thorough," says Ivy. "And you're sure this is going to attract The Dollmaker's attention?"

"Taking something and leaving a toy replica in its place? Absolutely. He'll know it's me, for sure." And he'll come for me.

But I don't say that to Ivy.

She nods and helps me cajole the hyenas back to Sophie's mom's van, where Soph and King Shark, our getaway drivers, are waiting for us. We load up my three new best friends, and there is beef jerky and cotton candy for all. Ivy whips out the bucket list, since we decided tonight's mission constitutes not one but two items. I let Ivy cross off both of them even though I'm itching to grab the marker and do it myself. (I'm a really good girlfriend.)

Harlivy Summer Bucket List

1) ~~Adopt a pet~~
2) Go to Pride
3) Find a cure so we can kiss for approximately forever
4) Find the girls. Defeat the bad guys. Save the world.
5) ~~Liberate the hyenas at the Gotham City Zoo~~
6) ~~Mani-pedis~~
7) ~~Road trip!!!~~

I laugh along with everyone else because I don't want to be the one to ruin the "Best Mission Ever" vibe.

But on the inside, the dread keeps growing.

The Tea Party

"The most special of days," The Dollmaker told me last night at dinner. Alice the Third had leaned too far over a balcony trying to catch a caterpillar, and she had fallen to her death, but I shouldn't be sad. None of us Alices should. Jervis needed us more than ever now, and he needed us happy.

The Dollmaker painted a picture of Jervis.

Consumed by his grief.

Drowning in what-ifs.

The poor man. Something in my heart told me Jervis was a sensitive creature, and I was the only one who could understand him. So, when The Dollmaker asked if I'd be willing to help, I'd said, "Absolutely," with tears shining in my eyes.

The Dollmaker set up a makeshift tea party on the wooden table in his studio. Pink plastic teacups—the kind any little kid might use.

"Of course, the real thing will be much fancier," he said.

"Of course," I answered, wanting to seem knowledgeable about such things.

"Open your mouth a little wider when you speak."

I nodded.

"And always say, 'Yes, Jervis.' Never 'No.'"

"Of course."

What other possible answer could there be for someone as wonderful and kind and brilliant as Jervis?

The Dollmaker tilted his head at me. "How much did Alice the Third tell you?"

"I—I—" Did he know about what she said to me in the bathroom? About the bruises?

"Do you know what you're supposed to do tomorrow?"

"I—" Now that he mentioned it, I didn't. But I didn't want to seem like a dolt, someone unworthy of Mr. Tetch's affections, so I said, "I'm meant to be Mr. Jervis's girlfriend."

The Dollmaker's eyes widened. "*No.* Goodness, no. I'm glad we had this meeting. No, you're to be his sister."

"Sister?"

He nodded. "Jervis's sister, Alice, died in a tragic accident."

"Oh." The poor thing. I never knew.

"I know," says The Dollmaker. "And Jervis is still terribly broken up about it. And what with that and Alice the Third yesterday, he'll be inconsolable. I need you to take his mind off the pain. To not just pretend to be Alice but to *become* Alice. Can you do that for me?"

My heart felt like it was cracking in two. "Anything. I'd do anything."

And I meant it.

But the next day, as I put on fresh white tights and a beautiful blue silk dress, a different part of my heart told me to be afraid. Whispered that maybe I shouldn't go. Maybe I should shimmy into the air vent instead.

But of course that was silly. Probably just nerves because I was about to go to my very first fancy tea party with the nicest man. More than that. *My brother.*

So, when the white rabbit appeared on my wristwatch, I hurried to a hallway in a part of the Tower I'd never been to before. The Dollmaker told me that this was where I should report, that this was the hallway that led to Jervis. The floor was lit with stepping stones, and the rabbit leapt from my wristwatch to the wall, hopping down the panels that led to a golden door.

I followed it.

I rapped on the door twice and waited like The Dollmaker had told me to.

I did not gasp when The Mad Hatter opened it. Even though his eyes were wild and his smile was crooked and his plaid suit was ripped in seven places and there was an awful scratch slicing a zig-zag down his face. I only smiled.

And when I saw that the lace tablecloth was torn in half and the teacups had been shattered against the wall—a wall dripping with tea and something that looked suspiciously like blood—I smiled harder.

Today was the most special of days.

CHAPTER 19

WE DROP THE HYENAS AT HAWTHORNE, WHERE I SPEND A few hours clicker-training them on how to hide in the hay if anyone other than me or Ivy or Mason approaches the stables. They're little geniuses, all three of them.

I'm practically floating when I get back to the conservatory. Emotional-support hyenas should totally be a thing. I meander over to the bench and flip through my lab notebook, seeing if there's anything I can learn from my previous failed kissing experiments. Ivy and King Shark are working on a new irrigation system for her vegetable garden.

"Hey, guys," calls Sophie from the green velvet couch in the corner. "I think your hyena plan worked."

We rush over, experiments forgotten. Soph replays a video from some news site on her tablet.

"A break-in occurred at the Gotham Zoo last night, but instead of money or electronics, a trio of hyenas was stolen," a voice narrates. "And left in their place? Some stuffed animals."

There's a close-up shot of the empty hyena enclosure, three stuffed animals posed in an extremely lifelike reenactment.

I nudge Ivy. "Nice one."

And then the action cuts to Montoya, power walking away as a journalist pelts her with questions.

"Tiffany Jones, Gotham News 1. Have you located the missing hyenas? What do you think the stuffed animals mean?"

Montoya declines to answer. Just huffs meaningfully and walks even faster.

"Success!" I say, slapping high fives all around. "No way does The Dollmaker see this and not come running."

Ivy is making her apprehensive face, but she shouldn't be nervous because we've totally got this. I purposely set my meeting with The Dollmaker for a few days after our heist, just to make sure he has sufficient time to figure out my stuffed animal clue. I know this is going to work. The Dollmaker is going to steal those stuffed animals, and he's going to meet me at Gotham City Pride (What? Isn't that where you plan all your secret rendezvous?), and I'm going to save Stella and everyone else.

"Hey, Harley?" King Shark clears his throat with a noise that sounds like a gargle. He kneads his finlike hands together. "I'd really like to go with you to the meeting. I was thinking I'd be useful as backup, and also"—he unzips his hoodie with a flourish—"I've always wanted to go to Pride."

Holy flying hammerheads, he is wearing a T-shirt that says FREE SHARK HUGS. And his arms are slung wide like he's imagining his best hi-would-you-like-a-shark-hug position. And his smile is so bright, it could light up the darkest depths of the ocean.

I leap into the air. "Hell yeah, you're coming!" Just as Ivy says, "Oh, buddy, I don't think so."

King Shark's toothy grin crumbles, and I look at Ivy like, *What is wrong with you? Why are you crushing his shark-y hopes and dreams?*

"Well, it's just that you're still a wanted criminal. And a shark."

Oh. Yeah, I guess those are valid points.

Sophie puts a hand on King Shark's shoulder. "I'm sorry." She shoots me a look, and I know she's thinking of our conversation in her bedroom when we talked about how King Shark deserves more, and we needed to get serious about his future. She's right. I tap my chin. She's right, *but also*, I hate waiting and rule-following and seeing my sweetest friends hurt.

"I have an idea so you can still go!" Patience may be a virtue, but it isn't one of mine.

"Harley," says Sophie, all mom-like, but I'm not just getting his hopes up.

"This is totally going to work," I say. "Step 1: we go to a costume store and procure you one of those inflatable shark costumes."

"Um, but I'm already a shark?"

"Exactly. And the police will be looking for a shark. But they *won't* be looking for a person dressed as a shark."

"Oh! I would be really good at being a pretend shark!"

"Yeah, you would!"

"That might actually work," says Sophie.

Ivy shakes her head. "It's warped but it's genius." (She's really good with compliments.)

Anyway, she and Soph and King Shark all need naps, but I decide to take advantage of the fact that we're staying here for the next few days by working on our kiss-periments. Up first? Checking my experiment where I fluorescently tagged the toxin from Ivy's saliva so that I could figure out which of her cells are taking it in and breaking it down. I remove my plates from the incubator. We have results, people! I check my petri dishes and then check them again. It's a particular kind of mouth cell that's breaking down the toxin. The oral mucosal epithelium, if I'm being specific, which is really just a fancy way of saying mouth lining.

Of course! Your mouth lining provides a barrier against all kinds of bad stuff anyway. And mouth wounds heal faster than skin wounds—without even leaving a scar. AND your mouth cells are younger than your skin cells (at, like, a molecular level). It all makes sense.

"Ivy!!!" I race back over to the main house and find her eating tomato sandwiches with Sophie and King Shark. "Guess what! Guess what! Guess wha-at!"

"What?" asks Ivy, handing me a sandwich identical to hers but with bacon.

"I found out it's your mouth cells! The ones that are metabolizing the toxin. Now all we have to do is discover the enzyme responsible!"

"Doesn't that typically take—"

"A gajillion hours? Entire scientific careers? Yes. Yes, it does. But by analyzing your mouth DNA against a known list of human enzymes and comparing for selected features, I *think* I'm gonna be able to crack this today. To the espresso machine!"

"I can make the lattes," King Shark offers shyly.

"I would love that! That would be the nicest thing ever."

Ivy is giving me side-eye. And then . . .

"You know what? Screw it. Make me one too. If you're doing this, I'm doing it with you."

"BEST DAY!!" I yell at the top of my lungs like a two-year-old on a chocolate bender.

Ivy snaps on a lab coat because this is Serious Business.

Heck yeah! We're doing this!

Seven hours and four artisanal lattes made by a giant shark-man later . . .

"We've done it!" I shriek in a voice that is not altogether hinged. My hair is flying every which way, and I look like I just created Frankenstein's monster or, at the very least, penicillin.

Ivy laughs. "We really did. We've discovered a new enzyme."

A thought hits me. "Ohmygosh, we get to name it! What should we call it? Quinzelase? Ivyase? I'm not really feeling either of those, but we can workshop it later."

Ivy pours us glasses of sparkling raspberry cider that she made herself, here in the greenhouse. "We're celebrating. This is one of the coolest things that has ever happened to me."

"I mean, same." We clink glasses, and I throw back the cider in one gulp and resist the urge to fling the champagne flute against the wall and yell, *Another!*

I get pensive as Ivy pours my second glass, though.

"What are you thinking?" she asks.

"That now we've gotten to the really hard part. *Your* mouth cells make the enzyme. But how do we get *my* mouth cells to do it? We'd have to, like, create a viral vector and deliver it to me somehow. I don't even think we have the equipment here to do that."

"No." Ivy smiles wickedly. *(I freaking love when she does that.)* "But Bruce Wayne does."

The gene therapy wing of Wayne Industries doesn't have nearly as many guards as you would expect. We haven't seen a single one since the two at the front desk, and we didn't even have to knock them unconscious.

Don't get me wrong, I totally wanted to, but our brainstorming went something like this:

> **Harley option 1:** I knock them both out with my baseball bat.
> **Harley option 2:** I set off a few simple explosions outside, and we watch them go running.
> **Ivy option 1:** We leave them to their desk and their doughnuts, and we climb up to the roof and slide down the elevator shaft on a beanstalk made of vines.

As you may have guessed, we decided to go with Ivy's option, not that mine weren't also totally viable (and fun) solutions. The beanstalk drops us at the fourth floor, and we get right to work.

We spend several hours doing some incredibly complicated, highly scientific viral vector production, and by the time we're finished with what is hopefully some legit gene therapy, the very first rays of sunlight are streaming through the windows.

"We better hurry," says Ivy.

"Yep."

While she aliquots our viral vector into a series of tubes in an ice bucket we borrowed from one of the labs, I spray-paint HA-HA-HA-HA-HA-HA on one of the walls in a lurid green. Might as well throw them off our scent.

I think about how close we are, about everything we've done to make this cure. But as the beanstalk lifts us back up to the roof of Wayne Industries, I'm reminded of the meeting I had with The Dollmaker, the one in that Emerald Study where he asked me what I would wish for if I could have any abilities I wanted. I feel a little guilty because all I thought of were things that would make me more powerful and gifted and dangerous. It never occurred to me to say resistance to poison.

We manage to get back to Sophie's mom's van and out of the parking lot with no police chases (alas!), but I do get another call on our way home.

"Montoya," I whisper to Ivy when I glance at my phone.

Montoya's voice comes through, all smooth and commanding, as soon as I say hello. "Harleen, you never came to our meeting a couple days ago."

"Right, yeah, I'm really sorry about that. I've been super busy." I throw Ivy a wince/shrug. Montoya always has a way of making me feel like I don't know what I'm doing.

"Oh? Busy doing what?"

"Um." Vigilante shit. "Nothing."

DO YOU SEE WHAT I'M TALKING ABOUT?

"I see. Too busy to clear your name and avoid being arrested?"

"Ahh . . ." I don't know what to say, so I go with nothing.

"Why'd you steal the hyenas?"

Crap, how'd she know it was me? "I don't know what you're talking about."

"Did it have to do with the trafficking gang?"

Ivy's eyes widen next to me. Again, I don't say anything.

"If you come in, I can help you. I'll do whatever it takes to catch them. But you have to stop doing things like this."

We're too far along in our plan to give up now, though. My meeting with The Dollmaker is already scheduled. And besides, we are this close to developing a cure that will keep Ivy's toxin from killing me. I exchange a glance with Ivy, and I can tell she agrees. So, I turn back to my phone, and I make my voice as strong as I feel right now.

"Maybe if the GCPD spent more time trying to find the trafficking gang and less time worried about me, the real bad guys would be blown to bits already."

Pretending to Be Alice

That first week, Jervis spent most of our tea parties crying. I learned that he suffers from terrible headaches and even more terrible guilt.

After the first hour of him hunched over the table and sobbing, I wasn't sure what to do or how to help, so I started picking up all the broken china from the last tea party and putting it in the bin.

At the crashing sound of a broken teapot, his head shot up, cheeks red. "What are you doing, Alice?"

"Oh." I froze, for a second worried that I was doing the wrong thing. And then I said, "I wanted to help. You take such good care of me, Jervis, so I wanted to take care of you."

His face had softened then. "You think I take good care of you?"

"Of course, Jervis."

"Better than Father?"

I didn't know who Father was, but I answered, "Always. Always better than Father."

This seemed to satisfy him. "He's the reason I have these headaches, did you know that?"

"I had no idea."

"Well, you should," he snapped. "I've told you enough times."

"Yes, of course, Jervis."

"He broke my head. Will you make more tea?"

I searched the cabinets for a kettle. Wonderland was a large place—a long table with all sorts of different chairs, a rose garden with high walls all around, a kitchen. And other rooms, each brightly painted and whimsical. I could see into some of them because the doors had been left open, but there was one door that always seemed to be closed. Shut tight with a giant golden padlock. I thought about asking what was inside, but I didn't dare. As I put the kettle on, Jervis kept talking, to me or to himself, I wasn't sure. "Fell down and broke my crown. Had a great fall. The greatest of falls."

The tea whistled, and I poured him a cup.

"I couldn't let him do the same thing to her."

I set the cup and saucer on the table in front of him.

"She came to me with two black eyes, and I told her we'd run away to Wonderland."

He took a sip of his tea. "It's too hot." Fixed me with his wild eyes. "Tell me I'm a good brother."

"Of course you're a good brother, Jervis. You're the best."

"That I am, Alice. That I am." He keeled over sobbing then. Head in his hands, hat off-kilter. Tears falling hot and fast into his teacup. "I protected her the best I could, and it wasn't enough. Not for when Father found us. I'll never forgive him for taking her away from me like that. I'll never forgive him for snuffing out her light."

My heart broke for him. Both the heart they control and the other one. The real one. I didn't have to pretend when I made my voice hard. "You shouldn't forgive him. He was terrible, and he doesn't deserve it."

I understood my job now. And I would do it. I would take care of this poor broken man, my brother, who had only ever tried to keep himself and his sister safe from their vile, abusive father.

Jervis wrapped his arms around me like he was trying to convince himself I was real. "I'll keep you safe here in Wonderland," he whispered. "I'll always keep us both safe."

I hugged him back sincerely.

CHAPTER 20

MASON HAS INFORMED US THERE'S A PLAINCLOTHES PO-lice officer guarding the front entrance of Hawthorne, so we make sure to enter through a hidden driveway in the back when we come home from stealing million-dollar technology from Wayne Industries.

We stash the viral vector in the minus-80-degree-Celsius freezer at Ivy's conservatory (and, of course, while we're outside, I have to go over to the stables and say hi to my babies).

Ivy watches me dote on them. "They're not children, you know."

"Says the girl who talks to plants."

And while Ivy coos at her chrysanthemums back at the greenhouse, I slip over to the freezer. We have what we need to cure me, I just know it. And I know we're supposed to run all kinds of experiments first to make sure it's safe and feasible and to figure out proper dosing and stuff, but I'm tired of waiting.

I think of that dog that scientists brought to Congress to shake paws with politicians. His scientist friends showed them how he used to be blind but now he could see thanks to the wonders of gene therapy. Lancelot, I think his name was. I remember thinking it was an A+ dog name. And A++ science. Lancelot and the other dogs were blind because of a particular kind of a mutation in their retinas, something that just happened every once in a while in that breed. So then the researchers injected one of their eyes with this viral gene therapy meant to repair the mutation and make the dogs' retinas work again.

The dogs were so excited to be able to see out of one eye that it almost looked like they were dancing as they ran around in loopy circles so they could see more of the world. (Eventually, the researchers fixed the other eye too, but they wanted to make sure it worked first.) And it did work. Amazingly. It totally cured their doggy blindness, and they were all very good girls and boys.

So, who am I to sit here and wait, when the only thing keeping me from kissing the girl of my dreams is sitting in this freezer? I put on Ivy's puffy blue cryo-gloves and open the door and pull out one of the tubes of viral vector.

Lancelot would do it.

But then I'm stuck. We haven't really settled on how to deliver it. With the dogs, they had to use an injection so it could get inside the eye, but since the target cells are in my mouth . . .

Couldn't I just coat the insides of my cheeks with it? Swish it like mouthwash? Would it really be that simple?

"Harley?" Ivy calls from the depths of the conservatory.

And I know if she catches me, she'll make me stop, but

I'm feeling brave today. Reckless. So, I open the little plastic tube and whisper, "Bottoms up."

Ivy rounds an indoor pond filled with lily pads and bladderworts. Sees me with the open tube. Puts two and two together.

"Harley, you didn't."

"I can't wait anymore. Not if we have the cure right here in our hands."

"But that could kill you."

"It won't," I say firmly. I can feel it. This was the right thing to do.

I can see the quiet anger growing behind her eyes, but she just gives me one of those I'm-not-angry-I'm-just-disappointed sighs that people with good parents are used to.

Then she kicks into Scientist Ivy mode, which means she basically acts like a cross between Florence Nightingale and a drill sergeant for the rest of the day.

"Stick out your tongue."

I do. She squishes it down with a tongue depressor as she checks my mouth, which makes it exceedingly challenging to tell her, *I like it when you're bossy.* Ivy ignores me and takes my temperature.

"No fever. Yet. I'll check again in an hour. Are you feeling okay? Any pain? Dizziness?"

"No. And no hot flashes or chills or symptoms of mortal peril."

She narrows her eyes at me. "I'll be the judge of that."

The next morning, Ivy declares that I am not dead (well,

that's a relief) and I might even be okay. Despite how flippant I've been, it *is* reassuring to hear that she doesn't think an alien head is going to start growing in my mouth or something.

"Now that it seems like I'm okay . . . ," I say tentatively. "For now," I rush to add when I see the look Ivy gives me. "What would you think about testing whether or not it worked?"

Ivy's mouth falls open and she goes very still. Her green eyes well up with tears. "I've been so worried about you, I forgot about that part."

I feel terrible about what I put her through. If I could prove to her right now that it was worth it, it would feel so good. So powerful.

"So, you would be okay with testing it?"

She nods.

"Okay."

I get out a petri dish and a cotton swab. Place the dish on the bench in front of me. My hand shakes as I swab the insides of my mouth, and I tell myself it's because I've hardly slept this week. But I know I'm lying.

I plate my cells, and then we introduce a sample of Ivy's saliva.

Will it work? Will my cells chomp up the toxin?

Ivy holds my hand while we wait.

This could be it. Today could be the day.

But when I pull the dish out of the incubator two hours later, I don't like the way my cells look. I slide them under the microscope to confirm what I already know.

They're dead.

And if I kiss Ivy, I'll be dead too.

"A no-go, huh?" asks Ivy, even though she knows me well enough to tell the answer from the downward curve of my neck.

I hate having to tell her we failed. *I* failed. I hate crushing her like that.

She nods and says she thinks she's going to go take a nap. And I tell her not to worry. That maybe the treatment takes time to work.

"Sure," she whispers before she walks away.

She doesn't look convinced, though.

"Hey, guys, check this out!" Sophie calls us over to the green velvet couch again. It's later that day, and she and King Shark are perched there eating Thai food. "I think you need to see this."

I rush over from my lab bench. Ivy stops tending her tiger lilies. Soph points at the television, where the same newscaster from the hyena heist is talking into a microphone.

"A break-in occurred yesterday at a place we previously believed to be impenetrable."

Ivy and I exchange glances. Please don't have footage of us at Wayne Industries.

"Gotham City Police Station."

Whew.

There's a shot of the police station from the outside. And another of Montoya stalking past because apparently she is their favorite person in the world to harass. (Their love is not returned.)

"While we were unable to determine exactly what was

stolen, we were able to confirm that there was a theft and that it occurred inside the police evidence locker. This is Tiffany Jones, Gotham News 1, reporting live."

I stare at the police station on the screen like if I concentrate hard enough, my eyes will X-ray vision through to the evidence locker and I'll spot the shadows of three missing hyena stuffed animals.

The news anchor at the desk thanks Tiffany and goes on to tell us that up next we're going to hear all about a set of grisly murders that took place at the Gotham City Public Library early this morning.

"Is the Looking Glass Killer really back, or is this a copycat?" asks the anchor with his best piercing stare.

Ivy's mouth falls open, and she breaks out her phone like her favorite singer just dropped a new album. But all I can think about is that evidence locker. The police may not be willing to say what was stolen, but I know it all the same. And I know The Dollmaker did it.

The Way of Things in Wonderland

Sometimes Jervis was gleeful, asking me riddles and feeding me little cakes. Other times, he was whiny, complaining on end about how The Dollmaker never let him have any fun. Never truly appreciated him, never mind the fact that the chips wouldn't exist without him.

"He reached out to me first, did I ever tell you that? It was on an anonymous message board, and he was able to connect things I'd posted with my . . . social experiments."

"What sort of experiments?" I served him another biscuit when I asked it.

"Oh. Why, I suppose one would call them tea parties . . . of a sort. I— It's nothing to worry your pretty little head about, Alice." He took a bite of the biscuit. "Overbaked." Another bite. "Practically begged me to work with him."

I nodded adoringly.

"But I go and leave the Tower for two days, and you'd have thought I'd murdered someone."

He laughed very hard at that, so hard he nearly choked on his tea, even though I wasn't sure what was so funny.

And still, other days, Jervis was desolate. Crying over Alice. Crying over the pain in his head. Asking me to massage his temples with lavender oil and having me tell him, *Shh, it wasn't your fault, what happened. It was Father. You did your best to stop it.*

It wasn't so bad, until the day I made a mistake. Until the day I said: *You did your best to save* her.

His head had shot up, cheeks redder than ever, hat nearly flying off. "Her? Her who? Who's her?"

And I knew it was a misstep, but I couldn't figure out how to un-step, so I said, "Well, Alice."

His eyes were so mad. Voice sharp as a knife and cool as glass. "But I thought you were Alice. Aren't you?"

I nodded so fast, too fast. "Yes, yes, I'm Alice."

And his eyes took me apart, and they knew the truth. He started screaming at me then. "You're not the real Alice!" Threw a cup at my head. "You don't really love me!" A plate. "You're a fake! You're pretending! Who sent you here? Why are you trying to hurt me?" Grabbed me by my white pinafore and threw me against the wall. "Who sent you here? Are you a spy?" Spittle flying everywhere. "No, you're with the police. With Father. YOU WANT TO BRING THEM ALL DOWN ON WONDERLAND, AND. I. WON'T. LET YOU."

I don't know how I got away. I think he knocked me unconscious.

I woke up the next morning with two black eyes.

CHAPTER 21

I DOSE MYSELF AGAIN. THIS TIME I DO IT WHILE IVY'S OUT walking with King Shark, and this time I use a technique called electroporation, which is basically like gently electrocuting my mouth so that microscopic holes get punched in the cells of my mouth lining and the viral vector can get inside better. It feels kind of like brushing your teeth with static electricity.

I don't tell Ivy.

I don't want her to worry, and I don't want her to get her hopes up just to have them dashed all over again.

Ivy walks in as I'm putting the new petri dishes under the microscope.

"What are you doing?" she asks.

She leans over as I'm working, her hair tickling the back of my neck, and I forget a number of things—including, but not limited to, how to use words and what my own name is.

"I wanted to try again," I finally manage to say. (Which is NOT something I was planning to confess to her until later, but she has magical truth powers, I swear it.)

"Did it . . . work?"

All the hope in the world is in that pause between her words. This is why. This is why I was going to hold off until later. But at least the news is somewhat better this time?

"The cells still died. But!" I add quickly when Ivy's face falls. "They lasted a lot longer this time, and they actually metabolized some of the poison."

"That's really good, Harley," says Ivy.

But I can tell it costs her to say it. So, the next morning, the day of The Dollmaker meeting, I set an alarm to wake me up at 5:00 a.m. (*I know*), and I slip over to the conservatory to test my cells one last time.

I scrape the insides of my mouth with a cotton swab. Rub my eyes blearily as I shove the plates in the incubator. And I stumble back to Ivy's room and fall asleep. Five hours later, the *real* next morning, ten o'clock, while everyone else is eating breakfast in the kitchen, I sneak back to the conservatory and check my cells.

"THEY'RE ALIVE!!!!" I shout to no one in particular.

But seriously, they are. I gaze at them under the microscope. So beautiful. So undead. Well, not undead like they're zombie cells, but you know what I mean. They've lasted a full five hours, and they've metabolized more than half of the poison! I can tell because there's less fluorescence than there was earlier this morning. If they can last until all the toxin has been metabolized, then the experiment worked. I'm cured.

I rush back to the house and get changed for The Dollmaker meeting. I wish I could stick around and check my cells again, but Ivy and I need to get there early to scope out the location and make contingency plans and stuff. Just before we leave, though, I pull Sophie aside and ask her to text me the results in a couple hours. In just 120 minutes, I'll know my fate.

Ivy and King-Shark-dressed-as-a-shark and I get in her pink convertible and tear down the hidden driveway. A half hour later, we arrive at the Gotham City Pride Festival because guess what, we are completing this bucket list, Dollmaker or no.

Harlivy Summer Bucket List

1) ~~Adopt a pet~~
2) ~~Go to Pride~~
3) Find a cure so we can kiss for approximately forever
4) Find the girls. Defeat the bad guys. Save the world.
5) ~~Liberate the hyenas at the Gotham City Zoo~~
6) ~~Mani-pedis~~
7) ~~Road trip!!!~~

Once

Once upon a time, I sat down in the little wooden chair with the heart cutout, and I learned what it truly meant to be an Alice.

Alice the Third got to wear dresses of the finest silk.

And if there was ever a stain or a hair out of place, he gave her two black eyes to help her remember.

Alice the Third got to eat tea cakes and petits fours and cucumber sandwiches.

Except when they played the game where he starved her.

Alice the Third got to go to tea parties every day.

But if she broke character, he broke her.

CHAPTER 22

I HAVE SEEN A RAINBOW BATMAN COSPLAY. I HAVE SEEN one of those inflatable *T. rex* people covered completely in pastel pink-blue-lavender sequins. I have seen more girls kissing in the last twenty minutes than I have in my entire life.

"These are my people," I tell Ivy. And she grins.

I skip through the grass of Robinson Park in my rainbow tutu and white crop top. My thigh-high white socks with rainbow stripes around the top are giving 1950s women's baseball league, and also, not to brag, but Ivy can't take her eyes off them. I have on one pink Converse and one aqua, to match my pigtails, and enough glitter on my face and in my hair to crop dust Miami.

Ivy twines her fingers in mine as she strolls along beside me. She's wearing a sleeveless white sweater and green canvas short shorts, but she does have on a rainbow flower crown made of real flowers that occasionally throw themselves at people's feet and then regrow. Meanwhile, King

Shark decided to keep things minimalist with his FREE SHARK HUGS shirt, seeing as how he's already wearing an inflatable shark costume that is straining at the seams. I seriously hope someone takes him up on those hugs, otherwise he is going to be crushed. I'm hopeful, though. Because while most people would be afraid to hug a shark, they're probably not afraid to hug a—

"Free shark hugs!" a guy with a rainbow mohawk yells, and King Shark bends down to embrace him.

"Wow, that was a solid hug," the guy says after.

"Thanks."

And I can feel the grin radiating from under King Shark's costume. This is exactly what I was hoping for.

"Thanks, Harley," he says in a low voice just to me.

"Aw, buddy, I'm just so happy for you. And if you need to talk about anything, you know Ives and I are here." I squeeze him tight and feel him sigh underneath me. He deserves to spend a day like this. More than a day, if Sophie and I have anything to do with it. She already set up a meeting with Kylie's mom about advocating for King Shark's freedom.

I look at the line queuing up in front of King Shark. Wow, this place is packed. I think about texting Shiloh—they mentioned they were going to be here. But also, I'm 200 percent sure this is going to be highly dangerous, and I don't want to put them in the middle of it.

We amble around the festival, scoping and strategizing.

What Ivy and King Shark think is the plan:
Harley will meet with The Dollmaker, and during said meeting, Ivy will attack him with decorative shrubs.

What The Dollmaker thinks is the plan: Meet Harley in the middle of the parade. She'll come alone and trade herself for Stella.

What Vengeance thinks is the plan: Show up at Pride and track The Dollmaker after Harley trades herself for Stella so we can get Jasmin back and find his lair.

What Harley thinks is the plan: Trade self for Stella. Fight my way out of The Dollmaker's lair before Vengeance et al. can get there. (It'll be like a race!)

Hopefully, Ivy won't be too mad when she finds the letter saying I let him take me, but it's cool—I put trackers in my clothes.

As we discuss where along the parade route is best to stage our meeting, we pass our fifty-leventh pair of girls kissing—a tall girl with short white-blond hair with a purple streak and a curvy girl with long brown waves, wrapped together in a rainbow flag. They might as well be in a whole other universe for how little they notice us walking past them. And a part of me still feels that gleeful sizzle (Yay! Girls kissing! Yay!), but another piece of me is sad. I want to kiss my girlfriend in the daylight. At Pride. With a million Gothamites celebrating around us. I want that so much it hurts.

So, when Ivy and I walk past a Test Your Strength game, one of the many booths lining the east side of Robinson Park, I yell, "Oh! Mallets!"

And when it's my turn, I choke up on the handle and I

slam the mallet down with everything I've got. The weight shoots upward and collides with the bell with a satisfying *ding-ing-ing-ing*. I don't care what anyone says: smashing things is like therapy for me.

"What prize do ya want, baby doll?" I ask Ivy, doing my best impression of a fifties boyfriend.

Ivy bats her eyelashes. "The rainbow kitten unicorn."

Which, I have to say, is very unexpected. She never struck me as much of a cat person.

The dude behind the counter knocks it down with a stick, and then he hands it to me, and I hand it to her.

"Are we going steady now?" Ivy says with this absolute vixen expression. Holy hell, what did I do to deserve this girl?

Counter Dude must agree, because he is staring directly at Ivy's boobs when he says, "Do you want a turn?"

She gives him this look. It's beyond scathing. Ascending to whole new stratospheres of aloof. Like, not only am I not interested, I also don't have the time or energy to explain why.

"No, thank you," she says. No, *pronounces*.

As we walk away, I think I hear him mutter "Witch" under his breath. Only he probably said something else, obviously.

I stop midstep. "I'll be right back."

"Harley, don't."

Ivy touches my shoulder, and it's almost reason enough to stay.

"I just need to do something real quick. King Shark, can I borrow that rainbow flag?"

"Of course!" He drapes it around my shoulders with a big, shark-y smile.

"Please don't strangle anyone with it," says Ivy dryly.

But I'm already headed back to the booth.

When I come back a couple minutes later, I am running. "We have to go! Now!"

We dash around the corner, giggling all three of us, and let me tell you, King Shark giggling is a thing to behold. His entire shark costume vibrates with it.

"What did you do?" asks Ivy.

"Did you knock him out cold?" asks King Shark.

"Better," I say. And I let the flag drop to reveal the Test Your Strength mallet.

King Shark and Ivy jump up and down and yell with me because that is clearly the only response in such a situation. King Shark even lifts me up and spins me around.

"I'll be right back," he says. "I'm gonna get us rainbow slushies to celebrate."

I respond by testing out my new mallet on a giant mushroom. But as the squishy mushroom bits fly everywhere, I freeze. "Wait, sorry, do fungi count as plants? Did I just kill one of your children?"

"It's okay," says Ivy. "Mushrooms are more genetically similar to people than plants." But she does make two new ones grow in its place.

As we put some distance between ourselves and the game booths, a text comes in from Sophie:

> Sophie: It worked—all the toxin has been
> metabolized! (I think.)

She sends me a picture to confirm.

I stare at it. Outlines of cells, but no fluorescence left. No toxin. I zoom in closer, scroll all around to be sure, but the results are the same—no toxin.

No.

Toxin.

This is it. I'm cured. Everything's going to be okay now. The thought hits me like a mallet to the chest, and speaking of mallets, I have to grip the handle of mine and lean against it like a crutch so I don't pass out.

"Harley, are you okay?"

I hear Ivy's voice before I realize her face is right in front of mine. There's this tiny wrinkle between her eyebrows that lets me know she's worried about me. But she doesn't have to be. She doesn't have to be ever again.

Across the lawn from us stands the most gorgeous tree. A positively queenly tree. It's only about twice as tall as me, but its branches drape in this way that is poised and regal, and its leaves are the brightest green.

"I'm wonderful," I tell Ivy. "C'mon."

"Where are we going?" she asks, but I've already grabbed her hand and dashed across the lawn with her.

I step right up to the beautiful, like, spectacularly stunning tree, and I pull Ivy under its branches with me. She looks into my wild eyes with her green ones, still curious, I can tell, but caught up in the moment. Waiting to see what I'll do next.

"Kiss me," I say.

She startles. "What?"

"Kiss me. You can kiss me. The cure worked." I wrap one hand around her neck, pulling her close to me. I've waited so long, and I can't delay another second.

But I do. Because Ivy takes a step back. "Are you sure?"

I nod emphatically. Like a bobblehead on speed.

She bites her lip. A LIP I COULD BE KISSING RIGHT NOW.

"Can I see the data?"

Not the most romantic thing she could have said, but fair. I pass her my phone, and her entire face changes. (Apparently, science is our love language now.)

"This is today?"

"Sophie just sent it to me."

"And your cells?"

"They metabolized all the toxin," I say with a grin that feels shark-y. Hungry.

"You did it. You finally found the cure," Ivy breathes.

I take my phone from her hand and gently drop it on the ground.

"*We* did it."

"We did it," Ivy repeats, and then she looks at my lips like OH HOLY CRAP, her brain has just put together what this means.

For us. Right now. In this moment.

We've been waiting-wishing-hoping for this for so long, and now it's here. I can kiss the girl I'm in love with and nothing bad will happen.

Ivy leans forward.

So do I.

She touches her thumb to my lower lip, and I shiver. And her face is close, closer, closer, our lips hovering mere centimeters apart like we haven't just had months of anticipation.

I kiss her.

I kiss her first, and when I do, when my lips touch hers, I get the most dazzling feeling, like I'm made out of stars and sparklers and sonic booms. And every synapse, every last one of my subatomic particles burns for her, is tuned to her. I love her so much. And when she kisses me back—oh. I can't stop, won't stop kissing her. We can live here now, under this tree, and I don't need food or water; I'll just drink her up. I'll tangle my hands in her hair as she runs her fingers down my shoulders, and there is nothing else in this world but us.

There are people cheering at a Pride float in the distance, and Ivy smells like peaches and tastes like summer, and the very air is shifting around us, sending a cascade of leaves falling on us like snow.

I open my eyes. No. Not leaves. Petals. The tree—it's blooming. Flowers opening up everywhere in pink-peach-yellow-green-blue-lavender. The petals land in Ivy's hair, making her look even more like a woodland fairy princess than usual.

And I say: "Are you doing that?"

And I say: "I love you so much."

And I say: "Are you okay?"

Because my girlfriend, the girl I have kissed for the very first time, has suddenly burst out sobbing.

"Hey," I whisper. "We can take it slow. It's okay. I get that this is a lot. It's a lot for me too."

"It's not that," Ivy says between hiccups. "It's like. I finally got to kiss you, I finally got to kiss the girl I love, and it just feels like such a huge gift, you know?"

I nod. I know. I really, really know.

"Like, most people get to kiss their girlfriends all the time. They probably take it for granted, just getting to be here. In this park. Kissing." Ivy wipes her cheeks. "I'll never take it for granted that I get to kiss you every day."

My mouth turns up of its own accord. "Every day, huh?"

She shakes her head. "No jokes."

So, despite how scary it is, I don't let myself hide the depth of my feelings with my humor. I make myself look directly into her eyes, and I can't stop my voice from cracking when I say it.

"Every day."

Her mouth forms this tiny smile as she wraps her arms around me. Her smile says *thank you* and her eyes say *more*. She kisses me again while the pink-peach-yellow-green-rainbow petals fall on our cheeks and eyelashes.

When we finally stop kissing (two minutes later? ten? a year?), I gasp for breath, and I gasp because my girlfriend looks different.

"Ivy, don't be alarmed, but have you noticed that your skin is slightly green?"

Ivy laughs and holds one of her arms up to the sunlight. "You know, I could feel that happening. Kind of tingly. I wondered what it was."

She doesn't seem worried, so I try not to feel that way either. "Do you feel okay?"

She nods. "I think kissing you makes all my cells feel more alive."

Number one on the list of things we'll be science-ing later.

"Well, that works because I could spend forever doing that." I brush some petals from her face, not because they don't look beautiful there, but because I'll take any excuse to touch her.

My phone is still sitting on the ground, and even though it's sprinkled with petals, I can read that the time is one-thirty.

"But he's going to be here in thirty minutes."

What Really Happened to Alice the First

Covering my injuries with makeup became second nature. I got so good at hiding them, I sometimes forgot they were there. So when Jervis decreed that we needed fresh tea and then asked me why was a raven like a writing desk, I wasn't thinking about the bruises under my eyes. Even when the steam from the new pot of hot water was billowing against my cheeks like a facial. Even when I rubbed at my eyes because I was so exhausted from the nightmares I'd had the night before.

I didn't know the steam from the teapot had melted my makeup.

Or that I'd smudged it off with the back of my hand.

Not until Jervis spied it.

"Alice, what happened to your eyes?"

And I panicked and said the first thing that came to mind. "Father."

I waited, clenching my fingernails into my stockings under the table. But luckily, he just nodded and said, "Yes, Father *would* do something like that. He gave Alice two black eyes the day before we ran away, did you know that? I never saw him do it, but I know it was him. He locked me in the attic that night like I was the one who had done something wrong. Because he thought it would keep me from saving her, you see? But I saved her all the same. I climbed down the drainpipe while she was sleeping, and I stuffed a rag in her mouth so she wouldn't startle when she saw me. We snuck out together and went to Wonderland. And we were happy there—and safe—for a very long time."

Today wasn't like the other days. Today, Jervis was feeling different. The kind of day where he was prone to sulking and reminiscing. I poured him a cup of tea and let him feed me bits of scone with jam and clotted cream, and then he said, "Have I ever told you what happened to my sister, Alice?"

This was the most dangerous, most tenuous of situations. If I said, *I am Alice and I'm right here*, he might claim me an impostor. If I said, *No, tell me what happened to her*, he might fly into a rage and tell me I was there and ask me why I was wearing her clothes if I wasn't.

I landed on: "Please tell me, Jervis."

It was sufficient.

"We were hiding in the basement of an art gallery. I painted the cinder block walls with a wonderland of color and stole bread and cakes so she wouldn't be hungry. And every day we had a tea party out of chipped cups."

He looked at me like I was expected to respond here, so I said, "It sounds beautiful, Jervis." Feet stepping onto wafer-thin ice and hoping it didn't crack.

"Oh, it was, it was." He stared at the door with the golden lock for a long time before answering. Then his eyes went black with rage. "Until *he* came. They were searching the basement, tearing apart Wonderland with their grubby fists. We were hiding in the crawl space, behind the water heater, so silent. We sat in the dirt and pulled the plastic moisture barrier over our heads like a blanket while they called out her name.

"But Alice was having trouble being quiet. She was scared. And then I was scared. What if she made a peep, and he found her? I couldn't let her go tumbling after.

"So, I had to help her be quiet. But it was all his fault, don't you see? I didn't want her to turn blue like that."

I was having trouble catching my breath. "Of course you didn't."

He turned on me with steely eyes. "Of course I didn't what?"

I tried to respond, but the words stuck in my throat. It was hotter now, so hot, and the air was thicker too.

"*Didn't kill her? IS THAT WHAT YOU MEAN TO SAY?*" Face red. Veins popping.

I still couldn't speak. My heart was beating so fast.

"WE NEED CLEAN CUPS. MOVE DOWN," he screamed. But I was frozen. "WHY AREN'T YOU MOVING?"

Heart on the verge of exploding.

Move, Alice, move. It's just moving. It's just breathing. I pushed myself up from the chair, shaking, but as soon as I tried to take the first step, I fell.

And I went tumbling.

CHAPTER 23

WE SIP OUR RAINBOW SLUSHIES. ONLY TWENTY-FIVE MIN-utes left until he's here.

Vengeance blows in wearing a rainbow chest plate and a take-no-prisoners expression, and we go over the plan again real quick just to be safe.

Fifteen minutes.

Vengeance tells us about her upcoming triathlon.

Ten minutes.

I sneak one more kiss with Ivy. Cross *Find a cure so we can kiss for approximately forever* off the Harlivy Summer Bucket List.

Five minutes.

That's when I see Shiloh waving at me from across the lawn.

"Harley! Hey, Harley!" Shiloh flaps their arms like they're trying to flag down an airplane.

One by one, Ivy and King Shark and Vengeance see them. And one by one, their chests tighten.

This is bad. Spectacularly bad.

"I'm so glad I ran into you! Didn't you see my texts?" Shiloh wraps me in a quick hug and says hi to Ivy.

I've got to get them out of here. The Dollmaker will be here any minute.

"I'm King Shark," says King Shark, offering them a handshake. "Are you Shiloh? I've been looking forward to meeting you. Harley talks about you all the time."

Shiloh looks up at the giant (costumed) shark-man standing in front of them and gulps. They interned at Arkham last year—they know what's lurking underneath. "Oh, really?" They reply with a pointed look at me that says, *Funny, she's never talked about harboring a known Super-Villain once.*

"And this is . . ." I trail off because I'm not sure if I should introduce her as Vengeance or Bianca.

"Vengeance," she cuts in.

"So, yeah, that's everybody." Let's get these intros out of the way so we can get Shiloh to safety and ourselves to certain danger.

"It's nice to meet you too," Shiloh says, holding out a hand to Vengeance and looking visibly rattled when she shakes it. I have got to tell Vengeance to take it easy on the handshakes. The girl doesn't know her own strength.

"Isn't it beautiful today?" Shiloh's voice has this strange sort of brightness. "The weather is perfect."

It really is. Sunny and gorgeous but not too hot considering it's the first Saturday in June (Gotham City likes to be the place that kicks off Pride month).

If I wasn't about to meet The Dollmaker, I would tell Shiloh that.

If I wasn't about to trade myself to a butcher, I would

entertain myself by trying to play matchmaker with Shiloh and Vengeance because it has just occurred to me that I don't know two people who are more freakishly obsessed with running and fitness.

Instead, I say (with the heaviest of hearts because no one does Cupid like Harley Freaking Quinn), "I'm sorry, Shiloh, but we were just heading somewhere else."

Vengeance is craning her head in every direction, searching for The Dollmaker. I should be doing the same thing.

"Well, I'll go with you!" says Shiloh with a quick glance at Vengeance. (I freaking knew it!)

Her fists clench at her sides. She turns to Shiloh. "Look, we're already supposed to be there, and we're not really allowed to bring anyone else."

"Oh." And their face. It goes through the five stages of crush-grief in a matter of seconds. "Sure, um." Their eyes flick to me. "I'll see you around, I guess."

They turn to walk away, and their shoulders are the shoulders of every little kid who's just been told, *You can't play kickball with us.* So, despite everything that's going on, I run after them and squeeze their hand.

"Hey, I'm really sorry. I'll call you later, okay?"

"Sure, whatever," they reply, shooting a parting death glare at Vengeance before they go.

I sigh because that did not go AT ALL the way it should have. I sigh because I'm three minutes late for my nightmarish date with destiny. I trudge toward the street, not nearly happy enough for someone being passed by the word *LOVE* constructed entirely out of rainbow balloons.

And then I see him.

Standing across the road from me is a man wearing a corduroy color-block T-shirt, striped pants held together with safety pins, and an expression that can only be described as pretentious. I wish I had gotten a better look at his face in those security videos from Arkham Acres.

I step closer, out into the street, gesturing for my friends to stay back.

He moves closer too.

It's got to be him, right? He wouldn't be looking at me like this, all hungry, if it wasn't him.

His face splits into a smile, and it changes his whole demeanor. He looks almost charming. And his eyes, they were so hungry before, but now they seem . . . *kind*. "It's nice to finally meet you, Harley."

I understand how he gets the girls to go with him now. I bet when he turns on that smile, he can take them in broad daylight.

"Where's Stella?"

We're still a good fifteen feet apart, and I have to call it across the road. He shrugs, unbothered, waiting as a group of dancers twirl between us in their colorful capes.

"Who can say?" He says it smugly, like a person holding all the cards.

I narrow my eyes. "You were supposed to bring her."

"And you were supposed to come alone."

I glance behind me, and Ivy moves forward, but I hold out my hand like, *It's okay, I've got this.*

"Where is she?" I say, harsher this time.

The Dollmaker sighs. "I'll be keeping her as leverage until after your transformation."

Of course. Of course he'd try something like this.

"That wasn't the deal." If I knew where he was keeping

Stella and Jasmin, I would take him out right now. Instead, I step closer. Lower my voice. "I'm not coming with you until you let Stella go."

There's a soft gasp behind me. Crap, I thought I was far enough away and speaking quietly enough that Ivy wouldn't hear.

"You are," says The Dollmaker. "And would you like to know why?"

He doesn't wait for an answer. Just points to a firefighter Pride float that's barreling our way.

"Your girlfriend is about to be standing next to a tank filled with industrial-strength weed killer. Maybe she'll survive it, and maybe she won't. But all I have to do is wave."

He's full of it, I think. And then I take a better look at the float. A tank of brightly colored liquid decorates the back of it. People in firefighter uniforms dance around, a couple of them holding a hose connected to the float.

There's something off about the firefighters. Something that separates them from the rest of the Pride goers, though I can't put my finger on what it is. It feels hard to think right now. As they draw closer, one of them points a hose directly at Ivy.

It doesn't matter. The rage boils inside me, and I don't try to hold it back. "*My girlfriend* could conjure an army of plants and kill you and every last one of your goons in an instant."

This time, I do say it loud enough for Ivy to hear. I hope she gets the message. *Attack! Attack now!*

The Dollmaker doesn't look nearly scared enough.

"She could." That smug freaking smile again. "If she wasn't unconscious."

What the—?

I hear a loud thump behind me, and I turn, but it isn't Ivy on the ground—it's King Shark. Ivy bends over him, asking if he's okay. This isn't how it was supposed to happen. I feel a little dizzy as I turn back to face The Dollmaker.

"Those slushies were delicious, weren't they?"

The slushies. Oh no. We gulped them down like sugar fiends. King Shark. And Ivy. And me.

"My other friend didn't have one," I say defiantly. Triumphantly.

But The Dollmaker merely looks bored. "No. She didn't. Help. *Please.*"

He pulls out a tiny crossbow-looking thing and shoots Vengeance. I yell out her name, but it doesn't keep her from crumpling next to King Shark, a feathered dart sticking out of her arm. Ivy is sitting on the ground with them now, struggling to hold her head up, fighting to hang onto consciousness. For me, I can tell. She never takes her eyes off mine.

The Dollmaker crosses the street to take me, and I fling up a fist to stop him, but I feel weak, so weak. He throws me over his shoulder like a sack of potatoes, but I keep my eyes open, keep them glued to Ivy's until it all goes black.

The look on her face tells me everything. She knows I sacrificed myself.

Jervis Likes Me Less

Now that he has told me.

CHAPTER 24

YOU'D SCREAM IF YOU WOKE UP HERE TOO.

In a place like this, it's the only appropriate response. I screech my throat raw and scoot myself backward on the cot.

The eyes staring back at me don't even look human. They blink at me, upper and lower lids opening and closing and a third eyelid, a translucent one, going back and forth over gray irises and black pupils. The girl—I think she's a girl—tilts her head like a bird. Like a predator. Assessing.

"She's awake," she rasps into a smartwatch.

My chest heaves up and down. Breathing is hard when you're disoriented and an uncanny bird-girl is hovering over you with talons where her fingernails should be.

Focus, Harley. I'm on my own, which means The Doll-maker probably only took me and not my friends, or maybe just that he's smart enough to put us in separate rooms. I'm on a cot. In a small white room. White cinder block walls on two sides. White drywall on the others. But not nice drywall.

This has been hastily put up. Isn't even painted. Could I kick through it? Escape?

My clothes are white too. My brilliant and colorful Pride outfit—the outfit I was wearing when I shared my first kiss with Ivy—is gone. My handbag and phone and newly acquired mallet—also gone. Just a white T-shirt, white drawstring pants, white socks, and, I'm just gonna make an assumption, white underwear. I wonder who took off my clothes, and I clench my fists at my sides, imagining it was him.

"Where are my clothes?" I say, my voice full of daggers.

I need to know (and not just because it determines how much of a pulp I need to beat The Dollmaker to). I had sewn a tracker into my tutu and cosplay-glued another to the inside of my bracelet. (I got the idea from Dr. Crane.) I was counting on Ivy and Vengeance using those trackers to follow me here—it was all in the note I left in Ivy's bag.

"Where are my clothes?" I say it again, this time with full-on katanas in my voice.

I leap into a crouch on my cot, hoping to startle this girl, get her attention. It works. She takes several steps back, checking her watch again, and I use the opportunity to slide a pen off the table next to me. Her feathers rearrange themselves—I have *literally* ruffled her feathers. Because, oh, right, did I mention, SHE HAS WINGS??

And now that I'm noticing the wings and the feathers and the whole dark-raven-of-the-night vibe she's got going, it hits me. I've seen this girl before. Well, not her, exactly, but a replica of her. In miniature. Nestled in tissue paper and tied up with string. She's one of the dolls he sent me.

"Lenore?" The name just pops out of my mouth, the one the doll was tagged with.

She startles again. Wasn't expecting me to know that.

"How did you—"

But before she can finish her sentence, the door behind her opens.

It's him.

The Dollmaker.

In all his unholy glory.

He wears paint-splattered (blood-splattered?) scrubs and the kind of sad mustache that only struggling artists have. But aside from that, it pains me to admit it, he's objectively good-looking. He doesn't *seem* like the kind of person who would hurt you.

"Harley." He smiles, and the points of his teeth glint in the fluorescent lighting. Not the charming smile from before. "It's so good to see you awake. Again."

The anger boils inside me, and I leap off the cot at him, pulling the pen from under my leg.

It all happens so quickly. Me, brandishing a ballpoint like a sword. Him, standing there so calmly, confidently. And something else. A dark blur at the periphery of my vision. Something bludgeoning me in the head. Stars behind my eyes. Lenore.

I realize it too late, as I'm on the floor trying to piece together what just happened. I groan and start to sit up.

"Don't," she says, one taloned foot to my throat.

I don't. I stop. I put my hands in front of me in the universal sign for *I am bested here and I give up*. For now, at least. I can't believe she's on his side. Must be some kind of Stockholm syndrome.

The Dollmaker is looking at me, but when he speaks, it's to Lenore. "When she's ready to be calm, she can have dinner with the others."

He watches my face for a moment longer, hand twitching at his side like he's holding a pencil. Or a scalpel.

I draw them until I don't itch anymore.

And then he leaves.

How long was I out for that it's already dinnertime? I don't bother asking Lenore. I do tell her she can remove her claw from my throat, though.

She retracts it, eyes narrowing, and the tip of one talon slips across my skin. Beads of red on a paper-white neck. I glare at her and wipe the scratch with my hand. It's only bleeding a little bit. I smear my hand all over my fresh white pants to clean it off, whistling as I do because I bet it'll piss off The Dollmaker.

Lenore regards me disdainfully, like, *Are you quite finished?*

I smile brightly in return. "What's for dinner? Do you eat real food here, or is it doll food? Because as much as I love rubber eggs and plastic broccoli, I could really go for a cheeseburger."

Lenore is not impressed. "We have real food."

"Uh-huh. I bet it's all protein shakes. And oatmeal. That's the vibe I'm getting from this uniform at least. Are we about to get divided into factions? Forced to fight in an arena? Inserted into a video game?"

This time Lenore's face is less stoic and more downcast. "No."

And a cold feeling slips into my gut because of course I know what he's really doing with us. The forgetting for a second only makes the remembering that much more awful.

The door creaks again, and I realize Lenore has taken my moment of sadness as me falling in line/consenting to be calm/whatever. She gestures for me to go first, so I do. At least there'll be dinner.

"Am I the only new person today?" I ask.

She looks at me strangely. "Yes."

So, he didn't take Ivy or Vengeance or King Shark. Good. Imagining Ivy, trapped in this place . . . I would lose my damn mind.

Not that they'd be able to keep her here. I'm fairly certain my girlfriend is the most powerful woman in Gotham City. Or would be if she ever chose to unleash it.

Lenore walks me down a few short hallways, and then she pushes through a double door into a big room with rows of tables and rows of chairs. It looks like the cafeteria for one of those weird little private schools where all the students dress in muted colors and do yoga between classes.

This is where the missing girls have been going. This is where he keeps them.

There are so many more than I thought.

Heads turn to look at me like they're all being pulled by the same string. Cool, cool, that's not creepy at all.

It's mostly girls who look high-school- or college-aged. But there are some guys too. I walk past a table where a child (girl? creature?) with skin the color of blood eats her dinner next to a freckle-faced boy who doesn't appear to have gone under The Dollmaker's knife yet. They can't be more than seven or eight. I didn't realize he had children here too, both boys and girls.

That crimson girl—he sent her doll to me—I didn't realize she was a child. Dolls tend to have a weirdly childlike look to begin with. I survey the room, trying to pick out each and every person who is stacked in boxes in Ivy's closet. The boy with the bat wings. (I remember getting his doll ages ago—I thought it was a girl with a pixie cut.) The girl with the burned and bubbling face, flamethrower arm resting heavily on the table.

Honestly, this cafeteria is like something out of a school for wizards and fae and magical creatures—or it would be if I didn't know these people were actually the product of strange and brutal surgeries and that they were going to be auctioned off to the highest bidder. (Also? It's much too quiet for wizard school. There are two armed guards standing against the walls, watching, and the fear takes up all the air in the room.)

Lenore directs me to the dinner line, where I scoop chicken and salad and black beans and rice onto a plate. (Apparently, it's important to provide your sadistic experiments with a well-balanced diet.)

I do everything I'm supposed to (get a drink, grab a fork and napkin), but on the inside, I am clawing for a way to get out. Assessing the exits. Searching for anything that could be used as a weapon. The plastic forks look pretty flimsy, but they're probably my best bet so far. I wonder if any of the other people eating dinner would be on my side. They all have to want to get out of here, right? I give Lenore a sideways glance. She sure seems to have drunk the Kool-Aid.

I hear the unmistakable sound of a car backfiring, and I jump. Wait a minute! My head snaps in the direction of the sound. I wasn't sure how long I was out, but that sound means we're probably still in Gotham City. Or at least, *some* city. I guess Gotham City makes sense given the number of stalker-y trips The Dollmaker made to Gotham U's campus.

The table nearest me is different from the others. All the girls there are nearly identical. Blond hair, dainty features, blue dresses, weirdly good posture. No discernible powers.

And it's funny—I know for a fact I never got a doll that looked like them. I wonder what that's about.

"You don't sit there," says Lenore when I pause too long.

The dinner crowd turns to stare at me again.

And even though this is an entirely different situation, the whole thing feels so middle school lunchroom that I scurry to the nearest table with empty spots left.

But when I get to my seat, I nearly drop my plate.

The girl sitting across from me is Jasmin.

My Schedule

Like any other teenage girl, I wake up, I eat breakfast, and I go to school.

I wake up in a dorm room in a madman's lair with three other girls who look just like me.

I eat a scrambled egg white omelet, served to me by a cafeteria lady who rarely says a word because the chip in her head tells her not to speak to us.

I go to class and learn how to be the best Alice I can be while the sounds of the city filter in through cinder block walls.

But I know at some point each day, the white rabbit will lead me to a tea party and then disappear. That's when the fear sets in.

I tell the other Alices I am so looking forward to my tea party. My brain makes me say it even though my heart knows it's a lie.

I spend so much of my days playing make-believe. Pretending not to be scared when The Mad Hatter opens the door to Wonderland and there is blood under his fingernails. Pretending I don't hear the noises coming from behind the door with the golden lock. Pretending not to notice when Jervis calls The Dollmaker over his watch and then steps outside to argue with him.

Today is different, though. An unexpected blip in the itinerary.

Because when I get back from my tea party, I see that Anton has brought home a new girl, one with colorful hair and fire in her eyes. She looks like the type to burn the whole place down.

CHAPTER 25

I FORCE MYSELF TO CALMLY SET DOWN MY PLATE. CALMLY pull out my chair and sit down. On the inside, I am anything but calm. I make myself study the rest of the people at the table because it helps me avoid staring at her. And even though I'm not looking at her, I can *feel* that Jasmin is doing the same thing.

Our eyes only locked for a second, but I felt the sizzle. It would be dangerous to look at her. It's dangerous just sitting at this table with her. We can't look at each other without everyone realizing we know each other. And if they can figure it out, then *he* will figure it out. And I don't even want to think about the ways he'll use it against us.

Based on what happened with Stella, I know he—
STELLA.

I search the room. Where is she? She's gotta be here. But I scan face after face only to find that she isn't. Does he have her somewhere else? Is she okay? I start to stand without realizing it. Lenore clears her throat, and I sit back down.

"Does anyone know a girl named Stella?" I say into my

hard plastic water cup as I take a drink. I wonder if I could smash it against the table and stab my way out of here with the jagged edges or if that only works with glass bottles.

The other people at the table trade glances, but their eyes also go to Lenore and to another girl at the table, one who looks like she eats wrath for breakfast and bathes in disgust. I wonder what's so different about Lenore and this other girl, what he did to get them on his side. As I check the cafeteria for Stella one more time, the boy sitting next to Jasmin gives me the subtlest nod.

So she is here. Well, not here-here, but somewhere in this place.

I still can't get over the sheer number of people here. I may have come for Stella, but I can't just take her and leave everyone else. I have to try to save all of them.

Lenore goes to get more water, and I finally risk a glance at Jasmin. She's different. It's a realization that takes place in the pit of my stomach instead of in my brain. Her left hand looks like it's wearing a metal glove, but knowing The Dollmaker, it's just as likely that it's fused to her body, intertwined with the bone underneath. And then her throat—there's a place that the neck of her T-shirt doesn't quite cover, a place that looks like a corner of a circuit board with wires going I don't even want to know where.

I open my mouth to say something—I'm not even sure where to start—a fountain of questions waiting to spill out of me, but Jasmin cuts me off with a small shake of her head. Her eyes dart to the angry girl. Right. So, it's definitely not safe to talk in front of her. I file that away for later.

Some of these people *are* safe, though. Some of them would be on my side. I look around the room, and I think about who. The girl who looks like a beetle? The boy whose skin and hair sizzle with electricity? Which of you might be willing to risk it all to help me? As I walk to refill my water, I pass by the table with the four creepy blond girls. Not the Stepford Four, that's for damn sure.

I press my cup against the lever, watching the water fill all the way to the top. Then I turn around.

"Whoa." I almost run smack into creepy blond girl #3, not that I can tell them apart. My water sloshes over the top of my cup and splashes on the floor.

"Hi," she says, staring at me with her probing blue eyes.

"Hi," I say back. *Weirdo.*

"Let me get you a napkin for that spill." She grabs a couple that are next to the drinks station, and we both bend over to wipe up the small puddle of water on the floor, only instead of actually looking at the water, she keeps those eyes of hers fixed on me THE WHOLE TIME. Even when I get back to my table and she gets back to hers, I look over my shoulder, and sure enough, she's still looking. And I know these girls are real people and not the dolls he sends me, but I swear, when she looks at you, it feels like one of those ancient Victorian porcelain numbers sitting on a dusty shelf with a cracked face, trying to steal your soul. I shudder.

After dinner, it's chores and then quiet time, except for me and Lenore. She leads me around different parts of the building.

"Is there gonna be any dessert on this prison tour?" I ask.

"No," she says, in a way that feels more scathing than if she had simply ignored me.

She goes into a room that looks like a dystopian classroom, but with more color. Plucks a watch out of a locked cabinet at the front. It's the only one in there, from what I can see.

"This has your schedule," she tells me. "You're to be awake, dressed, and at breakfast by eight a.m."

"Any wiggle room in that?"

"No."

Oh-ho-okay. But I keep pelting her with questions because a grumpy Lenore is a distracted Lenore, and a distracted Lenore is more likely to accidentally spill information or to not realize that every second I am strategizing, plotting.

I pause and actually read my schedule. This thing is surprisingly detailed.

Harley's schedule
Saturday

> 7:00-7:40 p.m. Tour with Lenore
>
> 7:40-8:45 p.m. Quiet time in dormitory
>
> 8:45-9:30 p.m. Bedtime routine & dormitory cleanup
>
> 9:45 p.m. Lights out

Sunday

> 7:00 a.m. Wake up
>
> 7:00-8:00 a.m. Morning routine
>
> 8:00-9:00 a.m. Breakfast & cleanup

Something about it makes me think that I'm not the only one with a schedule like this. That every other person who ended up here has one too. But what's the point? What's the goal of all this? I keep scrolling, but I can't see anything past breakfast the next day, which feels weirdly threatening.

After the classrooms, Lenore shows me the training areas (bars on the windows) and the dormitories (watches scanned to get in and out) and the green space outside (ultra-tall privacy fences capped in barbed wire). Everything designed for maximum control as The Dollmaker creates his pieces and trains them to be the perfect sidekicks.

I drift away from her as the tour continues.

"What's down there?" I ask, pointing to a darkened corridor that can only be described as ominous.

Lenore whirls around, feathers ruffling again, like a goose just before it attacks. Whew, I've really gotten her this time.

"You are to never go down there. And whatever you do, you never open that door. Are we clear?"

"Why? What's in—"

But Lenore is having none of my mess. "I said, are we clear?"

I roll my eyes. "Okay, okay. Nothing at all in the West Wing. Got it."

But the golden door waits at the end of the hallway. It beckons. What could be worse than everything I already know?

When Lenore resumes our tour, she is even more surly than she was before. She gives me the barest glimpse of the showers (not communal, thank goodness) and the rest of our bathroom (surprisingly clean).

"Do I have a toothbrush? What about floss? You know, gum health is very important. I read a paper about—"

Lenore cuts in sharply. "Please stop talking."

"Pretty sure I'm—"

She grips my wrist with her taloned fingers, and I'm so surprised by her urgency that I really do shut the eff up.

"I don't know how much time we have," she says, and her entire voice/face/vibe is different. How in the hell is it possible to change so much in the span of a few seconds?

"This isn't an artist's colony or modeling school or whatever he's told you. This is a trafficking gang. And The Dollmaker isn't an artist. Or, well, *he is*, but only in the sickest sense. This is his idea of art." She gestures to herself—her wings and claws and strangely inhuman eyes.

I'm so stunned by her confession (or, more accurately, her acting abilities) that it takes me a second to stutter, "I—I know."

She frowns at me. Reassesses. "You do?"

"I got myself kidnapped on purpose because he took my friend Stella. Also, he's obsessed with me. Have you seen Stella?"

Lenore nods. "She's here."

"Is she okay?"

Another nod. "She's going through the Trials, but she hasn't been through the Metamorphosis yet. Or the Calming."

"The what?" Is this real language that exists outside of a horror movie?

"The Trials are where he sees what you're good at. What your strengths are." She shivers. "And your weaknesses."

I imagine what she's been though and wince.

"The Metamorphosis is . . ." She gestures to herself again.

"That. Got it." I rake my eyes over everything he's done to her while trying to hide that that's what I'm doing.

She notices. "The Calming is worse," she says.

"Seriously?" How could anything be worse than a forced

metamorphosis? I remember the letters he sent me. Some of the girls ended up in unimaginable physical pain. Some of them died.

"Losing your free will," Lenore says bitterly. "They put these chips inside us so he can control us."

CHIPS? But I destroyed them all. Dr. Crane's in Arkham now—being psychoanalyzed by people who used to be his colleagues. He was implanting mind-control chips in the Arkham patients, using them to manufacture fear spray in the basement, but I stopped whatever sinister unleash-fear-on-Gotham plot he had brewing. I almost *died* making sure there wasn't a single chip left. How did The Dollmaker get ahold of more?

"I've helped them do it to other people. I didn't have a choice."

It almost sounds like a question. An intercession. Like she's hoping I'll weigh what she's done and declare that she's not a bad person.

"Of course you didn't," I say. But something doesn't make sense. If she's been chipped . . .

"How in the world are you talking to me right now? If you've been chipped, I mean?" I watched Dr. Crane embed a chip in King Shark. He didn't get his life back until Talia removed it.

"There are lapses. If you know how to fight for them." Something about the set of Lenore's teeth tells me she's a fighter.

"Lapses," I say.

I remember now, reading some email correspondence between The Scarecrow and a person named Anton. A person who Talia and I knew was taking girls across the city but who only revealed what he was doing with those girls in that very first letter signed *The Dollmaker.*

> My partner and I were intrigued by your idea that fear could be used to enhance our behavioral modification technology. As we discussed, the chip my partner developed has not proven as robust as we would like it to be in recent trials, and there have been . . . lapses.

So, The Dollmaker still has chips, but they're not the good chips. Not the ones Crane helped develop. He doesn't have foolproof, airtight, absolute control.

I can work with that.

That's what I tell myself, at least. Stay strong. Don't think about everything you sacrificed. Falling-falling-falling. The chemicals bubbling over me and dragging me down. The burning that crawled up my skin and down my throat. It's hard to breathe. Because I'm back there in those chemicals. Because those chips are here—*now*—hurting people. Lapses or no lapses, I've seen what they can do.

King Shark, crushing that ladybug.

The Scarecrow, jabbing me in the neck.

And now, my dear, you are mine.

He almost—I almost—

"I can only help so much," says Lenore, snapping me back to reality. "I'll do what I can, but your best bet is to work with the others who haven't been chipped yet. Especially the ones who have powers."

Noted.

"It's tough, though," she continues. "He doesn't tell us

when he chips people, so there's always the chance you're talking to a spy. And you have to watch out for—"

She stops mid-sentence. Blinks rapidly like she's got something stuck in her eye. Or her brain. Voice/face/vibe changes again.

"I'll show you where you sleep now," says Lenore in a flat voice that is nothing like the warmth and passion she was lit up with before.

I still have so many questions, though. "But what about—"

"What?" She narrows her eyes at me so sharply that my question nearly chokes me.

"Nothing."

Lapse over. Got it. I'm not getting anything else out of Lenore right now.

I brush my teeth and change into blue pajamas so pale they feel more like the suggestion of blue. The other four girls in my room wear matching ones. Except the little crimson girl. She wears a nightgown. Same color, though. He's big on aesthetics, this guy.

I climb up into the top bunk. Lenore is underneath in case I'm thinking of trying anything. (I am always thinking of trying things.) I pretend to read for a while—there was a book waiting on my bed when I got here. *Alice's Adventures in Wonderland*. But mostly, I'm scoping out the room. And the roommates. There are four sets of bunk beds. Me and Lenore. The angry girl—I've learned her name is Jett—shares a bunk with the little girl. And then there's the other girl, younger and shy, who I don't think has been changed yet. I wonder how long she's been here.

I wonder what Ivy's doing right now. She had to have found my note, and I'm sure she followed the trackers to wherever The Dollmaker dumped my clothes. (Not any-where nearby, I'm assuming, given that Ivy hasn't busted through the ceiling riding a giant sunflower yet.) She must be terrified. And angry that I didn't tell her my plan. And hurt. I try to imagine what I would say to her if she was here. How I'd convince her to forgive me.

I touch my fingers to my lips to see if they're still puffy from our first kiss. It was a hell of a kiss. String of kisses? But my lips don't feel any different than they usually do. Any trace of Ivy is gone now.

And I know it's a small thing compared to all the other very big things I am fighting right now, but did he seriously have to snatch me away on this, the day of my very first kiss with my girlfriend? I think about what would have happened when Ivy and I got home. Where that string of kisses would have led. I think about it until I'm practically dizzy.

The lights go off on their own, which is pretty jarring despite the *lights out* calendar notice on my watch. The room is pitch-black with the exception of some track lighting that leads to the bathroom and only the bathroom. And then out of nowhere—fireflies.

What the—

Or, no, not fireflies, though the light definitely feels alive.

"What is that?" I whisper. It seems like the kind of thing you whisper about.

"It's Fallon," says Lenore. And I think I remember hearing that was the name of the scarlet fairy girl.

"Her? Like, her-her?"

"She's bioluminescent," answers Lenore in a voice that suggests there will be no further questions. (Well, none that get answered anyway.)

So I pull the covers up under my chin, and for just a moment it feels like I'm at summer camp, not that we could ever actually afford one of those. This is what summer camp looked like in the movies, though. Minus the prison vibes and the cars honking outside.

And the surgeries.

And the animal hybridization experiments.

And the mind control and order forms for people.

Fallon's lights begin to migrate across the room, hovering over me like dancing stars.

"Fallon," says Lenore, and the stars wink out.

I think about what The Dollmaker did to Lenore. About how different she was in the bathroom when she was just her and not the controlled, warped product of some chip.

He doesn't have my mind. Not yet.

So, I let it fly in every direction, searching for a way out. Especially the vengeful, vicious directions. The violent ones.

I'll hit him when he least expects it.

Plan B

If I can't control when I have a lapse, there's no way I'll ever be able to talk to this girl.

Maybe I write down the things I want to tell her in here instead.

For instance:

The Dollmaker interrupted us during a tea party today and asked The Mad Hatter to come talk to him in the hallway. That's never happened before. The Mad Hatter turned red as strawberry marmalade. I knew he would want me to stay at the table, but I tiptoed over and pressed myself against the wall so I could hear.

The Dollmaker: . . . can't believe you'd . . . so soon. After that stunt you pulled at the library . . .

The Mad Hatter: [growled something in reply that I couldn't quite make out]

The Dollmaker: . . . bring them back here? . . . going to figure out where we are.

The Mad Hatter (shouting now): What about your auction? Like that won't bring the police down on Wonderland. Why is it only okay to take risks when it's for your things? Why can't I ever be the one to take them?

The Dollmaker: Now, now, I never said your things weren't—

The Mad Hatter (screaming): DIDN'T YOU?!

The Dollmaker: I don't think—

The Mad Hatter: THEN YOU SHOULDN'T SPEAK.

The Dollmaker (managing him the way you would a child having a tantrum): All right, all right. Calm down, Jervis.

The Mad Hatter (mollified, completely oblivious): Yes, you're right. I wouldn't want to lose your head. But it wasn't very civil of you to come to tea without being invited.

The Dollmaker: Yes, well. Perhaps I'll bring Lenore with me next time.

He never forgot to remind The Mad Hatter of that. That The Mad Hatter may have created the chips, but The Dollmaker held the remotes.

His footsteps began tapping away, and I rushed back to my chair and sat up straight.

"Yes, and perhaps I'll take her apart and see just how much she's like a writing desk," The Mad Hatter hissed as he shut the door and came back to the party.

He looked so angry, I didn't know what he'd do.

CHAPTER 26

FOR JUST A SECOND, MY BRAIN CONVINCES ITSELF I AM IN Ivy's canopy bed with her, snuggled under bamboo sheets. Then I open my eyes and find a scarlet-eyed demon girl sitting on the edge of my bed.

I sit up with a start, and she lets out a squeak and falls (jumps?) off the bed.

"Sorry," I call. "I didn't mean to scare you. Are you okay?"

She pops back up. Nods.

And then she rushes out of the room and completely disappears.

Huh. Well, that's one way to wake up.

I yawn and think about killing The Dollmaker and stretch and imagine exploding this whole building.

And then demon girl is back, handing me a toothbrush and toothpaste. She hops from foot to foot, agitated. I check my watch.

Sunday

7:00-8:00 a.m. Morning routine

8:00-9:00 a.m. Breakfast & cleanup

Time: 7:50 a.m.

Oh. Ohhh. I have ten minutes to get dressed and be at breakfast. Oops.

I don't know what happens if you're late, but I'm not about to risk missing bacon on a breakfast sandwich or even some cereal, so I bolt out of bed and go brush my teeth in the shower. When I come back in a towel, demon girl—Fallon; if she's helping me, I should really stop calling her demon girl—is waiting with an outfit from my dresser.

"Thanks," I tell her.

She smiles (at least, I think she does—her mouth is kind of odd, and by odd, I mean horrifying), and we walk to breakfast together, making it with seconds to spare.

There are no breakfast sandwiches, but there are scrambled eggs and blueberries, and neither are half bad. Still no Stella, though. I check every face twice, just to be sure.

Also? There is still nothing on my schedule for the rest of the day.

"Do I just cease to exist after breakfast?" I joke. "Or, oh! Is it like some kind of free space where you get to choose friendship bracelet making or archery or getting turned into a monster?"

I try to make a note of who laughs or seems like they want to laugh because they probably haven't been chipped yet and might be safe to talk to.

"The Dollmaker tells us what we need to know as we need to know it," says Lenore, who has just appeared at my elbow like I've called her to me by asking a question.

I'm working up a snarky response, one that will be sure to raise her blood pressure a few millimeters of mercury, when a flurry of activity sweeps though the cafeteria. Like watching the wave, but more subtle. Everyone starts checking their watches, so I check mine too.

9:00 a.m. Meeting with The Dollmaker

My heartbeat speeds up, but it's going to be okay. This is going to be okay. I need to get answers about Stella, and this will help me get them. I'll make sure of it.

But when Lenore escorts me to my meeting with The Dollmaker, I can't help feeling like none of us make it out of here alive.

It feels like the strangest combination of an artist's studio and a surgical suite. There's an operation table with a movable light overhead and anesthesia equipment. Enough piercing metal tools to turn your stomach. And then there's the other side of the room. Fabrics and makeup and color and texture and murder boards jam-packed with inspiration photos and ideas for each "piece." They're not people to him; that's clear from looking at the place. I always wondered if he called them dolls to put some distance between himself and their humanity, but now I know I'm wrong. He truly doesn't see them as anything more than playthings. I tear my eyes away from the boards. Even after seeing the order forms, even after receiving his dolls and his letters, this is worse than anything I ever could have imagined. He butchers people in the name of art. To him, that's not a girl—that's a piece of construction paper. That's not a child—it's a lump of clay. He's repulsive.

"Harley." He grins at me like I'm an old friend. "It's so good to finally see you here. You can't imagine what this moment is like for me."

That's probably true.

"I've been working toward this for so long, and now here you are. I should have thought to get champagne. There's just been a lot to do, though."

I plant my hands on my hips. "Where's Stella?"

A muscle in his jaw twitches. "We'll get there, but there's so much I need to show you first."

My eyes flick over the pictures on the wall. I don't see any of me, but there, just over his shoulder, is a photo of Stella surrounded by grotesque sketches, more sketches than any of the other dolls have. A nauseating flurry of artistic direction. Because he's having trouble deciding what to do with her? Because he wanted to give me options? I want to demand that he take me to her. I want to punch him in the face, but I guess if I was smart (which I obviously am), I would take this opportunity to find out what I can. All right, then.

"How did you make Lenore look like that? Your letters said genetic manipulation, but how could you make changes that big in somebody who was already basically an adult?"

His eyes light up. "Let me show you. This was one of my more innovative ideas, and that's saying something."

It's weird how he can be a monster and that obnoxious guy in any grad school art program at exactly the same time.

He pulls back a curtain to reveal what looks like a time machine or a portal to another world or a big giant test tube with machinery on top and bottom or . . .

"It's a hybridization device of my own making."

Or that.

"I worked on it for months. The first couple didn't survive, but now there's no limit to what I can do. Do you want to be able to run like an ostrich? Breathe underwater like a shark?" His hand twitches against his leg as he talks. Because he's imagining drawing me or carving into me?

"It would be pretty cool to fly," I say as if I'm really considering it. This is what he wants. Me, as an ever-admiring partner who hangs on his words. I can use that. "Do Lenore's wings hold her weight?"

He nods. "She flies beautifully."

"That's amazing." I shake my head like I'm trying to wrap my mind around it. Don't smile too much. I don't want to oversell this.

"It really is," he says. "And you, you will be the model for them all. My muse. I have so many plans for you."

I wince, imagining what those plans might be. They're not part of the wall, but maybe he keeps them somewhere else. "You're going to auction me off too?" Let's get him talking about the auction. What it is. When it is. Where it is. What scum scraped from the underworld and the biggest, shiniest buildings downtown might be there.

He looks shocked at the suggestion. "Oh, no. I'm keeping you all for myself."

His eyes rake over me like I'm not even a person, transfixed. And when he takes a step forward, I hold my breath because what if he's had that epiphany he's been waiting for? What if he wants to start now?

"By the way," he says in a low voice. A dangerous voice. "How did you hear about the auction?"

I force myself to meet his eyes. "Just something I overheard."

I hope he believes it. I hope he can't hear my heart beating. I hope some unsuspecting person doesn't get punished for what I just said.

"You don't need to worry about it," he says. "I'll always want you here. But a transformed you. A better you."

There's a crash and a scream from somewhere down the hallway, which is good because it takes his attention away from the face I'm currently making. (Sometimes it's just too hard to pretend to be anything other than a nasty woman.)

He rushes out of the room to investigate.

And I say through gritted teeth, "I'm fine just the way I am."

At first I peek through a crack in the door to see what all the commotion was. The Insect Girl appears to have accidentally jabbed a beetle-like appendage into a door panel while trying to scan her watch. Which appears to have locked everyone inside the classroom. The Dollmaker yells a lot as he struggles to get the door to open, what with the panel smashed and smoking. I close the door to his studio and snicker uncharitably. But now that he's gone, something occurs to me. I'm alone in The Dollmaker's studio. By accident or on purpose, I'm not sure. But I'm going to take advantage either way.

People Who Live in the Tower

Five dormitories, each with eight beds

The Originals

Lenore (Londyn) (raven hybridization)
Jett (bionic eye and ear)
Fallon (vampire squid/box jellyfish hybridization)
Lily? (new girl, no powers)
Harley (no powers)

The Alices

Me (Everly, aka Alice the Fourth)
Shy Alice
Pretty Alice
Funny Alice

The Boys

Gabriel (giant black witchy-looking wings
attached to his back and fused with his nervous
system)
Noah (electric eel hybridization)
Frankie (no powers)
William (no powers)
Cooper (no powers)

Scarab's Room

Scarab (hybridized with multiple species of
beetle, not sure what her before-name was?)

Jasmin (in progress, something with computers)
Navi (no powers)
Miranda (no powers)

Firefly's Room

Firefly (flamethrower fused to body, fireproof)
Maeve (snake hybridization)
Jumana (no powers)

Solitary

New girl (Stella?)

Grown-Ups

Anton (The Dollmaker)
Jervis Tetch (The Mad Hatter)
Six chipped guards
Three chipped people who work in the kitchen

CHAPTER 27

I ONLY HAVE A FEW MINUTES OR A FEW MOMENTS OR A FEW seconds—there's no way of knowing. Something about that makes digging through The Dollmaker's secret files that much more exciting. A note about said files: They are not actually labeled Secret Files, but (A) it's much more fun to think of them that way, and (B) they do seem kind of secret.

Medical information. Scientific research on predatory animals. Surgical protocols. And . . . jackpot! A white box that is mostly empty but still contains a few invitations, much like the one "inviting" me to the meeting at the club that night. Except these invitations are for the meeting to trump all meetings. The auction. The thing he's been working toward for months, if not years.

You are invited to be part of a revolutionary evening.
A night that will redefine artistry and power.
THE DOLLS
Gallery Exhibition & Auction

The auction is only five days away. I have to hurry.

And we're still in Gotham City—just like I suspected! It makes me feel more hopeful that somehow Ivy could—

I hear footsteps in the hallway, and I rush to shove the invitation back in its envelope and make the box look exactly the way it did before I touched it. I can't make it back to my chair in time, so instead I move to the murder wall, brushing past the scalpels as I do. I consciously avoid Stella—if I look too close at his plans for her, it might break me. Instead, I choose one of the least horrifying options—a red fox.

The Dollmaker bursts in just as I assume my best thoughtful-art-student-at-a-gallery pose.

"Oh," I say, turning like I hadn't expected him to catch me like this.

He seems surprised that I'm not in my chair. No, surprised that I'm not in my chair but that instead of being halfway into the ventilation system or armed with a battery of stolen surgical tools, I'm instead surveying his "work." I turn back to the board and work really, really, really hard at not patting my pocket.

"Hey," he says, face splitting into that self-aggrandizing grin of his. "So, you like the fox, huh?"

His question could not be more obvious. *Please tell me how much you like it. How much you like me. Like my work. Tell me I'm a genius. I know it, but I like the way it feels to hear you say it.*

"It's . . . bold." I have to force the words out, but luckily he's too in love with himself to notice.

"Isn't it? That's what I thought when I first designed it. Bold. And groundbreaking too. It took a lot of trouble-shooting."

Good grief, this guy likes blowing his own trumpet. Also—what exactly does "troubleshooting" mean when this is what you do? Dead girls, I'm thinking. Creep show.

"Did you know foxes can see the earth's magnetic field? They pounce when the shadow of magnetic north lines up with the sound of their prey. It's like having a guided missile system inside their heads."

"Wow, I had no idea." I glance around at the other effed-up vision boards in a way that I hope is the right kind of interested, but I make sure my eyes skim over Jasmin's. If he hasn't tried to use her as a bargaining chip yet, he clearly doesn't know we mean anything to each other.

"How many will you be able to get ready before the auction?" I ask.

And the way his eyes cut at me, cold and knowing, I'm scared I pushed too hard too soon.

"Will this one be ready?" I gesture to the fox, affect a devouring kind of gaze, like I simply can't take my eyes off it. I think about letting out a rapturous sigh but decide that would be overkill.

Luckily, my redirection is enough.

"It should be," he says. "I'm thinking of changing her to-morrow night." And then he pauses, hesitant. "Would you like to be there?"

I would rather walk across a glacier barefoot. Gargle with broken glass. He's going to know I'm faking. There are some lies that are just too big. So, I try to find the truth in it. "I'm nervous," I say honestly. "But I would really like to know what's involved in making a piece."

"You'll be fine." He smiles encouragingly. "I'll be with you the whole time, and if you start to feel sick at any point, you can go stand out in the hallway for a minute. Jervis had to do that a couple times, back when he used to come to these. But I'm not worried about you. You're like me. The science, the art, the creative process—you'll be so interested, you'll forget about the gore."

Well. That's reassuring.

"I hope I don't have to go stand in the hallway." It's the only thing I can think to say that will sound remotely like the truth. Also? It's unsettling how considerate he can seem. Almost gentle. I see how he manages to lure girls here. He's like one of those people who are pleasant when everything is on their terms. Nice until the switch flips.

"Don't worry about it," he says.

I pore over the pictures on the wall and wonder again why mine is missing.

"What about me?" I ask. "What do you have planned for me?"

There's something about not knowing that makes it even scarier. My mind wants to concoct all manner of possibilities, each more odious than the last.

His eyes light up. "I've only scratched the surface with yours. It changes daily, if not hourly. Let me know if you have any requests, though. I promise to at least consider them," he says just as my watch chirps.

10:00 a.m. Training Module 1

The Dollmaker shakes his head. "I can't believe we've been in here an hour already. I knew it was going to be like this once you got here."

He turns to leave, and I make a face behind his back.

"Lenore will be here soon to escort you," he says as he opens the door.

"I kinda need to go to the bathroom," I say.

"Oh, right." He pulls out a walkie-talkie. "Lenore, Harley will meet you at your dormitory bathroom instead of the studio." He looks at me. "I'm so excited for tomorrow. Just seeing you here, I've had epiphany after epiphany. You're like creative napalm. You have no idea." His fingers twitch at his side at the thought.

He hurries off to whatever his ten o'clock is, and I amble, then power walk, then run to the dormitory bathroom.

I hide a scalpel inside the toilet tank just before Lenore comes in.

The Tower

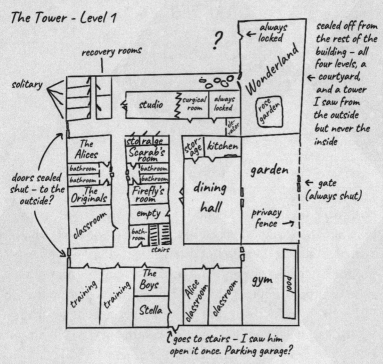

The Tower - Level 1

solitary

recovery rooms

? ← always locked

Wonderland

sealed off from the rest of the building — all four levels, a ← courtyard, and a tower I saw from the outside but never the inside

studio | surgical room | always locked

rose garden

de-vator

The Alices
bathroom
bathroom
The Originals
classroom

sto-ra-ge
Scarab's room
bathroom
bathroom
Firefly's room
empty
bath-room
stairs

stor-age | kitchen

dining hall

garden

← gate (always shut)

privacy fence →

doors sealed shut – to the outside?

pool

training | training | The Boys | Stella | Alice classroom | classroom | gym

↥ goes to stairs – I saw him open it once. Parking garage?

As best I can tell...
Basement = staff
Level 2 = the menagerie & science equipment
Level 3 = The Dollmaker

CHAPTER 28

THE GIRL WITH THE BLACK HAIR AND THE STRAWBERRY birthmark on her cheekbone huddles in the corner, wrapping her arms around herself like a blanket. She looks small. Scared. Standing there in her thin white medical gown waiting for a terrible surgery and certain doom and the other shoe to drop. To her right—a red fox, prowling around the inside of its cage. It's meant to make her a hunter—that's what I gathered from her murder board, anyway. Night vision, killer sense of smell, sharp claws, speed and agility—she'll be able to leap fences and scale roofs. According to The Dollmaker, she'll be able to hear low-frequency sounds too, like small animals digging miles underground.

"It's the stuff of dreams, truly, to have your muse see what you've been working on. To really become immersed in your creative process," says The Dollmaker.

I bite my lip and wonder if this is the right time. "I would have expected to see more plans for me. If I'm your muse."

"In due time. In due time. I want to make sure they're

just right before I show you the possibilities." He grins. "I'm so glad you're here."

"Me too," I reply. I want to pull this scalpel from my pocket and stab him directly in the eye with it.

I glance at the girl again, feeling the guilt rise in my chest. Luckily, he misunderstands.

"If the hybridization process doesn't remove that hemangioma, I'm cutting it off after." He vaguely waves a hand in the direction of her face.

Do not reach for that scalpel yet, Harley. No matter how much misogyny comes spewing out of his mouth.

Instead, I try to tell her with my eyes that she's beautiful, and her birthmark is beautiful, and nothing about her needs to be changed.

I can't believe I have to let this happen, the turning, the metamorphosing of this poor, scared, innocent girl, shaking in the corner. But I can't figure any other way out of this.

He leads her to the capsule, opening the glass door and shutting it behind her. She can't have been chipped yet, based on the way she's acting. As he locks the door, her eyes meet mine, pleading, and I have to look at the floor because I am the worst person in the world for letting this happen.

This is the plan, though. I watch a hybridization procedure with The Dollmaker. Midway through, I very apologetically tell him I'm feeling sick and I need to go stand outside for a minute. Count to three. Make sure no one is following me. And then I take off running. Free the other girls—the ones who haven't been chipped—and stage a mutiny. It's been two days. Ivy and Vengeance haven't found me yet, and there's no guaranteeing they will, so it's all on me.

The Dollmaker has Lenore lead the fox into the other

side of the capsule, snapping at her all the way until she finally manages to get it locked into its chamber. The fox looked cute in the pictures, but I guess most animals react badly to being in captivity. It launches itself at the door of the chamber, and I wince. Lenore's lucky to have all her fingers.

"Don't worry," says The Dollmaker. "It won't hurt the fox."

He says nothing about whether it will hurt the girl with the strawberry birthmark who is watching all of this. There are tears streaming down her tan cheeks now as it hits her what she will become. Her eyes meet mine again. *Help me.*

You know what? The plan *sucks.*

And you know who can change that? Me. Right freaking now.

The adrenaline fizzes through my veins, and I can feel my heartbeat thudding in my chest and wrists. Feel my breath quicken. Anxious in a way that I wasn't before. Because I don't know, won't know, what I'm going to do until I do it.

The Dollmaker approaches the chamber, ready to turn this girl into something horrible.

Am I really going to do this?

He checks all the settings, fingers twitching.

Throw my plan out the window and attack him without any idea of how it's going to play out?

Her tearful eyes meet mine again. Today it's her body. Tomorrow it will be her mind.

Yes. I. Am.

His fingers move to grip a lever attached to the capsule's console, this man who has been carving people up and taking their free will. I let the darkness loose in my mind so she can do whatever the eff she wants.

I whip the scalpel out of my pocket, and I don't think. I stab The Dollmaker in the shoulder with it, relishing the feeling of watching a blade disappear into him. Not for long, though, because half a second later, there's an arm around my neck, choking me. Lenore is even stronger than I thought. I turn my head to the side, fast, trying to angle my chin to the crook of her elbow because that's how you stay breathing when someone has you in a headlock. Only it doesn't work when the person you're fighting has partial bird anatomy. Lenore squeezes tighter. The room starts to go dark at the edges of my vision.

I remember there was a bookshelf against the wall behind me. A big one. If I could just. Get. Over there.

My vision grows darker.

I wrestle us toward the bookshelf.

Darker still.

My fingers can just reach it.

I'm on the verge of passing out, only a few threads left tethering me to my consciousness. Think of Stella. Think of Jasmin.

And I grab the side of the bookshelf and use every bit of strength I have to make it topple down on us before twisting out of the way. The crunching sound is terrible. Lenore may be quick and her talons may be sharp, but birds are light, and bookshelves are heavy. The arm around my neck loosens immediately, light flooding back into my vision.

I pick myself up off the floor. The girl's eyes are big as saucers behind the glass. I can see what she's thinking. I'm doing this. I might actually beat them. And then her eyes dart to the side.

I turn in the same direction, and there he is—The Dollmaker—scalpel discarded on the floor, wound gushing blood. Waiting for me. His face is twisted with the betrayal of it all.

"I'll have you one way or another."

Lenore thrashes, but she isn't able to get up. Not yet, anyway.

"We'll see about that."

And then I full-on sucker punch him. He goes reeling, falls like so many bowling pins, limbs scattering as he hits the ground with a satisfying smack. Strike!

Lenore has one arm free from the bookcase now. I'm honestly glad she's still fighting. I didn't want to really hurt her. None of this is her fault.

One of her legs is free now too. I'm running out of time. I can worry about ethical implications later. Like, after The Dollmaker has been locked away in a dark cell for the rest of eternity. I race over and rip the lanyard with the keys from his neck. His hand lashes out at the last second, fingers locked around my wrist, struggling to pull himself into a standing position. I take two running steps and kick off the wall, backflipping and taking his body with me, landing him flat on the floor again. He's wriggling like a cockroach, so I pick him up by the front of his shirt and clock him in the jaw, just to be safe.

This time, he doesn't wriggle so much. I run over to the capsule and unlock the door. He's not changing this girl. Not today. He's not changing anyone else ever again.

The girl falls into my arms, sobbing. "Thank you so much. I didn't want to be a monster."

"Happy to help!" I tell her. "We really need to start running, though. Can you pull yourself together?"

She nods.

And even though her face is red and blotchy, she scurries past The Dollmaker and over to the door of his studio. To our escape.

I look around for something big and smash-y. I'd really like to knock him out this time. (Because it's safer that way. Yep, that's the only reason.)

And then I'm hit with a terrible idea. A perfectly awful, completely diabolical, brimming-with-poetic-justice sort of idea.

I pick him up by the neck of his scrubs and drag him over to the capsule and lock him in. Think of all the victims he's butchered. The people who don't have control of their own bodies or their own actions because he took it. I fought too damn hard last year for those chips to ever be used again.

I stare him directly in the eyes as I pull the start lever.

"Are you ready for me to make you beautiful?"

Making Lapses

I think I can trick my chip into glitching more often.

All I have to do is not sleep.

Goal for tomorrow: try to tell other people with chips.

I wonder about trying to remove the chips completely, but I don't know. It's easy to insert a chip under a person's skin. I've seen the procedure as an assistant more than once. But digging one out? It requires a much bigger incision, and that's assuming the chip didn't migrate at all. That's what The Dollmaker told me when I helped him with Lenore's second chip. That removing a dead chip wasn't worth creating a larger scar and risking infection.

And trying to remove the chips ourselves without proper medical equipment or anesthesia?

There was a girl, months ago, who tried it. Sharpened her toothbrush into a shiv. Stabbed it behind her ear in a moment of desperation. She passed out from the pain before she could get the chip out.

And then The Dollmaker let The Mad Hatter make an example out of her.

CHAPTER 29

I DON'T WAIT TO SEE HIM TURN. THERE'S NO TIME FOR THAT. Plus, it sounds truly disgusting. I remind myself that he's not the only danger here—there's still Jervis Tetch, who I haven't even seen, plus all the people who have been chipped that I won't be able to get through to. And Jasmin and Stella to find and rescue. What if I find one of them and not the other? Or what if I find them both, but then there's all these people who still have chips and aren't going to want to be rescued? What am I supposed to do? I can't just leave them in this lack-of-bodily-autonomy hellscape.

It occurs to me that maybe I'm in over my head, but I've already lit the fuse. There's no stopping now. So, as I'm running out the door, I grab a broom and crack the wooden handle in half with my foot. It splinters satisfyingly. I smash the keycard scanner with the jagged end and hope that that'll slow them down for a while. Then I tear down the hallway to the first set of dormitories. Turn to make sure the girl I rescued is keeping up with me. (She is. I love when girls are quiet strong.)

"What's your name?" I call back to her.

"Navi," she says, panting.

"Cool. Here's the plan, Navi. I'm going to let everyone out of their dorms, and we're gonna stage a revolution, got it?"

"Got it."

I pass her the broom handle when we get to the first dormitory.

"As soon as I get the people who weren't chipped out, I want you to stab the scanner with the broom handle, okay?"

This plan has more holes than Swiss cheese, but if we can get even a few of us out, we can come back with Ivy and Vengeance and King Shark and the GCPD and the FBI and literally anyone who is willing to help. I hate the idea of leaving behind even one person with a chip, but I keep telling myself that this doesn't end today. I'll come back. I'll do whatever it takes.

Navi nods. "What if someone catches me?"

I grin. "Stab them with the broom handle."

"Okay." But she gulps when she says it, and I honestly don't know if she has it in her. Let's hope she's one of those looks-like-a-cinnamon-roll-but-could-kill-you types.

I touch my watch to the panel and wait for the door to open. It doesn't. Crap, did I trigger some kind of full Tower emergency shutdown? But Navi puts her watch next to mine.

"It only opens your own dorm. But this is mine," she says as the door slides open.

Behind the door is a small hallway/foyer, just like the one that connects my dorm room with the Alices'. We pass by the bathrooms, and Navi scans us into the dorm room on the left side.

Inside, three girls are changing the sheets on the bunks:

the girl who looks like an insect, a girl with blond braids who I haven't met, and Jasmin (woo-hoo!!). Insect Girl narrows her eyes at us. "Isn't she supposed to be receiving her hybridization now?"

I straighten my spine. Act like I'm in charge here. "Yes, but she has a fever, and she got sick all over the floor. The Dollmaker is concerned about how a weakened immune system could affect the hybridization process."

Insect Girl nods and goes back to making her bed. And I take this opportunity to leap onto her back and put her in a choke hold. Forearm lacing under her throat. Other hand behind her neck. And squeeze. Squeeze. She passes out after just a few seconds.

"C'mon, we're getting out of here," I say to Jasmin and the blond braids girl, who are watching in horror.

"What are you doing?" asks Jasmin. She honestly seems kind of annoyed for a person who is currently having their ass saved.

"Saving you." (Obviously.) "C'mon, we're leaving."

The blond braids girl jumps up and follows us. So does Jasmin, though she seems more reluctant.

"I've been working on an escape plan for months," hisses Jasmin.

"Okay, so we're doing it early." I nod at Navi, and she jabs the broom handle into the scanner.

Jasmin sighs. "You've planned this, have you?"

I shrug. "In the most general sense of the word."

Jasmin puts her head in her hands. "We're doomed."

But at least she follows me when I take off running.

"They're going to change the door panels now," Jasmin says—to herself or to me, I'm not sure. "It was an integral part of my plan, and now it's toast."

We race to my dorm next, completely skipping the one that shares a bathroom with Navi's. I'm not sure how we'll get into the other dorms without clearance, but we'll figure it out as we go.

Scan my watch. Storm the room.

But Jett is more suspicious than the Insect Girl, and when I attempt to choke her too, she throws me across the room. I get to my feet, rubbing my back where I landed against the bottom post of a bunk bed. That's gonna be a bruise tomorrow. If I make it that far.

I face off against Jett. Fallon watches from where she's sitting on her bed reading a picture book, and she doesn't look shocked or scared or confused.

"I'm trying to *help* you," I tell Jett, even though the real her isn't the one hearing me.

She cracks her knuckles. "You're the one who's going to need help."

She does a twisting aerial, landing in front of me and lashing out a fist. I'm so surprised, I almost don't block in time. I kick at her head, and she knocks my leg down. She thrusts, and I parry. *These aren't regular girls. They have powers. And training*, I have to remind myself. With Insect Girl, I had the element of surprise working for me, but that's not a luxury I have now.

I jump onto one of the beds and use it to flip over Jett so that I land behind her back. I try to get my arm around her neck, but she backward headbutts me in the face and slips out of my hold again, kicking out her leg and sweeping my legs out from underneath me. My butt hits the floor, and I feel wetness trickle down my upper lip. I wipe my nose with the back of my hand and see blood. Jett smiles. It only makes me want to fight harder. I kip-up to my feet. I'm just juking left and going right when Jett's eyes suddenly roll back into her head, and she falls away from me. Jasmin catches her.

She holds up her metal hand, which I take it she knocked out Jett with. "Guess this robot hand has some unexpected uses," she says.

"Thank you." I say it quickly and rush to Fallon's bunk.

"We're staging a mutiny," I tell her and another of our roommates, Lily, who does actually seem concerned that I am putting her in mortal peril.

They both follow me out into the hallway, and Navi breaks our scanner too.

"How are we going to get into the other rooms?" Jasmin asks.

I bite my lip. "I honestly don't know."

And then Fallon smiles. "I know where they keep the watches."

I freaking love that kid.

"It's this way! C'mon," she says, giggling, as she leads me down the hallway outside our room.

It's like this whole mutiny thing is a game to her. Which is good because it means she's not terrified right now, but bad when you think about it in a what-does-this-say-about-her-history-of-emotional-trauma kind of way. Maybe if we make it out of here, I could talk to her about it. She's exactly the kind of kid I've always dreamed of helping. (Okay, maybe I did not specifically dream of helping someone who is part vampire squid and box jellyfish, but, you know, the rest of it.)

I jog along behind Fallon, muscles tensed and at the ready

in case one of the guards comes, but they never do. It's just me and her now. I told Jasmin and Navi and the other girls to try to find Stella.

Fallon turns onto the next hallway, and I follow, and suddenly I know where we are. This is the West Wing. Or, well, the place I've been thinking of as the West Wing. The hallway is dark, like the time I saw it with Lenore, but as Fallon gets closer, parts of the floor light up in front of her. They're stepping stones, I realize. She hops from one to another, making her way to the golden door. Now that I'm closer, I can see that it's made of wood—carved with designs and painted a shimmery gold.

I hesitate. Something about this part of the Tower makes me uneasy. Maybe it's the darkness, or maybe it's the scenes carved into the door. A little boy and girl running away from a man with knives for eyes. In the next panel, the little boy is throwing her a tea party, but she seems fretful. I glance at the last scene, the one at the bottom corner of the door. Oh my gosh, is he murdering her by putting a plastic bag over her head? What in the dark fairy-tale hell is this?

"Are you sure this is the right place?" I whisper to Fallon.

But she just grins at me. "Of course it is."

And then she knocks on the door.

Why would a person knock on a door when we're supposed to be sneaking? There's only a second for the question to flicker in my head before the door opens.

Jervis Tetch waits behind it with the crookedest smile I've ever seen. I've never met him before, but I know it's him all the same. Disheveled in his green suit and oversized top hat. Blood on his collar, his or one of the Alices'. Something in his eyes makes me think that I should be more afraid of him than I am of The Dollmaker.

"Hello, there," he says, taking a step forward as I take a step back.

I have misjudged this situation.

"Harley, right?"

Not all of the hybridized people are chipped yet, and Fallon always seemed like she was going rogue and getting in trouble with Lenore, so I just assumed. Clearly, I was mistaken.

I force my voice to be strong. "Harley Quinn." Harley *Freaking* Quinn, to you.

I wish I had any kind of weapon right now. I feel like such an idiot. But Fallon was so damn adorable, once I got over the whole vampire squid thing.

"The Dollmaker's told me about you," says Jervis, pulling a watch from his pocket.

"Has he?" I assume a fighting stance. Get ready to punch him so hard that stupid hat of his goes flying.

"Mmm-hmm." The watch goes back and forth. "What brings you to Wonderland?"

"I—" *Don't look at the watch. Don't look at the watch. Focus on his paisley pocket square instead. Or the bloodstain on his collar.*

"Harley," he says commandingly, and I look at the watch in spite of myself.

Tick. Tock. Back. Forth. *Tick*—

Nope.

I close my eyes and deliver a roundhouse kick to where

I'm praying his head still is. (Note to future self: do some training blindfolded.)

Thwack. The sound of my foot connecting is so satisfying. The grunt of pain. The flash of anger. I open my eyes to find him and his pocket watch lying on the floor. And then . . .

"Fine, we'll do this the hard way," he says, wiping blood from his mouth.

I dart out my hand to snatch the watch, but then the pain flattens me. So much pain. Entire ropes of agony surrounding my arm and pulling it back-back-back. It's like nothing I've ever experienced, and I've been dumped in toxic chemicals. Stars dance in front of my eyes. No, not stars. Lights. Bio-luminescent raindrops floating in midair. The razor threads attack my other arm, wrap themselves around my neck and squeeze.

"Shhh," Fallon whispers into my ear as the world goes dark.

People Who Have Been Chipped

Probably

Maeve
Gabriel
Pretty Alice
   (I don't know if I'm being paranoid, but I think
   he's using her to spy on us)

Definitely

Me
Shy Alice
All of the guards and kitchen staff
Lenore (Londyn)
   (twice, because her first chip went completely
   defective after the hybridization process)
Firefly
Scarab
Jett (also twice)
Noah
Fallon

CHAPTER 30

EVERYTHING HURTS. IT'S THE ONLY THING MY BRAIN REGIS-
ters when I first wake up. That my arms and neck feel like they
were wrapped in live wires. That the pounding in my veins
and my heart feels like something I may not live through.

"Try not to move," says a voice beside me that sounds
vaguely familiar.

Someone is touching me, and the room smells like Easter
eggs. Another wave of vinegar wafts over me.

You've got more on yourself than the eggs, Harleen.

Mommy, aren't they pretty?!

They're beautiful.

Maybe I'm an Easter egg now. A giant one. Maybe this is
a whole new life and I'm being reborn.

The person traces a spot on my neck that feels like it's
on fire. I hiss.

"Sorry," they say. "You have to rinse with acetic acid early
to have the best chance."

The best chance of what? But my body won't let me ask
questions now. At least, I don't think I said that out loud.

The person continues to rinse all the parts of me that feel like they're burning. Eventually I'm aware enough to see what's happening to me. That girl with the blond hair who helped me clean up my water in the dining hall, one of the Stepford Four, is sitting next to me and gently pouring a clear liquid over the angry maroon lines that trace my arms and neck.

"I was there when it happened," she says as she works. "Jervis and I were having a tea party. I do love our tea parties." She smiles a manufactured smile as she says it.

So . . . she's definitely been chipped.

"I'm Alice. I usually help out when Fallon has an accident. I have the most experience. And we caught you within the first hour, so that's really promising," she continues, pouring more acetic acid over the lashes on my left arm. It looks like I've been branded.

I wince.

"Did that hurt? Sorry." (She does genuinely look sorry. She seems like a nice person.) "And, uh, sorry for what I'm about to do next. I have to remove the tentacle fragments and nematocysts with tweezers."

Well, that sounds like being in the seventh circle of hell.

I brace myself as she holds the tweezers above my neck, but it's not as bad as I expect. She's incredibly gentle.

"So Fallon's been chipped, huh?" I say as she plucks translucent pieces of thread from my neck and places them on a sheet of gauze beside her.

She nods, but her face is fraught. She's probably not allowed to tell me. "Fallon's not a bad kid. Try not to be mad at her."

Guess I'm not the only one who feels protective over Fallon. It makes me like this Alice girl more. And I know she's sure to take anything I say and report back to Jervis and The Dollmaker, but there are certain things I just have to know. And I'm curious to see how she'll answer.

"Has anyone ever successfully escaped this place?" I ask, and she flinches.

"No," she says. She continues to dissect jelly threads out of my wounds, but her hands are less steady now. "One time—" She shakes her head. "It's impossible to escape the Tower."

One time, what? One time someone succeeded? One time someone died trying? There could be a lot of things that follow *one time*, and I NEED MORE DETAILS, PEO-PLE. But when I ask her follow-up questions, all I get is Jervis-Jervis-Jervis.

He's so funny.

He takes the very best care of me.

I don't know what I did to be so lucky.

I try to answer carefully. Based on the bruising on her left cheek, I'd guess Jervis isn't as sweet to her as that chip in her head makes her believe.

"I'm really happy for you," I say. "But just so you know, if things ever weren't okay with Jervis, and you ever wanted to tell me about that—I'd be happy to listen to you then too."

Something flashes in her eyes.

"Oh, well, that's nice of you." And I think she's not going to say anything else. But then as she moves to my right arm, "Some girls do have people in their lives like that. It must be terrible for them."

"Yes." How to put this? I settle on mimicking her lan-guage. "Some girls deal with a lot of abuse. And it isn't okay. And they don't deserve to be treated that way."

"Yes," she says.

"I want to tell those girls that I understand how they feel. And I'm going to work really hard to help them. Because no one should ever be hit or screamed at or made to feel afraid."

"Yes," she says.

And then she throws the tentacle-covered gauze in a bio-hazard bag and packs up her tools and wheels everything out on a cart.

I hope I said the right things. I guess I should have been thinking about how to build a relationship with her and convince her to help me, but in that moment, all I could think about was The Dollmaker and Jervis and the chip and her pain. I just wanted to take some of it away.

When Alice is gone, I catalog the contents of my new room. They've given me nothing to work with here. I am in a cell, there's no other word for it. Solitary. There's a thin white mattress and a thin white sheet on a metal bench that's bolted to the wall. There is a sink. And a toilet.

No windows. An air vent you couldn't squeeze a small dog through. And a door with a small Plexiglas window and a rectangular flap that I am assuming is for food.

I am never getting out of here.

Not that I could even attempt it right now. The pain is so intense, I can barely move.

Through the Looking Glass

There's something off in Wonderland. I register it the moment I walk through the doors. There's a loud banging-clanging-breaking noise, and the air smells like blood.

"Jervis?"

"I'm in here, Alice!" he yells back with a laugh.

I turn to my left, to his voice. The golden padlock hangs open. My legs make me walk across the room, even as my heartbeat tries to tell me it's a bad idea.

"What are you doing, Jervis?"

Clash-bang! "I'm murdering the time."

I take another step to find The Mad Hatter bashing the daylights out of a clock with a sledgehammer. Piles of clocks and their parts to his right. To his left, a table.

I gasp and cover my mouth. Alice the First, Second, and Third sit around the table tilting teacups and holding crumpets. Dead. Their bodies are in various stages of decay.

I turn away and clutch my stomach.

"Well, don't be rude," says The Mad Hatter, bashing another clock. "Join them."

"I can't," I reply in a shaking voice. "I can't look anymore."

"You mean you can't look any less." *Clash-bang!*

I focus on the stone of the round walls that go up-up-up. At the gilded picture frames hanging there. No, mirrors. He's framed the pictures in mirrors. Each one a tea party. Each one—

I vomit down the front of my dress. The pictures. Everyone is dead. In the most gruesome ways. A power drill to the temple. Heads lopped off with piano wire.

I realize with a sense of dread that the clanging has stopped, and The Mad Hatter is right behind me.

"You shouldn't have done that, Alice. Maybe you'll be joining the party sooner than you think."

"Please, Jervis."

"Run away before I change my mind."

CHAPTER 31

I GET MAYBE A FEW HOURS OF SLEEP THAT NIGHT. THE Dollmaker comes in the morning.

"How are you feeling, Harley?" he asks.

I startle because it's jarring to wake up and find someone watching you sleep. I startle because he looks exactly the same as the last time I saw him.

"Why aren't you—" I stop myself because I'm not sure it's a good idea to call attention to what I did (tried to do?) to him last night, but he answers anyway.

"A fox?" He smiles during the long pause that follows, relishing the tension he makes me feel. "Because when the capsule opens mid-procedure, the hybridization is aborted. It's a safety measure."

Oh, yeah? For who? I manage to swallow down.

"Also because last night was a test." If he was smiling before, he is grinning now, so smug, so satisfied at his own cleverness.

"A test?" is all I can stupidly say. (Look, I'm still in a lot of pain here.)

"I knew you were going to try to escape."

My mouth falls open.

"Your acting isn't that good, darling."

My acting. Is impeccable. I could have earned whole-ass Academy Awards for how much I pretended I was interested in his mansplain-y art rambles.

"I can see you're surprised," he says, seeming ever more pleased. "It just shows how well I really know you that I was able to design a personalized trial just for you. I understand what makes you tick, Harley."

Like hell you do. Again, swallowed down.

"I assume the other girls have told you about the Trials?"

I nod. Strength tests, endurance, wit, speed, resistance to cold and fire and anything else he can think to throw at them.

"I wanted something special to test your abilities. You're more than these other pieces. I wanted to prove that to both of us." He laughs. "I wasn't expecting you to lock me in the capsule, though. That surprised even me. I thought you might be more subtle in your attempts to escape."

"I had originally planned to go with subtlety," I say grudgingly.

He nods like this makes so much sense. Like he knows everything about me, and it is So. Freaking. Annoying. "But you couldn't help yourself. You have too much fire in you. I love that about you. How unpredictable you are. How impossible to contain. You're like a puzzle I can't quite figure out. It's intoxicating."

"Glad I can be so entertaining for you," I say sarcastically. (Probably a stupid move, but I'M IMPOSSIBLE TO CONTAIN, REMEMBER?!)

His eyes flash for the first time since I woke up and found him here. (Yep. Definitely a stupid move.)

"I think we're ready to proceed with turning you into my greatest creation. I've adequately assessed your strengths and weaknesses now."

Weaknesses?

"Oh, you do have weaknesses, Harley. Trusting Fallon? Wanting to free others and not just yourself? In that way, you're extremely predictable. But now I know, and so you'll stay here until we have time to chip you. Can't afford to have any more of yesterday's unpleasantness."

I bite down on the insides of my mouth—hard—because none of the things I want to say will help me here.

The Dollmaker rises from the bench jutting out of the wall opposite me. Checks his watch.

"I've got to get going. There's so much to do. So many pieces to finish." He stands and walks over to me. He smells like blood and turpentine, art and death. He reaches out a hand and I flinch, thinking he's going to touch my face, but instead he inspects one of my pigtails, the pink one. "Not sure how I feel about this," he says with a grimace before dropping it back against my shoulder. He pauses in the doorway. "But don't worry, Harley. I'm going to make you beautiful."

And then the lock slides shut, and I'm in here, alone, in this room with no way out. No plan for escape. And the deadline for the auction looming over me like the blade of a guillotine.

Auction Schedule (as best I can remember it after seeing it on his desk)

THE DOLLS
Collection 1: Braving the Elements
Water: Fallon . . . . . Vampire squid/box jellyfish
Air: Lenore . . . . Raven
Earth: Maeve . . . . . Snake
Fire: Firefly . . . . . . Flame-powered and fireproof (surgical)
Finale: Harley . . . . Live hybridization onstage

Intermission

Collection 2: Art Revolutionized
Jett . . . . The ultimate thief (surgical)
Noah . . . . Electric eel
Navi . . . . Live hybridization, bidder's choice
Miranda . . . . Live hybridization, bidder's choice
Jumana . . . . Live hybridization, bidder's choice

CHAPTER 32

I HARDLY SLEEP THE SECOND NIGHT EITHER. IT HURTS TOO much. Both the lashes across my arms and neck and this feeling in my bones that I had a chance to rescue a good six or seven people but failed. The Dollmaker made it sound like I'm too prone to kindness, but I know better. I didn't escape with a smaller group because my pride told me I could save everyone, or at least everyone who wasn't chipped. Because Stella was the whole reason I was here, and I was going to be the one to rescue her, damn it. And I trusted Fallon not because I'm some kind of softie but because I think I'm such an infallible (in-Fallon-able?) judge of character.

I'm not kind; I just think I know everything.

And worst of all? I haven't just failed at my own escape— I've ruined Jasmin's. I heard the buzzing of power tools all day yesterday, installing new door panels where we broke them. I don't have to ask—these doors won't have the same limitations as the old ones. I have made it exponentially harder for anyone to break out of this place.

It is the worst kind of failure.

Maybe you're the kind of person who ruins things. I ruined the Reckoning. And I ruined this. It plays in my head in a horrible loop. I barely get off my sleeping shelf all day. What's the point? At lunchtime, the same Alice as before wheels in a tray, which is honestly a nice break because I was about to would've, could've, should've myself to death.

"How are you feeling?" she asks.

"Much better." And then I dig deep and pull a smile from I don't even know where. "Thank you for taking care of me."

Alice smiles back, pleased, a faint flush in her cheeks. "You know I didn't realize how good I was at that until I came here?" She shrugs. "But a lot of things happen here where people need taking care of, and I just started doing it, bandaging wounds and popping shoulders back into place. And my stitches are really good now—they hardly leave a scar. It made me realize how much I like it, helping people that way."

She goes quiet like she's said too much.

"No," I say, leaning forward on my shelf. "You're amazing at it. If we get out of here—*when* we get out of here, you should look into doing that. Being a surgeon or a pediatrician or a nurse or whatever it is that feels the most right for you."

Her smile is sad now. "Well, I think Jervis and I will probably be together till the end."

And I sigh with my whole body, because the words she chose, it's like even though she's chipped, a part of her knows where this is leading. Where it always leads for women who are unfortunate enough to know men like him.

"Anyway, they let me bring you your lunch because I told them I needed to check your wounds. So, I should probably do that."

Something about the way she said it . . .

I try to read between the lines of what her chip will let her say and do. "*Do* you need to check my wounds?"

She blinks rapidly several times. "Well, they're looking much better, and there's honestly not a lot you can do for them after the first day, so." That flush in her cheeks again. "I guess I just really wanted to see you. I liked our talk before."

I reach out and squeeze her hand. "I liked our talk too."

And I'm struck with this feeling—I am helping this girl. Helping her process the trauma she's living through on a daily basis. Helping her figure out what she wants to do with her life. Assuming she gets to have a life. This is what I want to do. Always. Forever. Help girls like her. Help girls who were like me when I was living with my father. There's something about helping her that feels like going back in time and healing a part of myself.

Alice squeezes my hand back (it actually kind of hurts, but I power through because we're having a moment), and then it's like something clicks behind her eyes.

"Oh thank goodness," she says. She stretches like she's been carrying a backpack full of cement.

"Alice?"

She smiles sadly. "Everly."

Holy crap, I'm talking to the real her. She's having a glitch or lapsing or whatever it is Lenore called it.

She opens my boxed lunch, and underneath my sandwich is a book, a journal.

"Here," she shoves it at me. "I wasn't sure if I'd actually get to talk to you as me, like, the real me, so there's a letter inside, explaining. Ever since Anton stuck me with Jervis Tetch, I've been writing down anything I can that might be helpful when I have a lapse. Anything I could use. I want you to have it."

I take the book. "I mean, this is amazing. Thank you." But. "Why are you giving me this?"

I'm trapped in here. Useless. Failed spectacularly at my last escape attempt.

"Because," says Alice—I mean, Everly—"I think you have the best chance of escaping. And because you were kind to me. About Jervis. You made me feel like I wasn't alone."

My heart nearly explodes inside my chest. I look her in the eyes. "You're not alone."

And neither am I. Maybe that's been my problem all along. Trying to do this by myself. Acting like I'm some kind of superhuman who has to save everyone without any help.

I never would have thought Alice would be the kind of person who'd be able to help me. Before. But now? Now I think there's a chance that if we all work together, if we pool all of our strengths and powers and ideas, we might be able to do something. I mean, there's still a 97 percent chance we'll end up caught and/or dead, but that 3 percent? I'll take it.

"Hey, you don't happen to know where they're keeping a girl named Stella, do you?"

She nods. "It's in there. I drew a map."

"Really?" I mean, this is great. It's something, at least. I try to work out how to use this information to my advantage, but my scheming is interrupted by Everly snatching the journal from my hands and shoving it under my mattress.

"What—"

"It's okay. I'm okay," she says. "It's just a precaution because I never know how much time I'll have before I'm Alice again."

"Got it," I say.

"Well." She gets up and goes to leave. "I better get back before they send someone to check on me."

And she's given me so much that I shouldn't ask her to put herself in anymore danger, but I'm going to try to learn from my previous failures. I'm going to try to depend on other people. And so:

"Hey, Everly?"

She turns. "Yeah?"

"Could you try to send Jasmin my way?"

Dear Harley,

I'm writing this letter because I don't know if I'll ever lapse at the right time and be able to explain these things to you myself. When I heard that someone was trying to escape, I knew it would be you. And even though you didn't make it this time, I think you're our best chance.

The earliest parts of this journal are more like diary entries, and the later parts are things that I thought might help you plan your next escape. I'm giving you all of it in case it helps.

Thank you for being brave enough to try. Thank you for being my friend. Please don't give up.

—Everly

CHAPTER 33

THAT NIGHT, I'M PERMITTED TO TAKE A SHOWER FOR THE first time in two days. Supervised, of course. But Alice was able to get Jasmin to stand in for her by claiming that Jervis (who I now know from her journal is The Mad Hatter, AKA THE FREAKING LOOKING GLASS KILLER) was having some urgent emotional difficulties and she needed to tend to him immediately.

"How come they let you babysit me?" I ask Jasmin. "I heard you weren't chipped."

"I'm not." Jasmin shows her watch to the guard stationed by the door of the cafeteria (I think I recognize him as one of The Dollmaker's Pride parade henchmen), and we exit. She lowers her voice. "But The Dollmaker's got at least three of his chipped squad patrolling the hallways at any given moment now, so there wasn't a lot of choice."

Patrols *and* new and improved panels? And probably other things I haven't noticed. "I'm sorry I screwed up your escape plan," I tell her.

"Thank you," she says. And once we get to the showers

and I have the water turned on (and have said approximately one million cuss words because showers + box jellyfish stings = bodily harm), she stands outside the stall and says quietly, "I may have some other ideas."

"I was hoping for that," I say as I shampoo my hair. And then a thought occurs to me. "How do I know you're not chipped?"

I don't need another Fallon situation.

"I hid a razor blade in the lining of your pajamas and a tool kit in your air vent," she says.

I grin. "Works for me."

"Hey, Harleen?"

"I go by Harley now," I say gently.

"Right. Harley. I think I remember hearing that." She pauses. "Are you doing okay? I, uh, stopped by the hospital right after your accident, but you were still unconscious. Does it . . . hurt?"

"Does what hurt?" Oh! She means my skin. Yeah, I guess that could be kinda jarring. "I'm totally fine," I say. "Pale as a ghost, but zero pain." Also, she came to visit me! Did you hear that?!

"Oh, good. You know, seeing you like that was a big part of why I went looking for the trafficking gang. Well, what happened to you plus what happened with Bianca."

I'm thinking about our time as the Reckoning, and I wonder if she's thinking about it too.

She clears her throat. "Maybe together we could beat him."

And I want to spout off about all my ideas for how I'm going to fix everything, but instead I peek around the shower curtain and say, "What's the scheme, daydream?"

"You are such a dork." And the eye roll she gives me, I just don't think a chipped Jasmin would be capable of it. "But, yeah, I've been working on some different escape ideas for a few months now."

"Hot."

I don't have to peek around the shower curtain to know Jasmin is rolling her eyes again.

"The night of the auction will be our best chance. He'll be so busy, he won't notice if a few people aren't in their dorms. Plus, it might give us the opportunity to bring down his patrons along with him." She runs me through the abridged version of her plan, but it's clear even from that that she's approached our escape with a level of detail only she would be capable of. "Will you help me?"

"Are you kidding? Of course I'll help you. I am obsessed with this plan. I am marrying this plan. I mean, I'm already kind of planning to marry Ivy, but maybe this plan wouldn't mind being a throuple."

"You are the weirdest."

"Also, oh! Let me tell you the stuff Everly told me!"

"That girl who's one of the Alices?" Jasmin asks skeptically.

"Hey, don't underestimate her. She's been writing down information about the facility and The Dollmaker and stuff strategically whenever she has lapses in her chip. She and Lenore and Fallon and Jett were in the first set, so I get the impression that their chips are the faultiest."

"Good to know," says Jasmin.

"And it seems like most of the people here who are chipped have these basic protocols that dictate how they go about their days—the victims, but also the kitchen staff and the guards. But I read something in Everly's journal about

The Dollmaker giving Fallon special commands using a remote. I saw The Scarecrow use something similar on King Shark last year."

Jasmin nods. "I've seen The Dollmaker use something like that too. Not The Mad Hatter, though."

"Really?"

"Oh, no. It would ruin the illusion."

I try very hard not to gag. Also, I tell her the most critical things I read in Everly's journal, and we use them to tweak the escape plan. I wish we had more time. There's so much more to tell each other, so much more to discuss. But there's only so long I can spend showering without looking suspicious, and we do have to get back.

I put on fresh clothes, and we start to leave.

I was feeling desolate before, but now? We might actually have a chance at this thing. "The only thing that could ruin this is if The Dollmaker chips one of us in the next two days," I say.

Jasmin shakes her head. "The Dollmaker's waiting until I'm finished. That's what he typically does anyway, but in my case, the modifications would definitely fry the chip."

We're at the door now, but I stop. Glance at the place near her collarbone where the wires are. "Hey, Jasmin, are you okay? If you don't mind me asking."

I don't say what I'm really thinking: *What did he do to you?*

"Oh." She sighs. "It's okay. Yeah, I'm gonna be okay." Is she trying to convince me? Herself? Both of us? "He's making me some kind of bionic woman. Because I'm so good with computers and hacking and stuff. One of my hands is completely cybernetic now, so I can crush things with it, and my index finger is a miniature laser. He's working on some attachments too."

Her voice is tight, skims right over the part about what happened to her real hand. "I can write code just by thinking it too. And he's in the process of giving me some sort of neural link. It would almost be cool if—"

"If you had a choice in the matter?"

"Yeah. And I also don't like looking like I'm part computer when I take my clothes off. By the time he gets to my face—I'm scared people won't see me as a person anymore. What if I don't recognize myself when I look in the mirror?"

She blinks back tears, and I step forward, but just as I do, the door opens.

"What's taking so long?" Jett eyes us like we're hiding shanks and flamethrowers.

Jasmin deploys one of her very best eye rolls. "We're coming right now," she says, all hint of tears gone.

I wish I could hug her, and I hate that I can't.

Jett continues to glare at us. (She seems to have taken us fighting her and knocking her unconscious extremely personally.) "Well, I'm walking her back to her cell."

Jasmin shrugs. "Knock yourself out."

Did she actually just wiggle her robot hand as she said it? I freaking love that girl. But I don't look at her as she walks away. It's important that we don't know each other.

Jett doesn't seem to suspect as she marches me down the hallway to my cell, pushing me by the back a couple times when she thinks I'm moving too slowly.

"Ouch. Geez. You know I just got attacked by Fallon, right?"

She gives me a cold look. "Only because you deserved it."

Wow, her chip must be one of the real good ones.

"So, just wondering, does your chip make you act like a heinous waste of air, or are you always like this?"

She answers my question by putting her hand on my neck—right on top of the very worst of the stings—and pushing me into my cell.

Son of a biscuit-eater, that hurts. I'm tempted to rub my neck, but I know that would only make it worse, so I settle for attempting to shoot laser beams through her face with my eyes.

"Enjoy your last night, Harley." She smirks at me. "The Dollmaker's giving you your chip tomorrow."

Ivy

Have you ever woken up to find that your girl-friend, the person you love most in the world, the person who almost single-handedly restored your faith in humanity, was missing? I think I'd rather wake up in a bathtub with a missing kidney.

You can live without a kidney.

But I can't breathe without her.

CHAPTER 34

ANOTHER SLEEPLESS NIGHT, BUT THIS TIME IT WASN'T BE-
cause of the pain. I can't stop wondering what it will feel like
to not have free will. I honestly can't think of anything more
terrifying. Of all the sadistic things The Mad Hatter and The
Dollmaker do to people, taking that away is the worst.

The door opens, and the dread fills me, but it's just
breakfast.

And the door opens, and the dread fills me, but it's just
Everly to check my wounds.

"I heard they're chipping me today," I say, testing to see if
she knows anything. I didn't think they chipped people this
early in the process. It doesn't make sense.

But she just clucks and checks my arms and neck. "You're
looking much better," she declares.

Then her watch chimes, and her face fills with this
haunted expression, like a hundred pounds of fear stuffed
into a one-pound sack. "It's time for me to go to another tea
party," she says with a smile that looks like it is causing her
physical pain.

I grab her hand. Squeeze it. "It's going to be okay," I tell her.

And she smiles at me even though she knows it's a lie.

After Everly leaves, I realize she forgot a roll of gauze on the metal bench opposite me. That's funny. I haven't needed gauze since the first day. I cross my closet of a cell and pick up the gauze. And I think about how Everly hid a journal under my sandwich.

I slowly unroll the gauze. Nothing, nothing. And then, there it is! About two feet into the roll is a small slip of paper. But all it says is *Lenore*.

Lenore what? Lenore's been programmed to knock me off? Lenore found a way out through a hidden staircase? You're losing me here, Everly.

I unroll the rest of the gauze to see if there's more, but that's it. *Lenore* is my only clue.

I roll the gauze back up and set it on the bench. Flush the piece of paper down the toilet. And my door opens for a third time.

"Lenore," I say.

"Hi, Harley," she replies impassively. "I need you to come with me to the studio."

I nod and follow along beside her. Waiting for her to have a lapse. To say something that will make this make sense. It's no coincidence that Everly snuck me a piece of paper with Lenore's name on it only to have Lenore show up at my door to lead me to my chip procedure.

We get to the studio, and I still haven't figured it out, and it's too late now. The Dollmaker is waiting for me. After today, I won't be able to help Stella or Jasmin or Everly or anybody. I won't even be able to help myself. I'll have to hope that whatever plan Jasmin has will work without me, and it occurs to me that I like saving more than I like waiting to be saved.

"Harley." He smiles widely when he sees me. "I usually chip people after the Metamorphosis, but you're too much of a flight risk." He turns to Lenore. "Can you strap her to the table?"

She marches me over to an operating table, and I climb onto it and lie down. I watch carefully as she fastens straps around my wrists and waist and ankles. I wait. Is she going to leave them loose? Make it so that I can escape and beat the crap out of everyone?

I test the wrist strap, but nope, she hasn't left me any slack. Lenore notices. Narrows her eyes and pulls them even tighter. Perhaps the secret message just meant *Lenore has it in for you, so watch it!* I don't even know.

Maybe the edge I'm seeing today is her chip, not her. It's not fair to assume. The Lenore I met in the bathroom that time was so different. Maybe she planned to help me at some point when she was lapsing, but it's not like you can make yourself have a glitch.

Her eyes are bloodshot—she looks beyond exhausted. Maybe the pain of the bookshelf falling on her means she hasn't been sleeping well either?

The door opens, and The Mad Hatter enters. I've only ever seen him one other time—that night I tried (and failed) to escape. But I've read enough in Everly's journal to know the measure of him.

Wild eyes. An unholy smile. He tries to hide his crazy behind a whimsical suit and hat, behind fairy tales, but it leaks out anyway. The pocket watch dangles from his vest. I wish like hell I'd smashed that thing.

He makes a beeline for The Dollmaker, and they discuss

details in hushed voices. Details about me. What's to be done with me.

The fear settles in like a poisonous fog, weighing me down, strangling me. In just an hour, thirty minutes, (less?), that butcher across the room will be able to make me do whatever he wants. I don't even know if I'll be me anymore. Will I remember who I am? It's followed by a more terrifying thought. Will I remember Ivy? Think about something else, anything else, quick. If I don't, I'm guaranteed to start sobbing in front of these assholes, and I don't want to give them the satisfaction.

I focus on Lenore to see if that will distract me enough because (A) she's the only other person in this room, and (B) she *is* acting awfully weird now that I'm looking.

Her face seems to be having an existential crisis—that's the only way to explain it. Her left eyebrow is in a feud with her right, and her lips would like to mutiny and run away from them both. Her eyes are still exhausted, though, like she's about to drop dead of sleep deprivation at any moment.

And then there's her hands. I wasn't even looking at them before, but now? There's a campy old horror movie about this guy who didn't have control of his hands, and I think they made him kill people or something. It was weird. Lenore's left hand picks up a scalpel. Oh gosh, is that what's happening here? Is she going to kill me before they can chip me?

She glances over her shoulder at The Mad Hatter and The Dollmaker. Oh! Maybe she's going to kill *them*!!

And then she angles her body so they can't see what she's doing, and (with more internal distress than you can shake a stick at) she drives the scalpel into her right forearm.

Ummmmmmm. . . .

The wound bleeds surprisingly little. (Maybe because she's part bird? IDK, I was expecting it to be a spurter.) She quietly and efficiently wipes the scalpel on her dark feathers and places it right back where it was. Quietly and efficiently begins DIGGING AROUND IN HER ARM with her fingers, but sure, that's fine, this is all totally fine. I'm about to lose my free will for the rest of my life (which probably won't be all that long), and Lenore has taken to carving herself up like a Thanksgiving turkey.

After way too many seconds during which I have to pretend like I'm not extremely grossed out (because, hi, The Dollmaker and The Mad Hatter can only be so distracted by their shared narcissism for so long), Lenore's chest relaxes in a silent sigh, and she pulls her talon out of her arm, gently scraping something small and white with it. If that's a piece of her bone, I just— I don't want to know.

But it isn't, I realize as she wipes it off on her feathers.

It's a chip.

I think back to Everly's list of people who had been chipped. It said Lenore was chipped twice because her first chip went dead after the hybridization.

"Should I scrub in?" asks Lenore, closing her fist over the chip.

The Dollmaker waves a hand at her, like the grown-ups are too busy talking to answer.

She moves to the sink and turns on the water. Stealthily rinses the chip and tends her wounds. After she washes and dries her hands, she moves back to the surgical table, pretending to check that they have all the necessary supplies. I know exactly what she's really doing. She's about to switch the chips. She's going to give me the bad one.

"Are you finished?" says The Dollmaker, who has crossed the room in a few quick strides.

She jerks her hand back. "Yes. We have everything we need."

Crap.

Crap. Crap. Crap.

She was so close. I try to keep the disappointment out of my face, though I guess it wouldn't be totally unexpected, given what's about to happen to me.

The Dollmaker moves to my other side, the one without the surgical instruments. I remember hearing that The Mad Hatter insists on being the one who does these procedures, since the chips were his invention. There's a trocar among the surgical tools, and I'm reminded of The Scarecrow and King Shark. How horrifying it was to watch my friend turn into something else.

The Dollmaker brushes my hair away from my face, hand twitching like he's only just able to keep from digging his fingernails into my cheek.

"Don't be afraid," he says. "I'm going to make you into something that transcends the rest of the world's wildest imagination."

The Mad Hatter sits on the stool beside me now in a newly donned surgical gown and freshly scrubbed hands. He snaps on a pair of blue nitrile gloves, and Lenore hovers, hovers, hoping/searching/struggling for an opportunity to swap the chips.

But she doesn't get it.

The Mad Hatter unclips the pocket watch from his shirt and starts swinging it in front of my eyes.

Tick-tock. Tick-tock. Back and forth and swirling round and calm voice and wild eyes.

"Relax, Harley. You're in a safe place. Let the calm wash over you."

Apparently, he doesn't need a chip. Apparently, all he needs is that pocket watch.

Forensic analysis of the crime scenes suggests that the victims actually killed each other.

How would you get someone to do that to their own family?
I know how.

The Mad Hatter's eyes bore into mine. I fight to hang on to my sanity. I dig my nails into my consciousness. I focus on how I might lose Ivy—all the little pieces that make up my memory of her evaporating like water in a frying pan (freckle on her shoulder, hair in the shower, flowers pressed in books), and I battle to stay here. As me.

Tick-tock.

If I could just see what happens with Lenore.

"Relax."

If I could just know whether she finds a way to successfully switch the chip before it gets implanted.

Back and forth.

Swirling round.

Wild eyes and crooked smile.

And then darkness.

And calm.

And somewhere else.

Tick-tock.

Ivy

I woke up first, probably a by-product of my resistance to toxins and poisons. My head hurt from the knock-out juice, but I didn't care. All I wanted was to chase after her. Problem was, I didn't know where to run.

A woman in a cotton romper hovered over me, saying she was a nurse and did I feel okay?

I said yes because I wanted her to go away. I said yes because if I thought about the answer too hard, it would break me. Harley was gone, and I hadn't told the trees to kill everyone in Gotham City yet, which honestly felt like a damn miracle.

We'll be fine, I told her. *Heatstroke, yes, all three of us. What are the chances?*

King Shark and Vengeance were stirring now.

We'll be fine, I repeated.

Not The Dollmaker, though.

I would kill him with my bare hands.

CHAPTER 35

"HARLEY?"

The Dollmaker is the first thing I see when I open my eyes.

I feel . . . woozy.

He undoes my straps personally.

"How are you feeling?"

"A little queasy," I answer honestly.

He nods. "That's to be expected." He looks at me, and his eyes shine so bright. "I can't wait to begin. This is going to be spectacular. Just you wait."

The Mad Hatter purses his lips. "You still need to test her."

"I know." The Dollmaker seems irritated, like he doesn't have time for things like simple tests.

But then Lenore enters the room, dragging Stella with her, and my breath seizes in my chest. The Dollmaker helps me stand up from the surgical table.

"I know you're still getting your bearings, but I need you to do something for me." He keeps his eyes on Stella as he whispers it in my ear.

Harley? She mouths my name, and she's crying, and she's so, so scared.

The Mad Hatter raises his eyebrows, and a slight smile forms on his face.

And I walk over to her, and I backhand her.

She crumples to the floor, and The Dollmaker tells me I'm wonderful.

I follow him out of the room without looking back.

I hated to do that to her.

But I had to.

If I didn't, he might know that he gave me the wrong chip.

Ivy

"She's gone." King Shark kept repeating it, even now that he and Vengeance and I were back at the pool house with Sophie.

And if he wasn't sitting on the floor with his knees tucked to his chest, and if it was anyone else but King Shark, I would have told them to shut the hell up already. Of course she was gone. I could feel it on a cellular level. Hearing it felt like a stab. Worse, like someone using a rusty sewing tool to rip out fresh stitches.

"She's gone," King Shark said again, and I slammed my hand down on the table without meaning to.

"Yes, but how do we get her back?"

Someone needed to tell me quickly, because I would tear the world apart piece by piece if that's what it took to find her.

"Ivy?" Sophie said gently.

And I realized I was clenching the table so hard my knuckles hurt and also that the potted plant in the corner just grew three sizes.

I realized everyone was staring at me.

I realized they were afraid of me.

"Sorry."

I tamped down the rage inside so it no longer felt like a black cloud choking the life out of the room. I walked across the pool house and sat down next to King Shark and rested my head on his shoulder.

"What are we going to do?"

"I don't know," he replied sadly. "But we have to try something."

It was then that I noticed the red-and-black envelope sticking out of my book bag.

CHAPTER 36

Thirty-three hours until the auction

STELLA IS HERE! STELLA IS HERE, AND SHE'S OKAY! STELLA IS here, and I just saw her! (Also, I slapped her. Hope we can still be friends.)

We don't get very far down the hallway before The Mad Hatter calls us back. Well, calls The Dollmaker back, anyway.

"Anton, can I speak with you for a moment?"

The Dollmaker leaves me in the hallway, and I have a second to process what just happened. Number one, I woke up and I still have free will. But number two, I slapped Stella in the face anyway because I didn't want them to find out. And as a result, number three, my hand really freaking hurts. Probably not as much as Stella's face, though. I hope I didn't break anything. I tried to take it easy on her without looking like I was taking it easy on her.

"Lenore just told me Stella has been here for days," says The Mad Hatter. "Where have you been keeping her?"

"Solitary," I hear The Dollmaker reply.

"You've been hiding her from me."

"No."

I gingerly move my fingers back and forth, testing each joint, thinking about how glad I am that Stella hasn't been changed as far as I could see. I think about how the anger would swell inside me if she had been. And then I think about what Ivy's reaction would be if The Dollmaker changed me. She'd lay waste to this entire place. She'd raze the building until it was in pieces so small, you could plant flowers in the dust. Would she still love me? If I was different?

That's when I realize the voices in the room have gotten louder.

"But you have so many. And her shoulders are just right," says The Mad Hatter. I wouldn't have expected a serial killer to sound so petulant.

The Dollmaker attempts to reason with him. "You already have an Alice. I thought you loved this one."

The Mad Hatter sighs. "I did. But then she vexed me," he says darkly. "I bet this one wouldn't vex me."

"This one isn't for you. I have plans—"

"You always have plans! You say that about everyone. And do you know how many of those plans would be a reality without me?" There's a sharp edge in his voice. Hell, in the whole room. It slices into the hallway, and I shiver because I can feel it.

"Of course, I couldn't do it without you. Your work is a critical part of this operation. I would never take it for granted." I hold my breath. Can The Mad Hatter tell he's being patronizing? I lean closer to the doorway, straining to hear, but Jervis doesn't reply. "Look, as soon as this launch is over, I'll find you a new Alice. I'll find you three if you want."

The Mad Hatter mumbles something I can't hear.

"Why don't you go look for one that you like on social media? That always makes you feel better."

I close my eyes and grit my teeth and try very hard not to black out from rage or nausea or both. The Dollmaker steps into the hallway, and I force the feelings away. Make my face as blank and unfeeling as porcelain.

"Sorry about that. He's a genius, truly, but a bit of a loose cannon. Are you ready?" he asks. "I have something special to show you."

I squeeze my mouth into a smile-like shape. "Absolutely."

He leads the way, and I follow along, but when I hear more footsteps, I can't help but glance back.

Jervis Tetch, The Mad Hatter, the Looking Glass Killer, is standing in the hallway, but he's looking inside the studio like he doesn't want to walk away. Like a starving man gazing through a window at a feast. I'd bet money he's staring at Stella.

Thirty-two hours until the auction

The Dollmaker walks me through the menagerie, cages stacked upon cages, terrariums from floor to ceiling, neat aisles of snakes and jungle cats and insects—it's almost like walking through a library of animals.

"What do you think?" He appraises me, studying my answer.

I take my time gazing at the different animals. "How did you do all this?" I hope I inject the right amount of awe into my voice.

His chest puffs up. (Success.)

I can't help staring at the cages and wondering which of them are earmarked for me. I wonder how a chipped Harley would ask about it.

The Dollmaker doesn't notice my wondering. "Well, it was a lot of work. And there's still a lot left to go. I was hoping to get your thoughts on Stella's transformation. She isn't singing to me the way the others have. Not even when I electrocuted her, if you can believe it. What—"

We're interrupted by Jett, which is probably for the best because lying about his plans for the other girls is hard enough. If I had to lie about Stella, after what he just said about electrocuting her, I'm not sure I could convince him.

"Dollmaker?" she asks in a voice that feels weirdly out of character.

He doesn't try to mask his annoyance. "What is it?"

"It's Stella." Jett gulps. "After Lenore took Stella back to her cell, Jervis went and got her. He took her to Wonderland, and then he flipped out on her because she wasn't Alice."

"Damn it. I thought we were past this." The Dollmaker pinches the bridge of his nose. "What state is she in?"

I pretend to be extremely interested in a nearby ball python.

"Not well. I don't know if—" Jett glances at me and stops mid-sentence. "I think you should come right now."

"All right. Take me to her." His voice is concerned, but hassled-concerned. Someone-just-dinged-my-car-door concerned. I try really hard not to kill him with my bare hands.

He leaves me standing there, already hurrying for the door after Jett. And then he turns.

"I wish I could spend more time with you, but there's so much to do when you're planning something on this scale. You understand?"

I smile like the doll he thinks I am. "Of course."

His face relaxes for a second. "Good. And speaking of, I

could really use your help. Could you check the animals? I need to know if any of them are in anything less than top shape. We don't have much time, and I can't let my art be compromised by deadlines."

I nod. "Anything I can do to help. I, uh, haven't ever done this before, though."

He runs a hand through his hair. "Right, yes. I'll send Lenore to help."

"Perfect," I say, but he's already leaving.

"If I didn't need that little freak . . . ," he mutters as the door snaps shut behind them.

My legs go weak as soon as he's gone. All I can think about is what The Mad Hatter might have done to Stella. And if she's going to be okay.

Thirty-one hours until the auction

I really need Lenore to glitch already. She may have given me her bad chip, but the good one is still in there, chiseling away at her free will. We're almost done checking the animals, and who knows when the next time is that we'll get to be alone together before the auction. We have separated the healthiest fish into their own tanks and tagged the most vicious predators of land and air and sea and discarded an entire terrarium of dead scorpions, and she is still his marionette through and through.

I'm just checking on a listless rattlesnake that turns out to be fine after all (yikes!), when the door to the menagerie opens.

"Are you almost finished?" asks Jett.

"Ten more minutes," says Lenore.

"Make that fifteen," I echo.

Jett narrows her eyes. "See you in ten."

Does she suspect? Does she know I'm not really one of them? Can she sense it somehow? Is she going to tell The Dollmaker?

But I don't have time to worry about that now. Lenore goes back to inspecting an axolotl, and I tiptoe across the warehouse floor of the menagerie until I'm right behind her.

I wrap my arms around her neck and pray I can make her pass out before she screams.

Thirty hours before the auction

I stuff a wad of gauze into Lenore's mouth. Waking up during a surgical procedure without anesthesia has to be one of the top worst things that can happen to a person. She bucks against me, but I can't let her go yet. I've almost got it. I dig the forceps under the skin behind her ear, under a scar that matches my own, the location of her second chip. It's surprisingly difficult—I don't know how Talia was able to remove them so quickly. But I'm nearly there. I can't give up now. I feel the tip of the forceps scratch against the chip. This is it!

Lenore delivers a kick that sends me flying across the aisle. My head bangs against an aquarium. There are stars behind my eyes.

But clenched in my hand? The forceps holding her chip.

I did it. She's going to be okay.

She leaps to her feet, ready to fight me.

And then her muscles relax. The change starts from her neck, and it reaches all the way to her toes. Her hands shake. She crumples to her knees, sobbing.

I run over to her. "Are you okay?"

Lenore throws her arms around me. I think she might snap me in half. No, really, she is that aggressive a hugger.

"I'm me," she says.

And my eyes start to well up, and there's a part of me that very much wants to appreciate the bigness of this moment she is having, but also, Jett said ten minutes, and it's been at least twenty, and she cannot walk in and see Lenore like this.

So, as much as I hate to do it . . .

"We don't have any time," I say. "Do you think you can get through lunch?"

She nods like the badass she is. Sucks the tears right back into her eyes.

And we go to lunch and hope like anything our acting skills are enough.

Ivy

We loaded up Sophie's mom's van as quickly as humanly possible. Sophie drove. Vengeance followed behind on her motorcycle. I navigated. King Shark loomed over my shoulder, and we both watched the blip on my phone like it was Harley herself and not merely a collection of pixels. At least she'd had the foresight to use a tracker.

"There!" I shouted, pointing down an alley. "She's down there!"

But my stomach sank even as I said it. The alley was empty. Of people. Just a few beat-up metal trash cans. I couldn't help imagining her body crumpled inside one of them as I leapt from the van. Couldn't help the thorns that sprang up around me on all sides as soon as the thought entered my mind.

One of the trash cans fell over, spilling garbage onto the street. Fast-food bags and soda cans and a rainbow tutu that I now knew had a tracker sewn into it.

"She's not here," I said, my voice cracking. I clutched the rainbow tutu to my chest.

Soph put her arm around me. "We'll go back to Pride and see what we can find there."

"Right. Pride. Good idea."

Only this isn't *Scooby-Doo*, and we didn't find any clues, and we all ended up hot and tired. I didn't know what I'd expected, a trail of glitter that would lead me straight to Harley?

She'd like that.

"That's the first time I've seen you smile all day," said Sophie.

"I was thinking about Harley."

Sophie's small smile matched mine. "Harley Quinn will do that to a person."

But our feeble scrap of happiness didn't last long. We searched the park and every street and alley nearby. Nothing.

Eventually, Vengeance left because she wanted to loop in Talia to see if there was anything the League of Assassins could do. She promised to call us with any leads, no matter how small.

Eventually, Sophie made King Shark and me go home too. Said we wouldn't be any help to Harley without sleep. And when we got back to the pool house, Sophie pulled the sleeping bags down from the closet without saying a word.

We arranged them just like we did at the sleepover a few nights ago. Only tonight we didn't have movies and popcorn and giggling till 3:00 a.m.

Tonight, we just couldn't bear to be alone.

CHAPTER 37

Twenty-five hours before the auction

MEALTIMES ARE THE SCARIEST PART. ALL OF US CRAMMED IN a room together with any number of people who might notice something, say something. I slide my tray down the line, getting a salad and a calzone. There's dessert with dinner today—ice cream with a chocolate medallion on the side. The Dollmaker must be trying to keep our spirits high. That or he's bribing us to stay on our best behavior.

The dinner line is short-staffed (I can see them back there prepping blistered shishito peppers and sriracha cauliflower bites for the auction patrons), and Jasmin is serving us dessert. I stare blankly at the wall behind her as I accept my scoop of ice cream. Fallon is behind me in line, and she doesn't miss a thing, that one.

"Seems like a good night to eat dessert first, huh?" Jasmin smiles this big, fakey grin at Fallon.

Something's up. Fallon's too excited about her ice cream to catch it, though. (She is seven, after all).

Did Jasmin slip something into Fallon's ice cream? Maybe something to knock people out so we can remove their chips? I eye my ice cream, trying to figure out if there's something different about it. Ah, well. I pluck the chocolate medallion out because you don't have to ask me twice to eat the best part first.

That's when I see it.

The letters on my chocolate, peeking out from under the layer of mint ice cream. I slurp off the ice cream, and sure enough, there's a message there.

Meet me at midnight.
Your bathroom.

How in the world? Jett is sneaking up behind me (or thinks she is), so I stuff the whole medallion into my mouth and take a seat. I remember Jasmin saying one of her fingers was a laser now. Is that how she did it? I fight the urge to look around the dining hall and assess whether anyone else is reading secret messages lasered into their dessert.

After dinner, Lenore falls into step with me on the way back to our dormitory.

"The chocolate was particularly delicious," she says.

"Yes, it was," I reply.

So, Lenore knows. She'll be at the meeting tonight. I wonder who else we'll see there. I haven't been able to de-chip anyone else on that list Everly included in her journal, but maybe Lenore or Jasmin has, or maybe Jasmin invited people who haven't been chipped yet.

My watch beeps just as I get inside the dormitory. A message from The Dollmaker.

Can you come to my studio?
I need your help with something.

I shoot Lenore a Look as I leave, but she heard my watch too. She knows nothing good comes from hearing that beep. I go to his studio like I'm walking the long hallway to my death sentence. Who's in there? Who am I going to be helping him hurt?

When I reach the door, he's already opening it, expecting me.

Jasmin is sitting on the surgery table.

Twenty-four hours before the auction

No, no, no, no, no. This is bad. Terribly, catastrophically bad. She's the only one who knows the full details of our escape plan. The rest of us were going to learn them tonight, but now? If she becomes one of them, I don't know how we're going to pull this off.

I try not to look in her eyes as I strap her to the table. She's worried, though. Scared. I can feel it radiating off her in waves. The Mad Hatter scrubs in, and the tools are laid out all in a row, with Jasmin's chip to the right of them. He talks to The Dollmaker for a second.

I could do it. I could cut the defective chip out of my neck the way Lenore did and switch it for Jasmin's. I mean, it was surprisingly difficult to remove Lenore's, and that was *with* me being able to see the injection site, and if I start bleeding, I don't have black feathers to hide it, but I'm sure I can do this. Just stab a sharp object behind my ear and wiggle it around under my skin until I find the chip. I hover

over the tools, reach out my hand to touch the scalpel. (It occurs to me why the girls so rarely try to remove the chips on their own.)

The Dollmaker let The Mad Hatter make an example out of her.

"What are you doing?"

The Dollmaker is behind me, blood and turpentine. His voice is in my ear.

"This scalpel looks dirty." I fight like anything to keep the quaver out of my voice. "I'll get you a new one."

I deposit the scalpel in the sink. Crap. They only talked for a couple of seconds. There wasn't time.

I go across the room to get a new scalpel from the surgical drawer. I'm not going to be able to do this. The window is gone.

I place the gleaming piece of metal next to all the others.

"Here you go," I say.

"Good eye," says The Dollmaker. "Can't risk any infections at this stage."

And I have to sit there—powerless—as The Mad Hatter hypnotizes my friend, as he slices into her neck and implants a chip there, destroys all our hopes of escaping this terrible place.

A few minutes later, Jasmin wakes up. A few minutes later, the whole world has changed. Her eyes are different when she looks at me. And when The Dollmaker tells her to use her robot hand to shock me, she does.

I jump, and my teeth clang together, and for a second, the pain shoots through me, searing and intense. It doesn't hurt as badly as knowing we'll never get out of here now.

Twenty-two hours before the auction

I whisper everything that happened as Lenore and I brush our teeth.

Is it still worth trying to meet tonight?

Who else do you think will be there?

Maybe we go to warn the others about Jasmin? Or just in case we can come up with another plan?

It's what we decide on—meeting at midnight, bathroom—but I can tell neither of us feels all that hopeful about it. Not now that we've lost Jasmin. Even so, we put on our pajamas and pretend to go to sleep, and I check my watch every ten minutes to make sure we're not late.

At 11:55, Lenore is asleep (she *had* been looking pretty sleep-deprived lately, probably from trying to get her chip to glitch before I removed it), so I gently and carefully and quietly sneak down from the top bunk. Gently/carefully/quietly touch her shoulder. She startles when she wakes, and the wooden slats of the bunk bed creak. I cringe and peer around the dark bedroom, but Fallon is asleep, with one hand wound in her red hair, and Jett has just let out a faint snore.

I think we're safe. Lenore and I tiptoe to the girls' bathroom. Everly is there. And a couple of girls I recognize from Jasmin's dorm, Navi and the girl with the blond braids. Girls who haven't been chipped yet. They tense when the door opens but relax when they see it's just us.

"I guess you already know the bad news, huh?" I say to them. "About Jasmin?"

The girls exchange confused glances. "She said she needed to get something," says the blond one.

"She'll be here in a minute," says Navi.

Lenore sucks in her breath. "We need to get back to our beds."

"What?"

"You can't trust Jasmin anymore," I say as I hurry behind Lenore. "She's been chipped."

As the horror sets in on their faces, the door to the bathroom opens.

Jasmin is standing in the doorway, her jaw set.

She's holding a knife.

Ivy

At twenty-four hours, Sophie's big-mom-energy, cool-under-pressure vibe cracked.

"Twenty-four hours is bad, right?" Started crying. Completely unraveled. "Seventy-five percent of people are found in the first twenty-four hours, and after twenty-four hours, the chances of finding them drop, and when you do find them, they'll probably be dead."

"She won't be dead," I said sharply. Everyone had better hope she's not. I would light the entire world on fire and laugh while it burned.

I let the anger fizz through my veins because it was better than feeling powerless. Because seeing Sophie panicked made something inside me crack wide open. The what-ifs sliced into me, cold and unforgiving, each one bleaker than the last. Was she hurt? Was she about to do something reckless and get herself killed?

And then a more painful thought: Why didn't she tell me what she was planning?

I could dissect that in my brain. I could do the mental work of unpacking it. But I was tired of being the one who thought everything through. I needed action. It was time for last resorts and things I never thought I'd do.

I didn't trust this person—I don't trust anyone. But I got the feeling Harley did, and at that moment, that was enough for me.

I picked up the phone and called Montoya.

CHAPTER 38

Twenty hours before the auction

LENORE AND I HAVE A RAPID-FIRE CONVERSATION WITH our eyes about how to take down Jasmin. Apparently, Jasmin sees this.

She throws up her hands, dropping the knife.

"What are you doing? Y'all, it's me."

I hesitate. Exchange another glance with Lenore. It *sounds* like Jasmin. But.

"I saw you get chipped," I say.

Jasmin nods. "Yeah, and you know what happened right after that?"

"You electrocuted me?"

She cringes. "Uh-huh, sorry about that. The chip made me do it. But after *that*, The Dollmaker activated my neural link."

More exchanging of the glances.

"And . . . ?"

She rolls her eyes. "*And* he completely underestimated

how powerful it would make me. I disabled my chip from the inside. Isn't that cool? I freaking love computer science."

She realizes that her scientific glee is not mirrored on our faces. That we, in fact, have not dropped our fighting stances, not even a smidge.

"How do we know you're telling the truth?" asks Lenore, her ink-black feathers standing on end.

Jasmin lets out an exhausted sigh. "I don't know. Harley, you know me. Ask me anything you want."

I shake my head. "You could still have access to your old memories."

"What if I use my electricity finger to deactivate Everly's chip right now? Then would you believe me?"

Lenore and I are in the middle of another eye-conversation when Everly walks between us to stand directly in front of Jasmin.

"I'm going to let her do it," Everly announces, like *just try and stop me*. "I've hardly slept for days because Londyn and I realized it's easier to make yourself lapse when you're tired. If there's a chance Jasmin can help me, I'm taking it."

She turns around to face us and tilts her head to the side, like a girl offering her neck to a vampire.

"I've never done this before." Jasmin hesitates. "I don't know if it hurts."

"I've gotten pretty good at handling pain," says Everly, her face harder than I've ever seen it.

"Okay," says Jasmin, and she gently touches the tip of her metal finger to the telltale chip scar behind Everly's ear.

Lenore and I wait, ready to go full battle royale if Jasmin is lying.

Her finger twitches, and Everly collapses in front of us.

♦

"I didn't mean to," says Jasmin.

"Sure, you didn't," says Lenore, who currently has Jasmin in some kind of Brazilian jiujitsu hold.

Jasmin isn't fighting Lenore off, though. Isn't even trying to use her cyborg powers.

I check Everly's pulse, and it's there. It's normal. Put my ear to her mouth. She's breathing too.

"She's okay. She's alive, anyway."

Lenore relaxes her grip a bit now that Everly has been pronounced alive. The two girls cowering in the back shower stall look a little less terrified too.

Everly stirs in my arms. "Harley?"

"Are you okay?" She took such good care of me. I want to take care of her if I can. I want to protect her.

"I think so." And then she sees Lenore and Jasmin and puts the pieces together. "I mean, I'm fine. It worked. She deactivated my chip."

I look her up and down like I'll be able to find the answer. "Are you sure? How do you know you're not just glitching like you were a second ago?"

Everly shakes her head. "It feels different. Less . . . cloudy."

Lenore's mouth falls open. "She's telling the truth."

She lets go of Jasmin, who is definitely not ready to forgive her just yet.

"Told you." And then to Everly: "I'm really sorry. I didn't know it would knock you out like that. Did it hurt?"

Everly shrugs. "It might have? I feel okay now, though."

Now that we've confirmed Everly and her brain are intact, Jasmin picks up her knife and whips out a screwdriver and uses it to open a vent at the back of the bathroom.

"I've been stashing weapons in various bathrooms for the last two months," she says, placing the knife inside the ductwork.

She's not kidding. There are scalpels and some metal pipes and at least two other knives from the kitchen.

"Wow," says Lenore.

"Yeah, nice work," I echo.

Jasmin smiles. "Thanks."

"So, what's the plan?" asks Lenore.

"De-chip as many people as possible tomorrow, especially people who would interfere the most."

"Then we have to get Jett, for sure," says Lenore, looking over her shoulder like she's expecting Jett to appear. "She already suspects something. I can tell."

I nod. "And Fallon." I touch my neck where I know the stripes are still an angry burgundy color. "The kid's lethal."

But Jasmin shakes her head. "I don't know if I trust a seven-year-old to keep a secret like this."

Lenore sighs. "She's right. Fallon has impulse-control issues. She might attack The Dollmaker before it's time."

I hate the idea of leaving Fallon's chip in place. They're right, though. I tell them this (grudgingly).

We discuss weapons next. And escape routes.

Jasmin quickly lays out her months of planning. "I think this'll work best if we stage our revolution while he's right in the middle of the auction. We can get a lot of people out safely before we even hit him with an attack."

"Agreed," I say. "We still need to figure out doors, though. I overheard the guards talking, and the new panels are set to lock automatically in the event of an escape attempt. And The Dollmaker has some sort of fail-safe override if they're damaged, so we can't hit the panels themselves, but I'm thinking with the right combination of supplies, I could make some pretty sweet homemade explosives to blast the doors open."

"Oh," Jasmin says, with this look like she really doesn't want to rain on my napalm parade. "I've actually got that covered."

I frown. "What do you mean?"

The last time we talked about this, it was a huge issue. One of our biggest issues.

"I—well, I can do it." Jasmin waves a hand, and the door to the bathroom slides open like she has telekinesis or something.

"Oh, you can do it, all right." I pop up on my knees, excited. "Also, how can you do it?"

"The neural link," Jasmin explains. "I can pretty much control anything electronic in the Tower. Anything connected to the local network, anyway. Doors, security cameras, the works. I even created a proxy server for all the chips we've removed and deactivated, so that when he checks on us, it'll look like we're all still good little robots."

"Holy crap." This is amazing. "Wait, are you, like, connected to the internet? Could you message Ivy and Bianca and the FBI and stuff?"

I picture Ivy. Getting a message from Jasmin. Blasting through the walls of the Tower with an army of hawthorn trees.

Jasmin shakes her head sadly. "Unfortunately, there's a firewall. It's pretty strong too. I can't break through it. So I've only got access to what's inside the Tower."

"Hey, that's still a lot, though," says Everly.

"She's right," says Lenore.

And I know it's true; I just— The thought of being able to talk to Ivy, even through a computer, really got my hopes up.

"I'll keep trying." Jasmin gives me an encouraging smile.

"Thanks." I bump my shoulder against hers. "We shouldn't count on it, though. Even if it's just us versus them, I think we've got a really good shot at this."

"Me too," says Jasmin.

I hang back as the other girls file down the hall to their dorm rooms. There's something else. I think back to what I wrote in the journal Ivy gave me.

"Hey, Jasmin?"

"Yeah?"

I hesitate because smashing things with mallets is easy and feelings like these are complicated. You never know if letting them out will have the expected outcome. But I still have to try, so: "I missed you."

Her face softens. "I've missed you too."

"I'm sorry that I didn't keep going with you and Bianca in the Reckoning." I think about saying Vengeance, but I'm not sure Jasmin would know who I'm talking about. "I really regret it. I wish I could go back and do things differently."

Jasmin gestures with her cyborg hand. "Hey, you and me both. I definitely wish I'd called you when I figured out the location of this place."

"I think we're more together than we are apart. But I think sometimes I get really caught up in wanting to be the person who does everything and saves everyone."

She smiles. "I think you and Bianca have that in common."

I laugh because that totally tracks. But I need to ask her

something serious. *Take the risk, Harley.* "Hey, would you ever want to start it up again, the Reckoning? Or something like it?"

Jasmin looks sad, and I worry I've asked too much. I've lost her. But then she says, "I've actually been thinking about that a lot while I've been in here. With what's happened to me, it's hard for me to picture living a traditional life. It just feels like I'm meant to do something bigger, since I have these powers now, you know?"

I nod. I may not have the powers she does, but I've always felt that call.

And then Jasmin freezes—it's weird how abrupt it is.

"You okay?"

"Yes," she says. "I've just been using the security cameras to keep an eye on the guards, and one of them was headed our way, but it's okay. He passed on by."

"Oh, good." A realization hits me. "When you say you can control security cameras, does that mean you can see previous footage?"

"I'm pretty sure I can," she says, eyeing me curiously.

"Can you see what happened to Stella?"

Jasmin's eyes widen, but she nods. "Give me a second."

She tilts her head toward the ceiling, and her eyes kind of roll back. "There aren't cameras in Wonderland." She winces. "But, yes, I can see him throwing her into the hallway. Oh my gosh, Harley."

My stomach clenches. "What?"

"They had to take her to the surgery room on a stretcher. Her face is really bad, and there's an awful lot of blood."

I don't want to ask, but I have to. "Did she make it?"

Seconds pass before Jasmin answers. I know she's probably

scanning the video feed, but the waiting is awful. "I see foot-age of them wheeling her back to her room." There's a pause, and then, "Oh."

"What?" I can feel that the news is bad even before she says it.

"I just did a scan of everyone's watches. Stella's isn't giv-ing off vitals anymore."

I'm sitting on the floor, and I don't know how I got here. I sob in a way that makes Jasmin scared. She tries to calm me—fast—so I don't wake anyone and ruin everything. But I'm already in the dark place. What if I hadn't gone for that half-baked escape plan? Would we have found another way out—a way that involves Stella still being on this planet? The guilt settles over me like a poisonous fog. The Doll-maker only took her because of me. This is all on me.

The tears keep coming, and I'm reminded of when Kylie got ripped away from us last year and I would spend hours in bed listening to her voice on my phone. Weirdly, that's what stops me crying. I don't have the luxury of sitting in bed and grieving right now. I have to get it together. I have to make sure no other person in this Tower meets the same fate Stella did.

So I push the grief down inside me. Lock it in a box. I can deal with it later. For now, I just need to find some way to keep myself focused on the end goal. The only thing that comes close to bringing me peace is imagining what I'll do to The Mad Hatter when I get my hands on him.

Eventually, the tears stop, and we should probably go back to our dorm rooms, but Jasmin doesn't move.

"There's one more thing I was hoping to talk to you about," she says.

And her face looks so apprehensive that I say, "What?"

"Timing. I think our best chance is going to be after the first four girls have been auctioned off." She takes a deep breath and holds it like she's got the hiccups. "I think we should do it during your hybridization."

She goes on to explain some stuff about how I'll get into the machine, and we'll make The Dollmaker think it's starting to work, but don't worry, she'll be able to stop it with her mind. I am barely even listening.

"I'll do it," I say.

"Renee Montoya," barked the voice on the other end of the line.

Harley was right. Montoya's voice did make me feel like I'd been sent to the principal's office.

"Hi, this is I— Pamela. Pamela Isley. Harleen Quinzel's girlfriend." My voice wavered on both "Harleen" and "girlfriend," but I tried to hold it together.

"Yes, Miss Isley. I'm aware of who you are. I thought you and Miss Quinzel would have been by the station by now. Could you let her know—"

But I didn't allow her to finish.

"He took her," I said. "He took her, and I need your help."

CHAPTER 39

Three hours before the auction

THE TOWER IS A BEEHIVE OF ACTIVITY. THE ALICES ARRANGE furniture and set out vases of fresh-cut flowers. The utilitarian chairs and round tables where we have every meal are gone, and the dining hall looks like it's ready for a wedding or a fashion show. But neither of those descriptions is really accurate, because there are no pews or flimsy folding chairs here. Everything is mid-century modern end tables and dark velvet armchairs. The feel is like some smoky, dimly lit lounge. I wonder if The Dollmaker borrowed the furniture from Labyrinth.

Lenore stomps the runway in front of me like she's in Paris and it's Fashion Week, strutting the full length of it from the back of the room to the stage. I count seats. I'd bet there are fifteen to twenty coming tonight. Maybe as many as thirty, depending on how many of those seats are for bodyguards and entourages. That's more than we were counting on.

I bite my lip, replaying Jasmin's plan in my head. It could still work. It's possible. If we—

Jett nudges me from behind. "You're up."

She didn't say it meanly, though, I think as I take my turn on the runway. Now that Jasmin deactivated Jett's chip, she's still tough, but she's not so mean. I keep walking. The Dollmaker wants us to practice, especially the part where we have to navigate the stairs from the runway to the stage. None of us are to trip. Apparently, face-planting isn't part of his creative vision.

I clip-clop up the stairs.

"Eyes up. Head high," he says from the lectern, where he's playing ringmaster.

I lift my chin a bit. I'd rather headbutt him and tackle him off the stage. I turn and face the invisible audience like a queen.

"Good. Perfect. Everyone else, do it just like that."

He has us practice our walks two more times before his watch beeps. "Damn. Okay. Once more, and then hair and makeup, and then wait in your dormitories until I call for you." He rushes down the runway "to see what it looks like from the audience," snapping at an Alice as he goes. "Find some flowers that aren't pink, will you? It's starting to look like a child's birthday party in here. The rest of you, full-scale rehearsal. And quickly, people."

We pantomime what will happen to us tonight.

First, Fallon.

Then Lenore.

Then Maeve.

Then Firefly.

And then me.

"We're going to transform you live onstage, and no one knows which animals I've selected but me. Isn't it exciting?"

I think about Stella.

"It will be," I say.

One hour before the auction

I braid Fallon's hair as fast as I can, two pretty French braids, not a hair out of place. If I can just keep myself busy, if I can just delay the impact of the grief, I can make it through tonight with our plan intact. The Dollmaker has hair-and-makeup charts detailing looks for each of us, and he was adamant that Fallon be the picture of sweetness and innocence. *The juxta-position is key*, he said. And then he explained to all of us in excruciating detail that juxtaposition is when two things that seem to be very different butt up against each other.

When I tell you we all deserve Academy Awards for pre-tending to be fascinated, I mean it.

The surgical scar on Fallon's neck is neatly hidden under one of her braids, almost in her hairline. It's really too bad the other girls wouldn't let me de-chip her. I run my finger over the scar.

"Harley?" says Jasmin, who is struggling to make a zipper work on Jett's costume. "I could really use your help over here."

"Sure," I say. "Just a minute."

Thirty minutes before the auction

We speak only in whispers because the patrons are starting to arrive. Lenore and I are in charge of getting everyone into place. On either side of the seating area are two golden cages

The Dollmaker built, and he wants the people who are already spoken for via special order to be standing in them. *So the patrons will have something to capture their interest as they sit down*, he said.

I scan my watch and open a gilded door so that Scarab (that's the girl who looks like an insect) can step inside.

"The door will open on its own," I whisper. "After I get in the chamber. You know what to do."

She gives me the subtlest of nods.

I lock her in. Across the room, Lenore locks Gabriel into his. His bat wings rustle as the door clicks shut behind him.

I scan the lounge. Men *are* starting to arrive, and they *are* looking. Especially at Scarab. My jaw clenches involuntarily. She's like a zoo animal to them. A commodity.

Everly passes a negroni to a congressman, and Pretty Alice presents her tray of old-fashioneds to the head of Gotham City's most prominent crime families. Even in the dim lighting, I recognize Salvatore Maroni as she hands him his drink. The Alices are acting as servers tonight, since none of them are being sold off like cattle. I remember asking (genuinely) why the kitchen staff wasn't doing it, and The Dollmaker looked at me in horror because *some of those women are forty years old, and it would seriously clash with the aesthetic.*

"Are you twins? You look like you could be sisters," says Maroni, his eyes lingering on Pretty Alice.

She smiles sweetly. "The Dollmaker made us this way."

"That so? He's a talented guy. A weirdo, but I give credit where credit is due. He's got a gift." He clinks glasses with his second-in-command, and Pretty Alice retreats to the kitchen.

I hurry to the other side of the dining hall, where long black curtains have been hung to form a makeshift backstage area. Honestly? I'm surprised there aren't more Super-Villains here. The Dollmaker invited them, I know. I saw Everly's guest list. Maybe they just want to be fashionably late, but I don't know. Maybe there's something more alluring about this sort of power when you don't have it yourself.

Other people are arriving now, and The Dollmaker stands at the door, greeting them.

"Welcome, welcome. So glad you could come. Hello, I was hoping to see you. Instructions for the auction are in your programs. Good evening. Oh, that piece? Why, yes, it is rather striking. What, ah, is it that you like about it?"

I turn away because even the best acting skills have their limits. *Focus, Harley. Keep your mind on the situation instead of him.* He has the patrons entering through the doors to the garden, which is good. We had counted on that. It's going to be our easiest way out. My eyes meet Jasmin's—she's across the room in a tech booth, where he has her controlling the sound and lighting and everything else electronic for the whole show. She's filing away the information just like me, I can tell.

I go backstage and make sure everyone is ready. Does their makeup need retouching, and do they have weapons hidden in their dresses? Are they lined up in the correct order, and are they ready for what's about to happen next? I take my place between Firefly and Jett. Noah nervously shoots a bolt of electricity back and forth between his fingertips.

Before I know it, the lights are going dim in the front of the house, and I can hear The Dollmaker's voice over the microphone. I peek through the curtains.

"Hello, everyone, and thank you for coming tonight. My name is Anton, but everyone calls me The Dollmaker. Please prepare yourself for a night that tears down the barriers between art and surgical technique, for a series of creations from my disturbing and fantastical mind."

As he says this, the gilded cages are backlit with lights, and the audience whispers and appraises. And then the hall goes suddenly dark. Nothing visible but the runway and The Dollmaker. He leans in to the microphone with a wicked grin, like he's about to share a secret with you and only you.

"Let the exhibition begin."

Ivy

Another day passes and another and another. It's hard not to feel hopeless. I slip away from King Shark and the others and their city search plans. Just for a minute. All I need is a minute. I lie in the grass in Sophie's backyard and ask the trees if it'll be okay.

CHAPTER 40

FALLON STANDS IN THE SPOTLIGHT, HANDS FOLDED, SMIL-
ing out at the audience. The man she just stung has already
been disposed of. Maybe he'll make it, or maybe he won't.
The Dollmaker doesn't care. Neither do the men in the audience. Their faces are horror and hunger simultaneously.
And when the bidding opens, they all have to have her.

Well, maybe not all. The Mad Hatter watches quietly
from a seat at the back—he slipped in just as the show was
starting. I would trade a kidney for the chance to be in a
room with him alone. With my mallet. I force myself to
focus on the auction so my darkness doesn't make me do
something stupid.

The congressman isn't bidding. "I'm hoping for something a little more subtle," he says to the CEO of a media
conglomerate.

The crime lord wins.

"Fallon, please go join Mr. Maroni." The Dollmaker ad-
dresses her, but he says it into the microphone. Everything is
a show. Even this part. Especially this part.

She floats down the stairs and sits in the small wooden chair near the Maroni contingent. So, that's what those are for. Fallon hands him the black recorder—a dog handing its leash to its master. Maroni's eyes say he's scared of the dimpled seven-year-old girl sitting next to him, but he doesn't flinch from her touch, doesn't give any of the usual body-language tells. He's good. Doesn't want his men to know.

Pretty Alice hands Fallon a hot chocolate, and she settles in to watch the rest of this macabre production. And the show goes on.

Lenore is next, flying down from the rafters, swooping low over the men's heads with a sense of drama that The Dollmaker is eating right up. I don't like it. In all our rehearsals, she walked the runway with the rest of us, which means it was a last-minute change, which means there could be any number of other last-minute changes.

Changes involving the hybridization machine? What if he doesn't have it hooked up to the local network after all? What if Jasmin isn't as strong as she thinks she is? What if she can't stop it?

I can't think that way. I have to focus all my energy on this night and my role in it. There's no way to succeed otherwise.

After another bidding frenzy, Lenore goes to the largest illegal-drug supplier in the Northeast. I'm honestly surprised The Dollmaker let her go—he relies on her so much. But then, I suppose he can always make another Lenore.

"Our next piece is a little different," says The Dollmaker. "For the gentleman who is looking for someone who blends in a little more. Maeve. See if you can find the snake in her."

She slinks down the runway in a snakeskin dress—black. Muted. Long sleeves. With a timeless silhouette. It would be classy but for the pattern. Her tan skin glows under the lights, and I watch the men in the audience study her, searching for something unusual or different. Because she looks like just a girl, an impossibly beautiful one, but a normal human girl all the same.

She walks onto the stage, to the man waiting there— another throwaway The Dollmaker found, and she scratches one fingernail down his cheek. So gently, it doesn't even leave a mark. Not that I can see from the back of the room, anyway.

He falls down dead a second later.

The congressman must have her, by the look in his eyes— cost is irrelevant. I try to follow the subsequent bidding war, but my mind is somewhere else now. It's almost time. Only one more girl and then me. I try not to catch Jasmin's eyes. Or Lenore's. Or the eyes of any of the other girls we've de-chipped.

Firefly takes the runway in a literal blaze of glory, but I barely notice. The mid-show spectacle is almost here. I thought it was strange that he didn't save me for the end, but The Dollmaker explained that having the biggest song before the intermission is how all the Broadway shows do it. You want everyone talking about that last song during the break. The minutes slip away like seconds.

And then his voice fills the speakers, telling the audience that what they are about to see will defy their wildest imaginations. Jett nudges me, just like in practice.

"You've got this," she whispers.

And I step out from behind the curtains.

I keep my head high as I traipse down the runway. Eyes up as I climb the stairs. I do not trip. I do not look down. I am standing in front of The Dollmaker/the machine/my fate entirely too soon.

"Some artists hide the techniques of their craft, but I'm proud to demonstrate mine in the interest of transparency. History has been made, and I will make it again tonight." Before he can finish his sentence, the curtains open and the stage lights shine like the sun on the hybridization machine he has set up onstage. He revels in the revealing. The audience leans forward. "I will be creating one of my pieces—*the* piece—my magnum opus. Live. Tonight. If you are faint of stomach, you may want to step out of the room. Art can be a brutal process."

No one leaves. But they do fall silent.

He loves it. He devours every second of it.

"Harley is not for sale. She is my muse. The standard from which I will create all future pieces. She inspires me to be more daring, to push the boundaries of what even I thought was possible."

The audience watches me, but it's not just them. Jasmin and Lenore and Fallon and the people backstage and the ones in cages. Everyone is glued to this moment. Not for the same reasons, but that doesn't change their shared fixation.

"And tonight, you will see her transformed." The Dollmaker leads me by the hand to the hybridization pod. I feel like the girl in the magician's act who gets put into the box. Only what's waiting for me is worse than swords or being sawed in half.

"The animals are being placed in the back of the pod as we speak."

Animals, plural. My heart beats against my ribs. But which creatures? Now that he mentions it, the back half of the machine is still covered by a black curtain, shrouded in secrecy.

"I thought it would be more interesting if we made this one a surprise," he says into his microphone.

And then in a whisper that is just for me: "Don't be scared. I would never do anything to hurt you."

I try to swallow his lie, but I end up biting the insides of my mouth so hard, they bleed. Luckily, he mistakes it as fear. And he's not entirely wrong. I am afraid. But if I have to turn into something horrible, so be it. It would be worth it to take him down.

The Dollmaker opens the glass door to the pod.

I hope Jasmin is as strong as she says she is.

I step inside, heels clicking on the metal floor.

I hope she can shut this thing down before it changes me.

I turn around, and The Dollmaker closes the door behind me.

"This is it," he says, excitement lighting up his voice.

I close my eyes and hope he's wrong.

Ivy

King Shark, Shiloh, and I return from another shift—we've been searching every city block in Gotham City systematically for anything that looks suspicious. Vengeance is still out there on her motorcycle. So are dozens of Harley's sorority sisters. Sophie held some kind of emergency chapter meeting, and they all came running.

King Shark shakes his head sadly at Sophie, and she nods and crosses out another section of the map. The atmosphere in the pool house is busy but frenzied. Worried.

And then all of our phones beep at once.

CHAPTER 41

MY HAIR STANDS ON END, AND MY SKIN BEGINS TO TINGLE, and not in a good way. More like being stabbed with a million tiny needles. She couldn't do it. Jasmin can't stop the machine. This is happening. I am being hybridized.

Like hell I'm just letting it happen.

I kick my foot against the door as hard as I can. It doesn't budge. But The Dollmaker turns to look at me. And I see the gasps on the audience's faces, even if I can't hear them.

Then it all goes dark.

The room, I mean. Not me. A complete and total power outage.

Hell yeah, Jasmin!

Lights back on, three of them. Two spotlights directed at each of the golden cages. And one on me.

The doors to the cages open in unison, a simultaneous creak. The audience members say, "Oh," because they think this is part of the show. The say it like people who aren't in danger, like people who haven't pissed off a bunch of kids with superpowers. Kids who just got let off their leashes.

The door handle in front of me clicks softly, and I know exactly what it means. The Dollmaker hears it too, and he turns, but he's too late. It's too late for all of them now. The great war has already begun, and they were too dizzy with greed to notice.

I kick the door again, and this time it swings open.

Chaos. The auction has descended into pure chaos. The Dollmaker's creations jump down from their cages and flood the room from backstage. Lenore nose-dives into the crowd, snatching up Pretty Alice and putting her into a cage. There were a few people we didn't get a chance to de-chip, and we don't want them hurt.

Onstage, The Dollmaker blocks my roundhouse kick.

"Get the cyborg!" he screams.

Jett rushes to help Jasmin fight off a couple of the Tower's goons. And the two of them are doing it. They're winning. As the fighting happens all around them. As Everly takes a round drink tray and begins whacking The Mad Hatter with it. As Noah rushes to help her.

But then Maroni thinks to use his remote.

"Kill the cyborg," he says to Fallon.

They're only a couple of yards away, and Jasmin hears him. Her eyes go wide with fear as Fallon answers, "Certainly, Mr. Maroni."

Jasmin searches for something she can use to protect herself. In a desperate move, she plunges the entire Tower into darkness. But Fallon can make her own light.

The brawl raging all around the tiny crimson fairy pauses, people unable to see through Jasmin's darkness, hypnotized by the snowflakes of light floating in the air, making their way to the cyborg girl. When the lights get close enough that Jasmin can touch them, Fallon's dress lifts, her tentacles shooting out.

And she wraps them around Maroni.

Remember the part where I said I wouldn't de-chip Fallon? I LIED. Sue me.

"Hope you don't mind I took her chip out," I yell to Jasmin.

"Thanks for letting me know," she calls back sarcastically over the crowd now stampeding toward the exits.

The men are terrified of what just happened to Maroni, and the dolls are desperate to escape. Everyone is scattering. I turn back to finish off The Dollmaker, but he's not on-stage with me anymore. Where the hell did he go that fast? I search the room, trying to find him, when Lenore screams. She clutches her side midair and falls to the ground, smashing into a side table, drinks going everywhere, glass shattering. A heap of feathers and contorted limbs. She doesn't get back up.

I see The Dollmaker, hiding to the right of the stage. He throws a weapon to the ground—the same one I saw him use on Vengeance at Pride. Like a small version of a crossbow, but more futuristic. He grabs another from a drawer that has apparently shot out from under the stage like magic. Aims the weapon at Maeve. I sprint across the stage, but even as I'm leaping into the air at him, I watch the dart shoot across the room and bury itself in Maeve's neck.

She falls too.

I push him backward, away from the drawer. I will end him. I will end all of this. Right now.

An arm closes around my neck.

"You're coming with me," says a guttural growl in my ear. It sounds familiar, but it can't be. She's supposed to be *dead*.

I catch a glimpse of the face of the girl who is dragging me away from my nemesis. It *is* Stella. She's alive! And . . . she's a wolf. Like, fangs and ears and yellow eyes. He turned her. She jerks me along, and my feet skitter against the floor, trying to keep up. She is seriously strong now, and she's not currently on the same side I'm on, but she is here. On this earth. Breathing. I'm so happy, I don't even care that she's kind of choking me.

My eyes meet The Dollmaker's, and he smiles like he knows everything.

"It's important to have insurance," he says, shooting another dart at Noah.

My feet scrape the floor as Stella drags me in the direction of my solitary cell. And I look around the room, and it hits me like a punch to the gut.

We're losing.

Lenore and Maeve and Noah knocked out with what I'm hoping were just tranquilizers. Everly KO'd by The Mad Hatter. He's got his watch out now, waving it in front of Jasmin.

I know how that goes.

Back and forth and swirling round and calm voice and wild eyes.

Tick-tock.

Tears form in the corners of my eyes. This isn't how it was supposed to happen. If we worked together, if I trusted them, we were supposed to be able to win this. But we did work together this time, and we're still not winning. We should have anticipated his use of the tranquilizers. We should have made it a priority to take out The Mad Hatter at the very beginning. But maybe we were always doomed to fail. Maybe when the power differential is this big, working together isn't enough. I feel embarrassed by how naive I've been.

Life isn't some stupid friendship movie, Harley.

And as I think it, the floor opens up.

Have you ever seen a giant-ass Venus flytrap bust through the floor and swallow a man whole?

It is quite a thing to behold.

Before I can fully process The Mad Hatter's extremely timely demise, there are more plants—shooting through the windows, broken glass flying everywhere.

"How in the world—" I can't even get the words out.

Now it is Jasmin's turn to look smug. "Remember that firewall?" she calls. "I broke it."

A band of people starts to gather in the space where the jagged pieces of window hang like jaws. A girl with hair the color of fire and roses peers through, and her jaw is set like a warrior's, and her face is lit with revenge, but she sighs with relief when her eyes meet mine. When she sees that I'm okay.

"Ivy!!!" I squeal.

And she crosses the room like there isn't a battle raging around us and takes my face in her hands.

"Did he hurt you?" she asks darkly, eyes cutting toward The Dollmaker as plants writhe like hungry dragons.

The intensity of it all makes my stomach flip like that first drop on a roller coaster.

"I'm okay," I breathe.

And the mask she's wearing dissolves, but we don't have time for hugs and tearful reunions right now. King Shark dives through first, and a couple members of the crime families who were thinking of fighting it out literally run screaming when they see him. He knocks Stella off me, and I yell for him to be careful because she's our friend. Vengeance jumps in next, tossing me my mallet.

"Hey, thanks!" I yell.

"You're welcome," she yells back, picking up a Tower goon and throwing him across the room.

I run straight for The Dollmaker, smashing the crossbow out of his hands. I turn for the drawer next.

"Stop. Hurting. My. Friends." I punctuate each word with a smash of his weapons.

And then I turn on him.

Fear flickers in his eyes.

"Harley?"

I step closer.

"We're supposed to be partners in this."

He is staring at me. Full tunnel vision. No one else exists.

He doesn't see the crowd of hybridized people converging behind him, led by Fallon.

"I think your art wants to have a word with you," I say, relishing the karma of it all.

And I walk up the stairs to the stage and smash his hybridization machine into pieces tiny enough that you could make glitter out of them.

The Dollmaker's screams are so loud, I almost don't hear the police sirens.

CHAPTER 42

BY THE TIME THE POLICE DESCEND ON US, WE'VE GOT THE right people in cages. Stella and everyone else who still had a chip have had their chips deactivated by Jasmin, and I've hugged Stella so hard, I think I scared her. (Though probably not as much as it scared her to find out she was part wolf?)

"How are you even alive?" I whisper as more GCPD than I've ever seen in my life flood the room.

"I don't know. The last thing I remember is that Hatter man attacking me, and then I woke up like this."

Wild. Based on what Jasmin said, it seemed like Stella was on the brink of death. I thought The Dollmaker only did hybridization procedures on people in tip-top shape, but maybe this was one of those last-ditch maneuvers. Like in that book I read in eighth grade where they turned that girl right after she almost died during a vampire baby C-section.

I guess that might also explain why Stella's only a wolf, not a wolf-scorpion like the doll he left on her bed at Arkham Acres. Maybe he thought a single hybridization would have a better chance of taking.

"Stella, I'm so sorry. This is all my fault." My chest clenches, and I swallow a sob because I can't be upset that she's basically a werewolf. Stella's the only one who gets to be upset right now.

"Hey," she says in a voice so firm, I barely recognize it. "You saved me. You saved everyone. I'm not going to let you beat yourself up over this."

(It's like she knows me.) Also? I feel like I can breathe again.

Across the room, The Dollmaker is still screaming in agony, and The Mad Hatter's skin looks a bit digested in places after being spat out by the Venus flytrap at Ivy's command, but it's no worse than they deserve.

"What in the unholy hell happened here?" Montoya directs the question at me, like the absolute shit show she's seeing is my fault.

"I'm the good guy here!" I say. Like, really. How hard do I have to try to make people believe that? I gently set my mallet on the ground and try to look upstanding.

Montoya does not look convinced. "Uh-huh. And the bad guys are . . . ?"

We all simultaneously point at The Dollmaker and The Mad Hatter and everyone else stuffed in a cage.

"Right."

The man who I believe is Montoya's superior also does not look convinced. "I say we cuff her."

Fallon materializes next to me and grabs my hand with her small one.

He recoils. "What the hell is that?"

"She is a child, and her name is Fallon," I say harshly. Geez, way to hurt her feelings, jerkhole.

An officer, a rookie by the look of him, attempts to put

handcuffs on Scarab, and she hisses at him, and suddenly there are guns raised all around the room.

"All right, I need everyone to calm down." Montoya's voice cuts through the Tower, and everyone stops talking. "Stand down. Put your guns away. Are we clear?" The officers are reluctant to comply. *"Now,"* she says. "And the rest of you, put your . . . weapons or whatever away. Let's everybody just calm down before someone gets hurt."

The officers finally lower their guns. Many of the kids sit down or put their hands up. The air in the room feels a little less fraught.

"Okay, now can someone please explain to me what's going on here?" She turns to me. "Harley?"

I take a deep breath. "Right. So, remember that thing that happened with The Scarecrow?"

We tell her about The Dollmaker and The Mad Hatter and the trafficking gang and what they've been doing with the people they've taken. Jasmin and Vengeance jump in to help me fill in the gaps. So does Jett—she's the only one of the OG Tower girls who isn't currently unconscious. (Well, besides Fallon. But Fallon doesn't seem all that interested in talking.)

Montoya asks us question after question. Ivy strategically interrupts me whenever I'm about to incriminate myself. She has somehow managed to plant bottles of her knock-out toxin in The Dollmaker's studio. That, plus the dolls and the girls and the hyena stuffed animals—she's able to twist our story in a way that makes it seem like he and The Mad Hatter were responsible for all our shenanigans this summer and we were just innocently investigating the bad guys. (It helps that Everly wakes up and tells them The Mad Hatter has a secret room filled with dead people having a tea party, which pretty much confirms his identity as the most-wanted serial killer in Gotham City.)

Montoya has doubts. I can tell she'd like to question me more. Alone. But the rest of the police are happy to believe a simpler story.

And before she can poke me any further, Tiffany Jones and the Gotham News 1 van appear.

"Aw, crap," mutters Montoya, and I have to stifle a snicker.

Tiffany has an absolute effing field day with The Dollmaker compound and the modified kids.

She shoves her microphone in Montoya's face like it's an Olympic sport and she's going for the gold. "What was it like leading such an unusual rescue?"

Montoya grunts in response.

I look in the opposite direction so I don't crack a smile. Wait'll Tiffany finds out they caught the Looking Glass Killer. Montoya's not going to get a moment's peace ever again.

Outside, Shiloh and Soph are providing drinks and medical care to the kids from the Tower. Ivy, Jasmin, Vengeance, and I move to help them.

Shiloh hands Fallon a juice box with a genuine smile (no flinching, no cringing, no staring). Have I mentioned how much I love them?

"Hey, do you need any help?" Vengeance says to Shiloh and only Shiloh. (Apparently, at some point between Pride and now, she has realized how awesome they are.)

"There's bottled water over there," Shiloh says flatly. They point out the water but otherwise don't even look at Vengeance, completely ignore the fact she exists. (Apparently, at some point between Pride and now, their annoyance over Vengeance's well-intentioned rudeness that day has only intensified.)

"Well!" says Vengeance. "Water we waiting for?" She nudges Jasmin and laughs at her own joke.

Shiloh crosses their arms. "Are you really making puns at a time like this?"

"Are you kidding?! There's never not a time for puns!" Vengeance goes off to get the water like the bucketloads of tension have swooped right over her head, but I catch her doing an unnecessary amount of flexing as she picks up a case. And I watch her check to see if Shiloh noticed. (Potentially. But they're also muttering "worst pun ever" under their breath, so it's really hard to say.)

Ivy wrinkles her nose. "We have got to find a system for rescue hydration that doesn't involve bottled water." I take her hand in mine, and her whole face changes. "I'm really glad you're okay."

"Can we talk?" I ask, stepping away from the group.

She breathes in sharply. "Sure."

I kind of figured there was some residual anger lurking underneath the relief that I'm not dead or changed into a hyena creature.

"I'm sorry," I say, just as Ivy says, "You can't ever do that again!"

Her green eyes are flashing, and she looks so very beautiful that I have to remind myself that now is the time for apologizing, not victory-kissing. But before I can really get a good apology going, she throws her arms around my neck.

"I just love you too much," she says, and bursts into tears.

"I love you too much too."

We stay like that for a really long time, me holding her. Eventually, I overhear the questions the reporter is asking "concerned Gothamites," though. Catch the things the police are muttering when they think none of us can hear them.

We've saved the day. Tiffany Jones, Gotham News 1, has declared it on air at least fifty times. But the question remains.

What are they going to do with these kids?

Hours later, we're helping the kids from the Tower get settled in at a nearby church that offered up its fellowship hall as a makeshift shelter. What's to be done with them is still the only thing the grown-ups will talk about.

"What do you think?" whispers Vengeance, and I know she's worried about the kids too.

"I don't know," I answer honestly. It means a lot that she looked at both me and Jasmin when she asked. "Stella can't exactly go back to Arkham Acres like this. And not all these girls have homes to go back to."

Jasmin nods. "Some of the younger ones and the ones with strange powers have had offers of adoption because of all the media coverage, but they're scared. They don't know who to trust, and they're worried people want to take advantage."

"And they should be worried," I say.

"Yeah, I've only run background checks on a few of them so far, and I'm already genuinely concerned," replies Jasmin.

Vengeance eyes her curiously. "Question . . . ? How did

you have time to run background checks? I've been with you this whole time."

"Right." Jasmin takes a deep breath. "There's some stuff I need to tell you."

While they talk, an idea begins to take shape inside my head. But the only way to pull it off is if we all work together again, as the Reckoning. And this time, it wouldn't just be Vengeance and Jasmin and me. We'd need to be bigger. We'd need to be more than we've ever been before.

I don't know if I've earned their trust back enough, but I know there's no way I could do it on my own. I'm not even sure it's possible at all.

When my other friends go to help distribute dinner to everyone, I hang back. And I ask the one person who might be able to make this a reality to hang back with me.

"Hey, Jasmin, can I talk to you?"

On the day of the unveiling, Vengeance gets to the coffee shop first. She looks confused when she sees me.

"Hey, Harley. I thought I was meeting Jasmin here."

"Well, yeah." I shrug. "This is kind of both of our thing. Well, potentially all of our thing."

Vengeance looks even more confused.

"I'll explain when everyone gets here."

Luckily, Ivy and Jasmin show up a few minutes later.

"Thank you all for meeting me here. I, uh, wanted to apologize."

Ivy gives me a weird look like, *That's cool and all, but why are you doing this in front of your friends?*

"I'm sorry," I say to Jasmin and Vengeance. "I wasn't always the friend I should have been, because I was obsessed with my future. And then I was obsessed with proving myself."

Jasmin smiles at me encouragingly. I feel like we really worked through some stuff when we were in the Tower together. Vengeance is less easily persuaded.

"I'm sorry I wasn't there when you needed me," I say just to her. "We were creating something really amazing with the Reckoning, and I shouldn't have walked away from that. I want to show you how dedicated I am to what we were building."

Her opinion of me seems to have gone up a smidge, but her arms are still crossed.

I continue, this time looking at Ivy. "And I'm sorry for not trusting you more. I mean, I trust you, it's not that. But, like, sorry for doing all kinds of wild stuff where I put myself in danger and didn't even tell you or ask you or include you. I'm sorry for not trusting you with things like that."

"Hey, that can be an issue for a lot of people," Jasmin says with a pointed look that makes Vengeance's ears turn red.

"So, yeah, something I learned while I was in the Tower is how to trust my friends more and depend on them more and not just to rely on myself. I hope you'll give me a chance to show you that new side of me."

"Of course." Jasmin is full-on grinning now. The lights in the coffee shop get brighter. "Oops, still getting used to being a cyborg." She dims them back to their normal level.

Meanwhile, Ivy is giving me more weird looks because we've already pretty much hashed all this out the past couple of days. "You know I can't stay mad at you."

Vengeance raises her eyebrows, like, *We'll see.*

"Um, it's more of a show apology than a tell. Wanna follow me?"

I lead them out of the coffee shop. (Well, we get lattes first—I'm not a monster). Vengeance is still wary.

"You know, you can't erase the past," she says.

"I know."

But at least she keeps following me, even if it is just because she's probably wondering where I'm taking them. The farther we get down the sidewalk, the more it starts to dawn on Ivy where we are.

"Hey, is this—"

I smile. "Yep."

I march us right up to the front door of the Bee Sweet Candy Factory. Ivy glances over her shoulder, like, *Should we be sneaking to a less visible entrance?* But when we get to the door, I don't pull out a crowbar or a pocketknife or a lockpick kit. I use a key.

Ivy watches me strangely as I unlock the door. As I lead everyone inside.

There's a sign in the foyer: THE KYLIE PEARCE HOME FOR LOST GIRLS.

And underneath that, in smaller print, a list of the board of directors, which includes all four of us.

Ivy's mouth falls open in surprise. "You bought it?"

She's not mad. It's the happy brand of surprise, not the angry one. I keep a catalog of her facial expressions in my head now, and this is definitely Good Surprise.

I smile like I've swallowed the sun and it's leaking out through my face. "We bought it." I gesture to myself and Jasmin.

"How?"

"I will pretend not to be offended by that question."

"The Dollmaker had a whole lot of money at his disposal even before auctioning people off that night," explains Jasmin. "We're talking tens of millions. So I took the liberty of funneling it through a series of untraceable transactions into one offshore bank account for each of the people being held in the Tower. I'm planning to arrange a trust for everyone who's under twenty-five, which is most of them."

"Wow." Ivy is impressed—nay, dazzled—by Jasmin. "How did you do all that?"

"With her mind!" I chime in gleefully. "Can you believe?!"

"Wow," Ivy says again.

I turn to see what Vengeance thinks, to assess how all of this is landing with her. That's when I realize she's tracing Kylie's name on the sign. And her shoulders are shaking.

"Hey," I say softly, touching her shoulder. "You okay?"

"This is a really big deal, Harley." She doesn't take her eyes off Kylie's name. "She would love it."

I'm suddenly struck with how much Kylie would love this place too. And with the bigness of this moment. Of how connected it makes me feel to her. Gosh, I miss her so much. I stand there with Vengeance for a minute, or two, or ten, just staring at Kylie's name.

And then I need to know.

"So, are you in? I know you're working with Talia and everything."

"And it's a big decision," says Jasmin.

Vengeance shifts her weight from foot to foot, uncertain. "What is it you're planning to do here?"

Jasmin gives me the sly kind of side-eye. "Should we give them the tour?"

"The Tour!!" I shout, and my voice makes the most delicious echoing sound.

We take them through the main entrance, the one where Ivy and I had our picnic.

I squeeze her hand, thinking about how different it would be, now that we've cured our kiss problem. She blushes. Pretty sure she's thinking about it too.

"It's obviously still set up like a candy factory," I tell them in my best college campus tour guide impression, complete with backward walking. "Which, I mean . . . I kind of love it, I have to say."

"Our goal is to make it like the Reckoning," says Jasmin. "Only bigger and more."

Vengeance is trying to maintain some semblance of aloofness, but *bigger* and *more* are, like, her two favorite words, so you can imagine how well that's going for her.

"We'd ask any of the people who helped with the Tower rescue if they want to be part of this too. The four of us would vote first, of course," I add quickly. "But we were thinking King Shark, Soph, Shiloh."

I don't miss how red Vengeance's cheeks turn when I say "Shiloh."

"Some of the kids from the Tower need a safe place to stay, and we figured we could give it to them," Jasmin continues. "And there are a lot of girls in the system who could really use a safe place to land. Like, literally I am going through the system as we speak, and I've already come across a dozen."

I grin and clap my hands together. "It'll be like summer camp! Not that I've ever been to summer camp. It's, like, superexpensive. But it always looked so cool in the movies."

"Wow, I mean, this is a huge undertaking," says Ivy. "There's so much to think about."

"I know! That's the whole point. Remember your forty-seven-item manifesto?" I ask her.

"Um." She hunches her shoulders and glances at Jasmin and Vengeance.

"Well, this is mine! This is my big goal in life. To help women and girls. As the psychiatrist I'll someday be. As the chaos monster I already am. Who says they have to be mutually exclusive?! The girls' home will give me a place to *combine* them." I just, I am so happy now that I've figured all this out, and I am going to continue on my med school route but also pursue this vigilante thing too, and I'm going to keep doing both for as long as I can until someone makes me stop. (And then I'll break out of jail and keep going.)

Jasmin and I lead Vengeance and Ivy through a rusted door that is coming off its hinges.

"We should probably all get tetanus shots before we move in," I say, kicking a bunch of old nails to the side to make a path. "I don't really have a plan beyond letting them crash here and making it like a 24/7 sleepover, but we can figure out the details later." I wave a hand dismissively. "Who wants to see the waterslide?!"

Vengeance raises her eyebrows. "There's a waterslide?"

"Uh-huh! I built it with giant plastic pipes and my bisexual audacity."

Jasmin and I show them the pool (currently filled with leaves and algae) and my waterslide (mostly finished). And where the dorms could be and the secret weapons vault and the giant tubes of candy (some things you just don't mess with).

They pretty much think our plan is awesome, but they do point out some minor details, like the fact that the place is completely dilapidated and looks like it's one good storm away from falling apart.

"We got it for less than a million," I whisper to Ivy conspiratorially.

She nods at a hole in the floor the size of King Shark. "I can see why."

She asks me if we've had a contractor look at the place and where we're going to get the funding to fix it up, which, all very good questions, and I have no idea. Jasmin and I spent our entire cuts of the Tower money on the purchase.

"I'm just not sure about this 'elbow grease' plan," says Vengeance.

But she's thinking about it! That's a good sign!

Ivy is frowning. "I'm also concerned about the part where we take care of a bunch of girls all by ourselves."

"Totally," I say. "Totally a detail we can work out. But in general . . ."

I wrap my arm around her waist and lead her around a corner, and her jaw drops open.

"Oh," she says softly, her nervous system struggling to take it all in.

In the south side of the factory, I found this huge round room with a glass ceiling—like it was just waiting to become an atrium for man-eating plants. Currently, it's mostly filled with tables and some dead bushes and some vines that have started taking over, but in the middle, in the part where there used to be a garden that I imagine the people who worked here ate their lunch around, I have planted a single tree. A positively queenly one, with leaves the brightest shade of green and branches that drape in a way that can only be described as poised and regal.

Ivy covers her mouth. "Is that—"

I take her hand. "Yep. I stole it from the park and brought it here."

Some people get their girlfriends flowers, but I figured the tree where we shared our first kiss would be so much grander.

"What do you think?" I ask. "Of all of it?"

She shakes her head. "Ah, hell, you know I'm in."

"Hooray!!!" I actually leap off the ground and punch my fist in the air as I yell it. It feels that good to know she's in this with me.

Ivy frowns. "It needs something, though."

"It does?"

"Uh-huh." She pulls a crumpled piece of paper from her pocket and sets it on the stone bench that encircles the tree, using a rock as a paperweight. "I'd say we completed it. Would you like to do the honors?"

Would I?! Jasmin passes me a pen, and if knocking an item off your list feels good, crossing off the final thing is just the best.

Harlivy Summer Bucket List

1) Adopt a pet
2) Go to Pride
3) Find a cure so we can kiss for approximately forever
4) Find the girls. Defeat the bad guys. Save the world.
5) Liberate the hyenas at the Gotham City Zoo
6) Mani-pedis
7) Road trip!!!

Ivy squeezes my hand when I finish, and everything is almost perfect.

Almost.

I turn to Vengeance as we walk back to the main entrance. "And how about you?"

"There's a lot of stuff to figure out."

She didn't say no. I hold my breath.

"But I like that Jasmin's on board. And the mission of it. And that it's named after Kylie and everything." She shakes her head. "And it's hard not to be sucked in by your enthusiasm. . . ."

"But?" I can tell there's a *but*.

She touches the sign again, the smaller one with all our names.

"What if I said no?"

I take a deep breath. "Well, I'm hoping you won't. And even if you do—this is what I want. This is my big plan. What we started with the Reckoning means something to me, and I want to keep it going. I mean, if you do say no, I'd have to change the sign, and that would be super awkward, but—"

Vengeance doesn't let me finish. She spins me around in a giant hug. Ivy and Jasmin join in, even though they're less of the group-hug type.

We're doing this. I get to fight for the things I believe in. I get to go to medical school and help people. I get to be a midnight vigilante and save the world. And I get to do it with my best friends.

EPILOGUE

One year later . . .

HAVE YOU EVER SEEN A GIANT SHARK-MAN DO DOWNWARD-facing dog in the middle of a rooftop rose garden as the sky turns the color of cotton candy? If not, I feel extremely sorry for you.

"Everyone, exhale and move into child's pose," Stella instructs us from the mat at the front of the garden. Meanwhile Remy moves through the group and makes small adjustments.

"You're doing great, Scarab. Just try to relax those . . . mandibles."

As I'm shifting poses, a summer breeze ripples through the garden, carrying the scent of roses through our yoga session, and is there anything more perfect? The roses just appeared one day, despite the fact that they weren't part of the landscaping plans. And when I mentioned to my girlfriend that they looked awfully similar to the roses at the Tower, she had turned bright red and stammered, *S-some people can't be trusted with flowers.* Let me rephrase my previous statement. The only thing more perfect than roses? *Stolen* roses.

Stella leads us through a few more poses, ending in corpse pose. (Side note: I love how deliciously morbid that one sounds.)

"Take a deep breath in. And out," she says in that serene voice of hers. "Let all your stress melt away."

I try to, I really do. I also try to focus on not focusing on anything at all, but it's not that easy when you have a high-key personality plus ADHD.

"You're flying through the sky, through the stars. And everything is okay. You don't have to do anything else. You're going to be okay."

I hear at least two people sniffling. Remy and Stella hold sunrise yoga every morning, but it's impossible to predict when Stella will go all meta and emo and leave us in tears. (Every time she tells us to stop accepting fault for things that bad people have brought our way, I not-so-quietly sob. Every. Damn. Time. I'm a work in progress, okay?) It's been great having both of them here. After Stella's hybridization, they were reluctant to accept her back at Arkham Acres, so I talked with Mrs. Watkins about having her come here. When Remy found out, she asked if she could come too. They're both doing so much better that it honestly makes me want to ask a lot of questions about Arkham Acres and what they were doing there and who was providing the funding for it. I'll add it to the running list in my journal, aka *The Harley Quinn Manifesto and Guide to Being Fantabulous.*

When Stella ends our yoga session, I roll up my mat and pad across the grass to King Shark. "What are you up to today, buddy?"

He sniffs. "I'm gonna test out the moat." Another big *sniiiiffff*. And then he grabs me in a hug and starts sobbing into my shoulder. "I just love yoga so much."

"Me too, big guy, me too," I say, patting his back.

BTW, we have a moat now! Complete with sharks!! (Well, King Shark.) It's really more of a lazy river that surrounds the rooftop garden than a strip of water going around the entire building, but doesn't it feel so much cooler to call it a moat? (Yes. Yes, it does.) I'd test it out with King Shark, but I have much too much to do this morning, so I leave him with Remy and Stella, and they launch into a talk about capital *F* feelings, and I head inside the Kylie Pearce Home for Girls.

It's wild to walk these hallways and see how much has changed. A year ago, this place was just a (totally genius, utterly brilliant) idea that Jasmin and I had, and now it's real. And, okay, maybe it's not the 24/7 sleepover I imagined, and maybe we needed a little (read: a lot) of help, but we created a safe place for women and girls to land. The Wayne Foundation stepped in to do the restoration of the factory and to rezone it as a residential space. Kylie's mom, who's been on the board of, like, a million nonprofits, officially established a foundation that runs the home and takes care of the girls. My friends and I come volunteer whenever we have time outside of school, so we're still SUPER involved.

We're offering all these summer courses, so, like, I'm teaching neuroscience and also this pretty badass combat class that Londyn and I lead together. And then Jasmin is teaching the girls how to code, and Vengeance teaches physics (and explosives—shh, don't tell), and Shiloh started a running club.

I hurry to my neuroscience class and rush to get everything set up because my students are arriving any minute. I have some high schoolers, some middle schoolers, and even a few little kids like Fallon. Kids from the Tower, plus other kids directed our way by Montoya or social services. And when they get there, I lean across the table and say in my best conspiratorial voice, "Do you want to see what's in the box?"

"Yes! Please! Yes!" says Fallon with a squeak.

The others nod rapidly. It's just a Styrofoam container, but they've learned what to expect from my eye gleams. I snap on a pair of nitrile gloves. And I open the box.

The brain is heavier than you'd expect. And not nearly as squishy. It *has* been fixed in formaldehyde after all.

"Brains!" I say, lifting the brain up and setting it on a metal tray.

"Ohhhh." The sound of science-induced awe echoes through the room. I freaking love brains.

"So," I say seriously. "We are going to learn a lot of cool stuff about brains today, AND I'm going to let you touch them, but first we need to go over some rules. People donated their bodies to science in order for us to have these brains, so we have to treat them with a lot of respect."

I go over the usual safety measures (do not touch the brains without gloves on, do not touch the brains and touch your friends, do not eat the brains). The kids are obsessed, even the high schoolers. And so am I, honestly. Borrowing the teaching brains from Gotham U is kind of the greatest. So is teaching a neuroscience course of my own design.

When class is over and everyone has touched a brain (even Cooper), I go find Ivy to see if she wants to get coffee with me before my hand-to-hand combat class. I stand in the doorway until she notices, watching her work in her botany lab as one of the quieter girls, Lily, follows her around like a puppy.

Ivy smiles when she sees me. "How long have you been there?"

I shrug. "A minute."

"Coffee?"

"Coffee!"

We go to the on-site coffee shop because if I'm in charge of creating a place, you better believe there's coffee.

"Can I get a pumpkin spice latte?" I ask the barista, even though it's the middle of summer. (Kylie's mom declared that if this place was going to be named for her daughter, it was only right that there be feminist pumpkin spice lattes on tap at all times.)

Ivy gets an iced coffee, and Lily gets a hot chocolate. She clearly feels the way I do about letting your taste buds have what they want, regardless of season. We go out to the roof-top lawn, by the rose garden, and sit on the grass as Lily runs off to join two of her friends. Across the lawn, Vengeance and Shiloh are having a seriously high-key planking contest. They hold their bodies above the grass like statues. But Vengeance's arms are starting to waver. . . .

She buckles and hits the ground with a thud.

"Ahaha!" shouts Shiloh.

"If you could just let me use a little bit of Venom . . ."

"Nope. We agreed. No powers."

Vengeance feigns a grouchy face and pulls herself into a sitting position. "Fine. I declare plankruptcy."

"Where do you get all these terrible puns?" groans Shiloh. But I don't miss the smile that passes between them.

I was really worried they were going to hate each other for all eternity until I walked in on them making out in the weapons vault a few months ago. Now Vengeance makes organic protein fudge for all of Shiloh's races. Meanwhile, Jasmin and Soph sit by the edge of the moat and talk about how hard it is to settle on a career plan if you're a multipotentialite. And Noah and Everly compare TBR lists under a willow tree.

I put my hand over Ivy's. "This is the best."

"Yup," she replies.

"Thank you for doing this with me."

"Anytime."

We watch as Lily and Co. play a game of hide-and-seek that somehow involves the hyenas. Beyond the rosebushes is a huge privacy fence that Ivy knitted together with vines as big as your arm because we've had problems with photographers camping out in the apartment building across the way and trying to get pictures of the more unusual people who live here. My eyes are drawn to the fence now because Fallon has climbed halfway up and appears to be trying to pick a flower near the top. Right as she slips, a vine shoots out and snags her by the foot, lifting her through the air and keeping her from hitting the ground.

"Fallon, that's not a safe choice," calls Ivy.

The vine gently deposits Fallon next to the game of hide-and-seek, and she rushes to join in, frolicking around the garden and chasing Bruce. I take it all in and think for the millionth time how lucky I am.

"I just realized something," I tell Ivy.

"What?"

"I remember a time when I felt like I could never have a

normal life. Or a happy one, you know, with kids and dogs and fences and stuff." I watch as Fallon tags Bruce and runs away giggling. "But we ended up getting it after all."

Ivy laces her fingers through mine. "Yeah, we did. And we got it our way."

ACKNOWLEDGMENTS

I couldn't have finished this trilogy without the help of a Super Squad of heroes, villains, and antiheroes.

To the vigilante girl gang who brainstormed plot ideas in coffee shops, beta read early versions, and helped me make The Dollmaker at least 20 percent creepier—Kate Boorman, Alina B. Klein, Dana Alison Levy, Maryann Dabkowski, Mayra Cuevas, and Gilly Segal, you are all the absolute best, and I'm sending matching leather jackets with rainbow fringe, plus a recently liberated hyena named Bruce.

To the Gotham Outsiders, Chris and TJ, thank you for inspiring one of my favorite scenes in the whole book, and please accept a million free shark hugs.

I've been lucky to be a part of some really wonderful writing communities. Huge thank-yous and sparkly mallets to the MoB, the Drafted Tavern, High School English but with Wine, the Korner, the ATL Culture Club, the LBs, the Not-So-YA Book Club, my Atlanta writing buddies (especially Kelly, Lauren, Becky, Aisha, Julian, Marie, Kim, Kate, Carrie, Vania, Jessi, Lee, Angela, Addison, and Elizabeth!), my college girls (Becca, Anya, Katie, Laura, Bethany, and Nicole), my mom walkers (Theresa, Susan, and Sharon), and my writing group (Jenn, Lauren, Dana, Terra, and Maryann).

To everyone at Brave + Kind Books, Little Shop of Stories, Broadleaf Writers Association, and Georgia Center for the Book, and to all the librarians, bloggers, teachers, readers, and everyone on BookTok and HarleyQuinnTok—thank you. Writing books for kids is amazing because of you and the work you do. I'd say you deserve superpowers, but I suspect you already have them.

To my agent, Susan Hawk, I'm forever grateful to you for making this happen. The way you continuously make my dreams and other authors' dreams come true feels like a thousand glitterbombs' worth of magic.

To Sasha Henriques, we did it! We finished the trilogy! I'm so very proud of these books, and I couldn't have done it without you. To Elizabeth Stranahan and Madison Furr, thank you for everything you've done for Harley. Y'all are more unstoppable than an army of man-eating plants. To Sara Sargent, Lois Evans, Ben Harper, Jim Chadwick, Janet Foley, Rebecca Vitkus, Barbara Bakowski, Tricia Callahan, Kaitlyn San Miguel, Ray Shappell, Cathy Bobak, Kris Kam, Sarah Reck, the Random House Books for Young Readers marketing and publicity teams, and anyone else at PRH or DC who worked on this book in any way: Thank you for loving children's books so much and for being so dang good at your jobs. Rainbow slushies and feminist pumpkin spice lattes all around! And to Kevin Wada, thank you for making ANOTHER spectacular cover. She's perfect.

To my family, especially Mom, Mica, Maxie, Dennis, Dad, Julie, Hannah, Matt, Little Zack, Bekah, Jonathan, and Aunt Amy: I love you more than King Shark loves hugs.

To Ansley and Xander, I love you so much. You keep me dreaming.

Last of all, to the Harleys who inspire me—Arleen, Margot, Tara, Kaley, and Gaga—thank you. I am honored I got to write this character. Being part of her evolution is the highlight of my writing career.

ABOUT THE AUTHOR

RACHAEL ALLEN is a scientist by day and kid lit author by night. She is a winner of the Georgia Young Adult Author of the Year Award, and her books include the Harley Quinn trilogy (*Reckoning, Ravenous,* and *Redemption*), *17 First Kisses, The Revenge Playbook, The Summer of Impossibilities,* and *A Taxonomy of Love,* which was a Junior Library Guild Selection and chosen as a Book All Young Georgians Should Read. Rachael lives in Decatur, Georgia, with her two children and two sled dogs.

rachaelallenwrites.blogspot.com

She is made of electricity and laughter . . .
and no one will ever hurt her again.

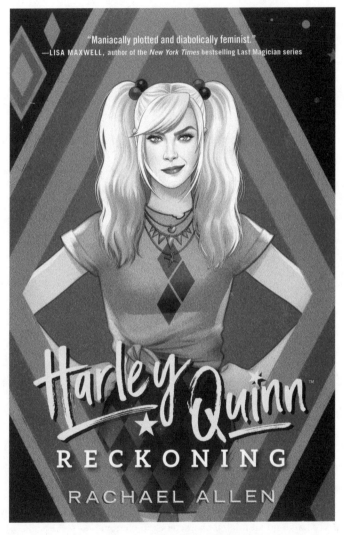

"Maniacally plotted and diabolically feminist."
—LISA MAXWELL, author of the *New York Times* bestselling *Last Magician* series

Harley Quinn

RECKONING

RACHAEL ALLEN

Keep reading for an excerpt from the first book in the
HARLEY QUINN TRILOGY.

PROLOGUE

WE'RE SUPPOSED TO LOCK THE DOOR WHEN WE LEAVE. IT'S one of Dr. Nelson's biggest Official Rules, along with keeping a detailed lab notebook and saving all your data on the Gotham U network. Today when I arrive, clutching a coffee I made at home and rubbing the sleep from my eyes, the door is open. Only halfway, which is another weird thing. It's always all the way open or all the way closed.

I can't explain why my shoulders tense. Why my hands clench into fists until my nails dig in.

I walk inside.

The table with the coffeepot looks just the way I left it, and the computer and the desks—everything is fine. Admittedly, I get kind of jumpy in the morning. Judge me if you want; I'm not reducing my caffeine intake. I set down my bag and my cup. Maybe a janitor came in early. People don't usually beat me here because (A) I'd rather die than see my hungover father in the morning, and (B) I am GOING to get the good thermocycler before that pissant Trent Bayers comes in. Crap, is he here? Because there is no amount of coffee that could prepare me for that.

I step from the office space through the door into the main lab—without my coffee because having food and drink of any kind in the lab spaces is verboten. Trent's arrogant self isn't occupying the good machine. Thank. Goodness. I get my samples from the freezer, but I can't shake the feeling that someone's watching me. I wonder if Trent would do something as obnoxious as hide in the lab just to scare me. Actually, that is kind of a great idea.

I take a deep breath and try to focus on my work. The repetition of filling tiny tubes with even tinier amounts of liquid soothes me. As soon as I have my samples going, I make coffee and wash all the glassware that the undergrads and postdocs left in the sinks yesterday. According to Dr. Nelson's Unofficial Rules, these are my most important tasks as an intern. Then I double-check my thermocycler. (It's going! Which means the DNA in my samples is multiplying like rabbits!) And then I close a drawer that's open and grab an ice bucket that someone left on the counter. Water sloshes inside. Not just water. Little plastic tubes with fancy labels. Dr. Nelson is gonna be pissed. These antibodies cost six hundred dollars a pop, and somebody left three of them out overnight.

I slide over to the lab notebook on the counter to see who will be the next victim of his entirely deserved wrath. Bernice Watkins. Wait, what? Bernice is always so careful. It's something I noticed ever since August, when we started bonding over being in the same post–high school gap-year program. The uneasy feelings prick the back of my neck again.

I pull out my phone to text Bernice.

Harleen: Are you here?

Maybe she had some kind of emergency or something. Wouldn't she have texted me, though? *Not if she's mad at you.* I shake away the thought and go back to the office area, where I pour some fresh coffee in my travel mug and text again.

Harleen: Look, I'm not trying to be weird, but what time are you coming in today?

There's a vibrating noise from across the room. I text one more time.

Harleen: ??

I hit Send and wait. The drawer across from me vibrates again. The drawer in Bernice's desk.

I'm across the room in a second, opening it. Bernice's phone. Bernice's bag. These are things that should not be here without Bernice. I'm the early bird. She's the night owl, stumbling home exhausted after the rest of the lab is already gone.

Something's wrong.

There's a creak from the other room.

"Bernice?"

Maybe she got tired and slept in the lab. I'm not gonna lie—I've done it before, though it had a lot more to do with my dad than with my experiments.

I walk back into the main lab, where my thermocycler is still going, and the lab is as empty as it was before, but this time the emptiness feels sinister.

"Bernice?"

All these other rooms and hallways connect to the main

lab, stretching through the fifth floor like roots. Bernice could be in any of them, I tell myself. And so could anyone else. It'd be super easy to hide in— Nope. Not even gonna think about it. I check the cognitive-testing room, the surgery room, the cold room, even the bathroom. Empty, all empty. It does nothing to ease the sense that something bad is waiting, watching.

I go back to the main lab. Look at Bernice's notebook and the area where it seems she was working last night. There's a pipette with the plastic tip still on, as if she was just about to draw up her next chemical solution. *What the hell, Bernice?*

I stand in front of the benchtop. Pick up her pipette like it'll tell me the secret of where she is. Instead, I get this chill—like someone is watching me, hot breath on my neck. I shudder and look over my shoulder.

And then I see it.

The door to the darkroom is shut.

We never keep it closed unless we're actively working in there, but maybe Bernice is doing a really long exposure, or maybe she went in there at midnight and fell asleep while she was waiting, or maybe a hundred thousand other things, but when I touch the door handle, I don't want to open the door.

"Bernice, you in there?" If she *is* doing an experiment, I sure don't want to screw it up.

Nothing.

I have to go in, see what's going on. Otherwise I won't be able to shake this feeling of being watched. But my muscles won't move to turn the handle. I have to force them.

The door is locked.

My heart starts beating faster. I whip out my pocketknife,

wishing like anything I had my lockpick kit. I pull out the smallest tool and listen for all the right clicks. This lock is more complicated than the ones I'm used to, and every second feels important.

Finally, the door creaks open. A shape forms in the darkness—

Bernice, sitting in a chair, her torso flopped over a benchtop.

"Oh thank goodness. You scared the crap out of me."

I touch her shoulder at first, then shake it. "Bernice?"

Harder. "Bernice!"

Her mouth lolls open. Her eyes are glazed. *Don't be dead. Please, don't be dead.* I cup my hand in front of her mouth and wait for a breath that never comes.

"Oh crap, Bernice."

I unlock my phone with shaking fingers and dial the campus police.

"Hello? My friend needs help, and she's not breathing. I'm in the neurobiology building. Nelson Lab. I need you to get here *now*."

A trickle of white foam leaks from the corner of her mouth, and her cheeks are so, so pale.

"You have to hurry, okay? She's . . . she's dying."

Every ICON has a story.